STEPHANIE KRENNING

Stephanie Krenning
Colossians 3

MILLENNIUM
GONE

**CREATION
HOUSE**

A NOVEL

MILLENNIUM GONE by Stephanie Krenning
Published by Creation House
A Charisma Media Company
600 Rinehart Road
Lake Mary, Florida 32746
www.charismamedia.com

Design Director: Bill Johnson
Cover design by Lisa Cox

Visit the author's website: Glorytogloryministry.com

Library of Congress Cataloging-in-Publication Data: 2014902929
International Standard Book Number: 978-1-62136-738-3
E-book International Standard Book Number: 978-1-62136-739-0

First edition

13 14 15 16 17 — 9 8 7 6 5 4 3 2 1
Printed in The United States of America

ACKNOWLEDGMENTS

I'D LIKE TO acknowledge my kind and giving husband, Jonathan, who finds it a great joy for us to stand side by side in all our visions and dreams together. He is a great support. I want to thank my resilient son Luke and precious daughter-in-law Becca for their support in this book project. Since Luke was quite young, he wanted me to "write more books and movies." Lord willing, so I shall! Zoanne Wilkie has also been a constant strength and joy in this book venture. My love to her and her husband David always.

The people of Creation House are people of excellence. Thank you for liking my book and working so generously and kindly with me.

Most importantly, I want to acknowledge the Holy Spirit who gave me jot and tittle with ideas galore! One scene in particular about the river of God and its many facets was confirmed just a few weeks later after I wrote about it. At that time I heard a person's testimony on TV who had seen the river of God on a visit to heaven when Jesus took him there. He described the jewels, sparkles, and other various features I wrote about. Only God can make life so exciting! Thank you, Father God.

FOREWORD

THE YEAR 3052 seems so far away and not real to us today. But if one considers the days of tribulation being a reality within the next thirty years, and this being the teen years of the Twenty-first Century, all one has to do is add a millennium of reigning with Christ, and "bam!" there you are! Even though the true City of God—The New Jerusalem—doesn't descend and hover above the earth until after the devil is thrown into the lake of fire once and for all, this story remembers the "camp of the saints" and the precious City of God mentioned in Revelation 20. Just in case John (who wrote the book of Revelation) was back-tracking and the City of God was there when the devil and his hordes came marching upon it, this story covers it all. The book of Revelation isn't absolutely clear to anyone yet, but there are many who have a good grasp on it. This book is to encourage and strengthen us in our everyday living while discouraging us from being "lukewarm," all while reading about the possible future of our seed's seed and the generations to come with the events that will certainly come to pass.

~ Chapter One ~

BURNING THROUGH OUTER space, a meteor of gigantic proportions hurled its way toward Earth. Scientists were confident it would burn up and dissolve when it reached the earth's atmosphere. Then to everyone's surprise, not only had it broken into scores of mini meteors, other meteors fell toward Earth as though angry hands hurled each one personally. Then it seemed as though more handfuls were thrown after the first dozen came, catapulting through what used to be Earth's protective band.

Large meteors broke apart, and some just downsized while raining upon the Southern Hemisphere. Trails of smoke and poisonous vapors filled the skies. Villages and towns disappeared in the snap of a finger. Tsunamis appeared on the coasts as fragments of destruction from the heavens plummeted into the seas. At first smaller waves twenty feet high would travel in a race to flee from the intruder that shot down to the bottom of the sea. Then all too dreadfully soon, other meteors slammed the oceans causing gargantuan tsunamis that nullified coastal cities, counties, and any sign of life as far as the eye could see.

Mountains that once stood as majestic monuments through the world got very angry and lost all control, spewing their fiery liquid fury. If life could have beheld the volcanic show, it would have surpassed all beauty and wonder before seen. But such was not the case as pyroclastic steam and hot molten lava went out of bounds, melting the geography for scores of miles. Fallout from the ash clouds covered the earth for months on end. Who could survive the days of death? Hailstones weighing one hundred pounds dotted the earth, and people did not know how to escape. Begging God to die from the horrors and pain, it was no use, for His fury and wrath had finally come to judge the earth just as He had warned for centuries.

There was no electricity to rely on. Roads and fields held feet of ash if not destroyed by earthquakes and all that was manifesting. Visibility was a luxury and food became a dream. Water became polluted over vast territories. Those who thought they only dabbled at moral compromise became evil beings. Terror had become their worst enemy and driving thought.

But there were those who believed what many persecuted men and women had warned: that such imminent events would take place, and people should prepare and organize to keep themselves protected. The government tried to keep these things hushed in fear of wide-spread panic and loss of control. Those who took the warnings had prepared and planned on going to their protective shelters or had gone into hiding already. Then there were those who repented of their sins and called on the name of the Lord. They clung to the memories of family members or close friends who had been believers, and who had tried to warn them beforehand of such catastrophes. Many such shelters had been built by God's people, and food and water sources had been stored in abundance. Miraculously, many of these shelters remained intact. But those believers were gone from the earth by an uplifting act of God. The new believers clung to the presence of God which is what kept them sane and peaceful far above any others that struggled to survive. These new believers and survivors were a remnant of God.

~*ᒲ*~

About a thousand years later.

"Misty! What are you looking at?"

The whimsical, puppy-like dog strayed into Krista's life just weeks before on a foggy Easter morning. Krista never ceased being amazed at her. Misty seemed like a mind reader. She always felt Misty was on the same page as her, which gave them an exceptional bond.

Looking at the foreboding sky, Krista knew all too well to call on the name of the Lord to keep her focused, especially with the challenges that lay ahead of her. Again Misty's dark brown eyes chased the cloud-ridden skies from left to right toward the wailing sirens in the far distant woods.

"Those sirens don't seem to want to stop, do they, Misty?" Sassy, blond haired Krista reached into her pocket and jangled her keys. Misty was already trained to know what jangling keys meant—a ride in the car for both of them.

"Let's go, Misty! This sounds like a local problem. If we move now, maybe we can be of some help." Krista reflected on the word *problem*. Problems had been escalating everywhere. But she would have to think about that later, for right now she needed to get going.

The wriggling little mutt resembled a cocker spaniel, and had already arrived at the door of the car waiting for her master. They each hopped in, and Krista turned the key.

"Ph-whomp!" The car was jarred as if it had been hit by something heavy and powerful, but what? It started to die as the two of them proceeded down the driveway in her mid-sized, red jazzy sports car.

"Satan! I bind you and your demons powerless right now in the name of Jesus! Father, please send your angels to be with us. We plead the blood of Jesus over us now! Amen!"

While Krista was surprised at her war-like prayer, she was not surprised as energy poured through her foot into the gas pedal, and the car sped off in its new energy as an answer to prayer.

Off they went into the dusk filled evening. Krista slid open the sunroof, and Misty seemed to bark her own orders in the lower heavenlies while Krista fought in prayer. They followed the call of sirens until they saw smoke just a couple of miles away.

Lately, she possessed a stronger ability to know, remember, and sense things more keenly. Even amidst the wail of the sirens, Krista had a deep peace enveloping her. She was drawn back to a time that often played in her memory.

In a time of desperation one night many years back, Krista lay out on her bed and called on the name of God. What happened next was difficult for her to explain. It was like a flash of light, and then a great peace had engulfed her. She sensed a great presence and knew right away it was the presence her aunt and uncle had told her about. Up until then, Krista was more into keeping up her physical strength and abilities than needing some other presence she couldn't identify. But that had all changed in the twinkling of an eye.

She had followed generations of military specialists and service minded grandparents, aunts, and uncles. But her mom was the ambiance of femininity. She was a "stay at home" specialist who could do anything. She was adept at cleaning, arranging, and cooking, but not just those tasks; she was a problem solver and managed her cleverness into every chore. She could fix the most mundane things about the house. To Krista, she was the most loving, wise, and full-of-fun mom in the world. Unfortunately, she died when Krista was fourteen.

Thinking she had been reminiscing for only a moment, Krista gazed with swells of love at her longhaired dog sitting acutely at attention, watching the road as though she knew where they were going.

Krista thought on how she had a clearer purpose that filled her since those days without the Lord. It was a purpose only God and his presence could give her. Thankfully, His presence seemed a constant in her life and many others she knew. Even though she wanted to be just like her mom, Krista's mind and body also computed with the remarkable talents of her dad, who had been a Navy Seal and later worked with a hidden branch of the Secret Service in the United States. She remembered him with a broad smile.

Abruptly, her thoughts were interrupted by Misty starting another barking jag. Krista looked around carefully in the direction Misty was looking. Misty's two front paws perched up on the front console as her tail wagged like a wind-whipped flag.

"Oh no, Misty, it's a fire. A big one. We better be careful where we park." Far in the distance, billows of smoke filled the air. Krista found an old dirt road and decided to follow it to keep hidden as much as possible. She couldn't explain it, but she knew she wasn't supposed to be seen yet.

The car fit neatly into a small turn-around off the dirt road nestled next to the woods. Misty bounded out of the car sniffing the air, her eyes danced while looking at the tops of the trees.

"You're spooky, Misty. I always think you're watching something." Krista looked up and couldn't see a thing except what she thought might have been a couple shafts of light.

"Naaah," she discarded that thought.

Misty turned her keen nose onto a path made only for chipmunks and barked back at Krista to follow.

"No, no, Misty, the action is up here." The silken, black dog barked again only to bound off down the forsaken path with Krista yelling as lowly as she could after her.

"Lord, what is all this mystery about? So much is changing," Krista mumbled while surrendering to her clever companion and trying to catch up with her. Some minutes into the thick brush, with her head down, Misty's tail was profusely wagging, announcing a new found treasure. Krista pulled back some branches, a large fir branch, and...

"Misty, just what are you do—"

Krista stopped short as she pondered upon Misty's latest find.

"Well, hi there!" She looked at two dirt-covered children clutching each other, looking awe-struck.

"Are you alright?" Wanting to calm the two shivering beauties, she said softly, "This is my dog Misty. She's always finding something wonderful." With her usual tender smile, Krista bent over to get a closer look at them. It was just like Krista to sooth and speak peace in the storm. "Here, let me take you to a safe place."

Oddly enough, they jumped into her arms, mastering a chokehold around Krista's neck in no time. Their clothing looked decent enough, but torn and dirtied just the same.

Krista did her best to not fall over and crush her little rescuer while the children wildly clung to her. Just then, Misty ran to the closest tree with her front paws stretching up as far as they could go while her back legs danced in excitement. Then as fast as she appeared at one tree, off she went to another and another, barking orders as though terrorizing every bird in the territory. But there were no birds.

"Misty! Quiet, Misty! Come here! Misty!" Krista yelled in her loudest whisper. Krista was mystified. *"I know we bound the demonic spirits. Could it be the angelic spirits?"* Krista pondered the thought.

"They *must* be angels, lady!" exclaimed the little boy as if he could read her mind. "Just like the one that told us you'd be here! Except, we saw *that* one!" The boy was emphatic.

Krista drew back and eyed each child carefully, rather wide-eyed herself. "Look, you guys, how about you tell me where you belong."

This time the tousled, red haired little boy pulled back and looked her square in the eye. With pompous authority, he was eager, ready, and willing. The roughed up boy took Krista's face gently in his hands to keep it toward him. "The angel told us you were to take us to our grandpa and grandma!"

"Whoa," thought Krista for a moment, startled by that statement. "What's your name, honey?"

"Rusty, and this is my sister Sissy."

"Well, hi, Rusty and Sissy." Krista grinned largely. "My name is Krista, and this is my dog Misty." Krista laughed, amused at how all their names sounded like they were all part of the same jingle family.

Krista gently put them down to get a better look at them with all of the questions that mulled around in her head.

What a lot of spunk for a boy in such tragic surroundings, Krista mused, making sure that eye contact was secure with the ruddy little boy.

"Where are your mom and dad, Spunky, I mean Rusty?" she said, quickly recouping.

"They got taken by some angry men!" Rusty flared.

"They were awful," Sissy added. She had been so quiet up to this time that Krista had only to wonder what they had gone through.

Krista observed Sissy's long, fine hair all matted. It was a beautiful, strawberry blond unlike Krista's thick, golden yellow hair.

Krista bent over with her hands resting above her knees to get more eye level with them, "Rusty and Sissy, listen to me. Let's all go over to the firemen, and let them know you're okay. They will know what to do."

"But the angel!" Rusty cried as he pushed back the hair from his eyes.

"What angel, Rusty?"

"The angel!" He was quite anxious over this, and Sissy was pointing up in the air.

Krista threw a quick look up, then over her shoulder and half doubtingly asked, "Are you sure you saw an angel?" Both of the children nodded so hard Krista thought their necks would snap.

Eyeing both of them carefully, Krista sent out a feeler. "Did you feel anything bad about this angel, kids?"

Both shook their heads no.

"Were you scared or did you feel peaceful?"

"We felt warm all over and peaceful, and besides, he said you and your doggy would come and help us. We felt the presence. You know... *the presence!*"

Well, that had answered some questions for Krista. Still, she would be cautious.

Krista had barely processed the thought when a swoosh of wind went over their heads sending chills down Krista's back. Krista finally realized that darkness had almost settled in. She could hear the commotion in the distance and made out lights reflecting in the sky near the fire, as it seemed to be lessening in intensity.

"You're not taking us to the firemen are you, lady?" asked Sissy in her little, heart-pulling voice.

Krista knelt down. "Don't worry, honey. I've got a plan that doesn't involve the firemen." She stroked little Sissy's face softly and prayed under her breath, "*Lord, help.*" Standing up with renewed courage, Krista offered cheerfully, "Come on, kids." She jangled her keys, and Misty answered with a prance.

"I'll take you to my car." Deciding to carry the children, Krista stretched out her arms, and they jumped right in. She could already feel a bond starting to knit them together as she balanced the two little cuties on her hips and watched Misty bound for the car.

"Pretty Kissta," said little Sissy, "Pretty Kissta." Sissy pulled back a few hairs alongside of Krista's face. She stared at Krista with total acceptance, and Krista smiled comfortingly right back.

With a happy, silent inward sigh, and in spite of the extra load, Krista's pace was faster than usual following her 'little general' dog, bounding with its black, curvy hairs fanning and waving in the breeze.

During their walk to the car, large angels that were propped in the trees above smiled at the little troop below. Swords were glistening, and if you listened closely, you could even hear a small orchestral humming coming through the swords. But one angel had his face toward a disturbance beyond this refuge. He nodded at the others, and they took off in flight, in the very direction Krista was traveling toward, as darkness came upon them.

Chapter Two

O KAY, GOD, WHAT *do I do?*" Right away, a deep assurance settled within as she thought about the children's plea to take them to their grandparents. The presence was strong about her. Now that she had decided to make tracks toward the grandparents, where did they live? Surely God would show her. She had learned about His guidance in one of the many classes she had taken with other believers over the last ten years, with plenty of the real-life experiences to test what they had learned.

She felt strangely excited but pensive. What was God going to do? Questions flooded her thoughts from day to day, but now she had even more. Why was the atmosphere so different? She knew in her heart the answer to that, but didn't want to accept it.

It isn't like they hadn't been told. God had frequently shown up to the many who had become believers these thousand years while the devil had been shut up in the abyss. Thankfully, many inhabitants of God's City were sent by God back into the earth to share what God had in store for those who would believe.

These people would be sent to any given nation that was still in existence after the great wrath of God. Though much of the earth had been destroyed, there were survivors who were eager to receive from those sent to them from the City of God. Yet all these centuries later, rebellion was a loud voice, and darkness was like a thick blanket over the torn and shaken earth, which had been totally revamped and was in full swing.

Instructions had been given to the Christians everywhere on how to prepare for this season of testing after the devil was loosened from the pit. Most everyone was experiencing visions, signs, and wonders. But something very different was in the air. Speaking of the air, it was thicker; the light was darker than usual, and uneasiness had become a bubbling caldron all over.

Were the thousand years truly up? Was satan loosed to deceive the nations as prophesied in Revelation 20:7–8? Would Krista and all her sisters and brothers in the Lord soon be going to the Beloved City, where they would be safe forever? Was there a further ushering—saving—of souls for the City of God to come? These questions plagued Krista.

The thousand years had to be up. No one was told everything. Then it occurred to Krista that she had taken authority over satan while leaving her house, hadn't she? Didn't they say *that* would be a sign? There were also other things she and others were told. Many were given specific assignments for this season.

A document existed that revealed some plan that had been written from a leader in the Middle East, and then stolen from an unknown person or organization. But what did the paper look like? Was it a scroll? Was it in a book? Krista had been given instructions to get this document and guard it—with her life if necessary. Just what it looked like hadn't been revealed to her yet, but she would know. She was promised that from the Lord.

That's all she knew about it except that God had told her that the enemy wanted this document badly and would be desperate. There was a satellite picture enclosed with this document that had a picture hundreds of years old since it was taken before all of the satellites had been destroyed by God's hand when the stars fell according to Revelation 6:13.

But now, Krista knew her mission was to get these children to safety. With a few questions to the children, Krista had a logical direction to follow. She needed to first head south, then west toward the ocean.

Up ahead Krista could see her car. Funny, it almost glowed. Was it that light again she had seen in the tops of the trees a little while ago?

Krista was deep in thought when little Sissy broke in, "Are you taking us to Grampa's house?"

Krista looked at Sissy with amazement and compassion; her eyes instantly brimmed, "Yes little, honey. That's exactly where we're going."

"Yay!" yelled Rusty and Sissy as the three comrades, plus one, piled into the turbo-powered car. Like Krista, the car was small but packed a lot of power. When it came to giving, it was generous, and when it came to fuel, it needed none. So were the days of innovation from about 3052 on.

Down the road they headed back toward the main thoroughfare when suddenly the headlights picked out two burly looking men. One man had two large German Shepherds held tightly on a leash. Krista felt uneasy, and Misty started a low growl. "It's okay, Misty. Let's see why they're flagging us down."

Krista put down a window as she rolled to a stop, and prayed out loud, "Lord it's only been a week and already things are getting eerie. Help me, Lord, *'For You have not given to me a spirit of fear, but of power, love, and a sound mind.'*"

Just then, Misty jumped out of the window racing past the two dark guard dogs.

"Hey!" yelled one of the men flashing his light on Misty as she scurried away. The other man struggled to release the brutal dogs to chase after her. Once loose, their legs took off—stretching in full stride—thankful just to run; their feet didn't seem to hit the ground. They thought of Misty as a delicious target to tear apart, which only added to their fervor. At that moment, the guard swung his light back around to Krista's side of the car when the noises of a dogfight ensued afar off, out of sight. His thick hands and fingers covered with glossy, black hair shared a grip of a wrestler. Krista fought to keep her thoughts on God and who He is rather than get caught up with the frenzied surroundings. So many wars so quickly!

"Misty!" The children yelled as they became frantic. Above the vicious growling and frenzied whining of the dogs, Krista joined the children's screams. The fight was so intensely ferocious that both men left her alone for a moment to shine their light on the fight.

As they struggled to find a fix on the dogs, a powerful urge came over Krista. Something told her to "Go!" so she stomped on the pedal and plunged forward, blasting out of the intersection, up the road quickly. Finding another road that was less traveled, she took it, hoping to hide in the hills while awaiting her flight of escape.

Flashes of the men's lights in her rear-view mirror were panicky. But soon the luminous fir trees on both sides of the roadway stretched out their branches covering her as if encouraging her along, waving her on by as she disappeared in the thickness of their embrace.

"What about Misty? What about Misty!" yelled the children.

"Lord, cover Misty! Be her help!" Krista prayed loudly as tears silently traveled their way down her face. She could only trust Him and His Presence. Krista turned to the children to calm them, but they had instantly calmed down after Krista's prayer.

Then, Rusty looked out the back window and said so lowly, "God, don't let Misty feel any pain."

~ Chapter Three ~

BRENT WAS A tall logger man whose love for the outdoors outweighed nearly everything he had ever been in contact with. That's why he chose logging. It was the best sport around, and everyone who ever encountered him outside the logging camp thought he worked out in the gym six hours a day. He did, but it was God's gym. The eight to ten hours spent daily in logging didn't pale in comparison to the indoor gym. Brent was thankful for having a gift that enhanced his life in every way.

"What more could you want? Clean air, working outside, keeping your mind clear, and feeling close to God. How I love the Lord God," Brent thought as he leaned up against a big old cedar.

Well, he didn't have time for women after he cleaned up with God before he got sent out to the Northwest and was planted in the hills of giant green timbers.

Timber laws were not too stringent just as long as trees were planted in their place. Because of the extensive damage hundreds of years ago after the earth was ruined, little evidence remained about the laws that had existed. The population had drastically decreased and slowly built back up. For years there were few people and lots of contaminated land. After about seventy years there was a lot of land to rebuild from plus the land that hadn't been destroyed. People were desperate to move on, but with sense and not silly regulations. There was a new spirit of joining together that lasted for centuries, but it seemed to get lost again over the past couple hundred years.

A lot of volcanic ash from some of the disasters destroying large parts of the earth had actually been a blessing years later, for it nourished the ground in richness and gave good soil in depth. However, many places had not inches, but feet of ash. When rains and seasons had come and gone, what was once dry desert and empty valleys became lush with growth and soil ready to be used.

Towns slowly sprang up in these areas, and it was as though the beginning of all time had rebirthed. A town could consist of twelve people, but to them it was a town. People did what they could with one another just to survive.

Forests of hundreds of thousands of acres were replanted, seemingly everywhere, and reserved for decades before they were harvested and replanted. But over the last few hundred years, the population had started to escalate, and to keep the greenery plentiful was once again a challenge in different places of the world.

Brent happily found himself right in the middle of a great forest that went on for miles all around. It would be his home for a few seasons.

Still, he pined away for his sister's family this past week. Their relationship was enough for him. God and, well, his dog Zipper and his sister's children were about the most satisfying relationships one could ever imagine. How he loved them. He knew he needed to keep his life simple for the time being, and he was right where he needed to be for that.

Brent overlooked a lush valley at the edge of the forest where he was working. This job had taken him to the other side of the world. Someday he would be reunited with his sister and brother-in-law and the little squirts, down the road in life.

Unfortunately, he had been transferred quickly just the last week from Wisconsin to the Northwest. Before that, he had been in Oregon. Deep inside he knew God had a plan, and God had even revealed some unexpected changes that were coming to him. Just what they were, he didn't know, but the peace of His Presence was ever with him.

"Hey, Brent! Are you going to stand there all day? We've got timber to fell! And it's Friday! You know what that means!" Mal, one of the supervisors for the crews walked up behind Brent swinging his axe and snickering. Giving any kind of gibe was Mal's favorite past time, and it often seemed aimed at Brent.

Mal equated it with being clever and witty.

Brent saw it as being lost and terribly insecure.

Mal took off into a different direction, and Brent secured his boots. Brent figured Mal was a man wandering with no satisfaction. He'd be a tough mission; and Brent knew there was a whole lot more of his heckling to come.

"It's Friday." He knew what it meant for some of the guys. Last Friday, his first day, they threw at him some mild earthy names and even cast a few jeers at him for not following their crowd. It didn't make sense to them that Brent wouldn't want to head to the nearest bar for a cool one at the end of a week of hard labor. That's what men did! Brent didn't fit in at all with them, and they were not going to let Brent get by with that easily.

Brent was amazed that the unsettling feeling and surroundings seemed to be growing by the day. Phew! This wasn't going to be as easy as he thought. But hadn't he been warned? Brent held onto God's presence, which is all that would keep him sane in a rough and lonely world ahead of him. Even though it had only been a week since the devil had been loosened back to deceive the nations, he saw too much rude harshness all around him. Darkness seemed to escalate and things just started to get plain weird.

Brent's deep, sky blue eyes were almost as sharp as the discernment that walked within him. It wasn't exactly time to throw his beloved ax over his shoulder; in fact, he had half an hour to show up for the job, but that still didn't stop Mal from finding an excuse to banter him. He felt like he was Mal's special project—disarm Brent. But Brent knew the Word well, and found it his constant companion. Nothing was going to distract him, outside or inside, from his commitment to God.

Mal wandered back through. "Better watch out for those hemlocks, Brent. After the cold winter we had, they are the most unstable toppers we've got. You just never know when an accident might happen. We lost four guys a few years back because of those greens splinting up on them. It would sure be a shame if one of them got ya. So you just watch out, ya hear?" It seemed like Mal couldn't ever walk away from Brent without snorting or snickering. The more he was around Mal in this short amount of time, the more his remarks seemed threatening.

"All right, Brent, keep your eyes on the bigger picture and be prepared for anything."

"Hey, Brent!"

Brent whirled around. "Hey, Darren, how are ya?" Pleased to see him, Darren met up with Brent, and Brent threw his massive arm around Darren's shoulders as they walked toward the truck. They had only met the day before.

They shook each other with a side to side hug, then Brent reached to pick up the rest of his gear and started to pile it into the back of Darren's two and half ton truck. It blazed blue like the color of Brent's eyes. "Nice taste in color here, Darren." Brent teased his smaller, yet bulldog built, friend.

"You've got some mean muscle there, Darren. Are you as tenacious as your build? I can see the timber has to watch out for you!"

Darren laughed, "It's the special few on the job I'd rather feel wary of me. I think a few have it in for me, to pound my frame into the ground, if you know what I mean."

"No way! What have you done to them?"

"Ha! What have I done to them? I showed up for work last Friday, that's what I did. They have their own little clan. I haven't seen you be a part of it. Maybe that's why I got detail to be your..." Darren searched for the right word, "...team."

"Hmm, now that's interesting." Brent rubbed his softening beard, just a week old. "I arrived last Friday too, and I've been thinking I'm their special project." That drew a laugh out of Darren.

"Rrrrr!" Brent and Darren jumped about a foot off the ground as Mal drove up in his black pick-up with oversized wheels, then blared the horn. "Change of plans! Get down to the third mile marker. Head north for thirty yards, and you'll see a clearing for parking. We'll be on the right with the equipment all set up."

Mal turned his head toward the road, and then turned back with a sneer on his face. "Oh yeah, and quit turning up fifteen minutes early! If you want to be any good around here, show up ten minutes early!" With that, Mal plunged into the gas pedal, his tires dug into the soft dirt, and debris sprayed a good fifteen feet around as he laughed his way down through the forest.

Zipper barked, and Brent and Darren brushed themselves off and had a good laugh. "Hmm, you'd think they didn't want us around or something!"

Brent gave Darren's remark a smile and agreed. "Wow, a real macho guy; like he came from some other days of old." Another hearty laugh came from the both of them, and they piled the rest of Brent's gear into the truck.

Knotty Pines, Douglas Firs, and a scattering of Hemlock were laid out from a replanting forty years ago. Brent could see clumps and dense pockets of growth. It was never safe in the logging business. Trees had their own minds when it came to falling from time to time in spite of the skill of loggers. He could see a Hemlock down from the weather. They weren't the sturdiest of trees.

"Hey, Darren! I'll watch your back if you'll watch mine, eh?" Brent didn't know Darren that well, but he had a strong hunch they should stick together.

"You got it, Brent." Darren lingered with an "I got it" grin and went immediately to pet Zipper who was eager to know his new-found friend better.

Brent looked around and gazed up into a forty-five foot Douglas fir, pure and beautiful. Instantly, perspective came rolling into his soul, and all felt well again. He whispered a "Thank You" to God and called Zipper to get into the truck. Zipper and Brent's special axe stayed by him everywhere he went.

The guys were quiet driving down the stretch to their next site. Each was praying about each other and the day to come as they committed to be a team. They knew it wouldn't be long before they would start praying together if truly they were on the same side.

Chapter Four

Bzzz! Bzzz! Crackle! Crack! The sounds of tall pines and firs were positioning for their journey to the earth with a calling all their own. The forest was alive with workers on this warm spring day.

Brent noticed they were on the outskirts of this particular forest ridge just about on the opposite side where they had been this morning. The last minute change of location was uncommon in this business. They normally liked to finish sections at a time. He kept his eyes and ears open. At least they were near a more traveled road to get to stores and rural businesses. *"Ah...Friday...fun in town."* That must be it Brent reasoned.

"Lunch! Lunch!" was the cry heard everywhere. The buzzes tuned out, and men went to their trucks while others went to one of the two trailers for refreshment.

Brent met up with Darren, and they were about to chow down when Jason, another one of the supervisors, came over to Darren with his back to the sun. This caused Darren to see more of a silhouette than Jason's face.

Brent could feel the hairs rise up on his back like a cat. He glanced at his watchful dog, then quickly over to Darren.

"Hey, Dare!" It was part of Jason's make-up to never call someone by their full name. "I want to talk to you tonight about something I heard about your family. Nothing horrible or anything, but I heard something I thought you'd like to hear and just want to pass it by ya."

Darren, trying not to slip into alarm, said without thinking, "All right. How about I meet you right here after work?"

"Nah, I can't do that. I'm called by the boss to be somewhere else. I can meet you at the Inn after that meeting. It's right in the village. There are only three hotels in the village, and this one is called an

Inn. It's on 4th Street. Head down the hill and go left at the first light. Think you can make it?"

Darren was really caught off guard now, but answered, "Sure. See you then…ahh, what time?"

Jason already turned to head back, "See you at seven."

"Okay." Darren just drew a blank.

Looking back Jason added, "Oh, and it's called the Tall Pines Inn." Then he went toward the trailers as others sat munching on snacks, sandwiches, and soup.

Brent and Darren stared at each other. Darren was still stunned. "What did you make of that?"

Right then, Zipper let out a big sneeze.

Brent raised his eyebrows. "Can't put my finger on it, Darren, but I don't like it. Before that guy opened his mouth, I could feel the hairs rise up on my neck. Something is not good with that man."

Darren reached into his cooler and robotically brought out some bottled iced tea to go with his sandwich. "It's like…it came out of nowhere! What could he know about my family?"

"I don't know. But whatever it is, I'll be in the background for you. Does that sound okay with you?"

"Yeah, that sounds very okay with me. I didn't want to go into town tonight. I just wanted to hang out here, block everything out, and just rest. I had plans to pick up a book tonight I've been carrying around. I only have time for books on the weekends because I stick to the Word during the week."

Darren had just rattled that out and realized he had just shared his faith openly without thinking. For a moment he was scared that his sharing had been so spontaneous. But hadn't he had a peace around Brent? Besides, he had felt no check in his spirit as he was sharing or was it because he was so vulnerable at the moment?

Brent came to his rescue immediately. "Hey, I understand. I feel the same way. I'm so tired at the end of the day, but can't wait to get into God's Word before my eyes close."

After hearing his confession and looking at Brent's big encompassing smile, Darren drew a huge sigh that was long in coming since Jason had invaded their space. When he let out his breath, blood came rushing through his body as if it had been held in suspense the whole time. He felt he had come back from somewhere dark.

"To tell you the truth, Darren, I don't like the idea of you going. Do you really need to go?"

As if a light went on in Darren's head, he said, "How about you and I pray about it right now and see what God has to say about this and how He directs us in the rest of the day? The thought '*bigger picture*' ran through my head just now. Strangely, I feel better about everything."

Brent grinned, "Now there's a plan I can sink my teeth into! Let's pray!"

The two guys sat there with their food, dog, and axes as they entered into a realm of the super-natural.

Zipper would always do a strange thing when Brent prayed. He would lie on his stomach and rest his head between his front feet as if to join in. When they finished praying, the atmosphere changed, and they recognized for the moment that a bigger plan was at hand. They may not like the plan, but trusted God that they would rejoice in the end.

"*Yup*," thought Brent, "*just like I thought. Tonight was going to be a long night of prayer.*"

Brent checked on Zipper's water, which he kept by the truck before heading back to his job. After a few good laps of water, Zipper led the way back into the woods.

~ℓℓ~

The trailers for showers and fellowship were always busiest on Friday nights. Thankfully it was specially designed for teams on the job away from civilization. There were two showers and two bathrooms all separate from the each other in each trailer, which was most convenient for the crew of a dozen men. The crew was divided into two groups as the second crew, who dealt primarily with the placement of each tree after it was on the ground, came in on the second shift for everything.

Most of the guys had gone on to whatever they did at the end of the hard week. Many didn't have family to go home to, so they headed to the nearest watering hole.

Meanwhile, Mal, Jason, and a third but newer supervisor that had come in from Montana, named Hank, were meeting in the office trailer sharing notes for the evening.

"I don't know, guys," Hank haltered. "The boss didn't say anything to me about that."

"I don't know what you're whining about, Hank," demanded Mal. "The plan is as smooth as the end of a polished hatchet."

Jason broke out in howling laughter. "That's it, Mal; keep those comforting words a'flowin'! Sheesh!" He just kept shaking his head, laughing.

"Hey guys, I don't mind getting the job done, but I usually hear it from the boss with the two of you. This feels like breaking rank." Hank just stood on what seemed like thin ground next to these guys. He felt uneasy, and that's all there was to it. Mal was no easy company to be around, and with his 6 feet 4 inches and runaway mouth, Mal was pure intimidation. He and Jason seemed pretty tight, and Jason had one stocky build, which was like looking at two bull-dogs all in one man. He could really push his weight around.

"Well, Hank," as Mal's piercing eyes shot through his own, "if you aren't going to go along with this, it could mean lots of trouble for that sweet little wife of yours. She seems a bit lonely, and we'd like to help you out as much as we can."

Instantly Hank's stomach churned. He knew exactly what they meant. He had only been with them for about six months, but felt he had been around them too long. Huh. He hadn't really formed that thought clearly before. But it hadn't hesitated to be clear to him now. What he would do with this insight, he wasn't quite sure, but it would have to be put on hold. He knew instinctively he needed to go along with them for now.

"Ah, guys, you don't need to get so ugly about me checking

protocol. You'd do the same thing, and you know it." Staying tough was Hank's salvation at the moment.

"Yeah, you're right, buddy." Mal went along. "You kind of had us wondering there for a moment. We gotta do what we gotta do!"

Keeping up the strong front, Hank swung out his hand to shake Mal's. "You got it, bud. I'll see to it and catch up with you guys after showers. Okay?"

Jason piped right up. "Yeah, man, see ya down at the Inn." He got up and stood by his tall friend Mal while Hank headed toward the door.

Hank reached outside and distanced himself from the trailer site in a reclusive frame of mind. Deep into the woods he went to clear his head.

Walking through the dense forest, he heard what seemed like a clapping noise high up in the boughs of the evergreens. He stopped. He was afraid to look up, but the noise persisted and even seemed to get louder.

Curiosity reached its peak, and Hank couldn't stand it any longer. He leaned his back against one tree as if to support himself and gazed upward. Flashes of light randomly spread high above from one side to the other in no special pattern.

"Looks like a storm trying to form somewhere up there, doesn't it?" Whirling around in stark surprise, the startled and now frightened Hank stood there facing Brent while trying to keep his knees from buckling.

"Oh, hi, Brent," Hank struggled to look composed. "I didn't know you were here. What are you doing here?"

"Well, my camp is just over there, and I saw something moving near here out of the corner of my eye. I came to investigate. So, what are you doing here?"

"Ah..." Hank really didn't want to let on, but felt the pull to let some excuse spill out incase great relief was on the receiving end of it all. "I just came out to look for my knife case. I dropped it around here somewhere the other day rabbit hunting."

"Hey, I can help you look for it then," answered Brent. But before he could get another word out, Hank broke in.

"Nah, that won't be necessary." Then still feeling the whir of the trees and noticing the clapping noise wasn't going away, Hank changed the subject.

"What do you suppose is going on up there? I don't remember ever hearing trees making clapping noises before. But come to think of it, I suppose they always have. Just can't remember making that connection before now."

Brent smiled and took a long breath. *"Okay, God, give it Your best, 'cuz I'm just taking this one by faith!"*

"There is a verse in the Bible that says," (Brent knew it would be a waste of time telling him it was found in Isaiah 55) *"You shall go out with joy and be led forth with peace; the mountains and the hills will break forth into shouts of joy before you, and all the trees of the field will clap their hands."*

"Go out with peace?" Hank chuckled, "That would be the day. You don't really believe all that stuff do you?" Hank paused for a moment, "But, the trees clapping their hands part, that's kind of cool."

Hank seemed to have that distant look in his eyes, and Brent could tell something was hitting him deeply.

"Yup, that peace stuff is for real Hank. And sometimes you just have to contend for it. So, I'll give you the shortcut for that." Brent didn't want to waste time doing a lot of witnessing, hoping his actions had spoken that in volume over the past week. And he had a sense this was a small crack in time for this divine meeting.

"The shortcut is quite simple, and here is how it's laid out. If ever you need peace, call on the name of Jesus, and I promise you, He will meet you inside and out. After all, He is God. And another thing, once you do that, and He reveals Himself to you—which He will do—thinking on Him and learning about Him will cause that peace to increase and pass your understanding totally and completely."

"Whatever," Hank piped up, "I don't need to hear that stuff. You guys are crazy! I'm getting out of here." Turning on his heels, Hank steamed off totally in the opposite direction as though he wanted to get lost in the forest forever.

Forests had a life all their own as far as Brent was concerned. For some people it was looking out onto the water, for others, it was hearing the gentle whir of industry, but for Brent, it was the thick green living timber that changed with the winds and the rains that ministered to him.

"Well, God, I tried! It sure felt like Your leading, but he sure rejected that whole sharing. Help me stay true to Your leading. I trust You any day over my understanding! Go with Hank, Lord. I can tell something is really weighing him down. Be there for him, God. Out of the greatness of Your compassions and understanding, Lord, be there for Him; reveal Yourself to him, In Jesus' name, amen."

Brent sank down with legs crossed under a wide evergreen wanting to reminisce and get lost in his own thoughts. He whistled for Zipper who promptly answered the call. He thought about the simplicity of his dog Zipper. With all of the upset in the atmosphere, it just felt good to get his mind off of it all and have this warm creature be by his side.

Zipper, however, found something to smell in a nearby trail close to Brent.

"You've got it good, you 'ol coot! Get over here!" Brent lovingly demanded. Zipper came wagging his tail and burrowed into Brent's lap waiting for his soothing voice to keep talking to him. Zipper could chase a stick and bring back a pile of firewood between his teeth. Brent laughed thinking about it. Well, almost a pile of firewood. Paul Bunyan had his Blue Ox, and Brent had his honey colored pure-bred; as big as they came. Somehow, Zipper would dump those sticks right onto the dead fire that Brent put out every morning when he chose to live and sleep outside. Zipper, or Zip, got his name from chewing on zippers when he was a puppy. Gold and silver were like a magnet to Zipper and resisting those shiny things was not in his makeup. He knew better now than to chew on the zippers, well, most of the time; but Brent would catch him licking or nuzzling them every once in a while. Must be some fond memory for Zip, Brent figured.

"I love ya, you rascal you. You're a good partner to have, that's for sure. Glad you're with me boy."

Brent deeply pondered the past several days, how surely different the environment felt. Things were changing rapidly from what he had been blessed to be a part of for such a long time. He knew the enemy must have been planning a fierce storm those years of being locked up. Why couldn't it just be all over with now?

But something was nagging him that took him past that question, and he couldn't put his finger on it. He knew tonight would have some long hours of prayer because Darren had a meeting with Hank, or maybe there was more to it, he wasn't sure. Brent continued to pet Zipper and was comforted just running his hand over Zips silky, honey-red hair.

Brent also thought of his struggle over when to be alone and when to be around his comrades who kept harping at him to be with them. Nothing was going to happen if he wasn't with them, but he had to draw a tight line. He was with them throughout the week, and that was proof during all the nitty gritty of the day's work that Brent stood out as different from all the rest. That's what he was hoping anyway.

Although, there were a couple of guys who caught his attention as men he should possibly try to hang out with. Thankfully, Darren had been one of them.

Now that God had brought Darren alongside him, it felt like a plan was coming together and it felt good. God would soon reveal to both of them why. But to get through this night...

~ Chapter Five ~

TREES RUSTLED A troubled breeze above Tall Pines Inn and the streets in the village leading up to the Inn. Darren had a good prayer time with Brent earlier, but was trying to practice closing his eyelids just a bit more, for when he was carefully listening for anything, his eyes always seems to be wide open and buggy looking, and he didn't want to give any hint that he was unnerved or disturbed.

Everything looked normal around him. Candy's Bakery Shop was kitty-corner to the Inn, and the name made him laugh as he thought, *"Shouldn't she be in candy?"* Someone had designed a large smoke shop that carried beer and other spirits resembling a memory of some gas station years before the millennium started. The walls around the front half of the station were some sort of super Plexiglas that endured wind and powerful gunshots. Everyone could see the front half of everything in the store because of the see-through Plexiglas. It was part of the novelty. Yet, at night, a steel mesh window covering would come down and lock the place up tightly only to open late the next morning for lunch to all who were thirsty and wanting a place loud and fun to get lost in. The wonders of the bright red and white rounded looking gas pumps, like retro gas stations from a millennium before and revolving doors into the other part of the store, made this place a curiosity.

Further down the street was a restaurant that made barbeque and smoked meats their specialty. That place was called Bear Pa's. Clothing stores and souvenir shops encompassed Darren's vision, and he thought it might be kind of nice to get to know this town a bit better sometime. He'd have to run that thought past Brent.

Nearly forgetting his appointment across the street, Darren shook his head and walked as casually as he could across the intersection to meander into the Inn. It was getting late, and he didn't want to be there. He looked around and didn't see anyone necessarily watching him. The Inn was about four stories tall and planked with what he figured was pine and high-tech stain. He recognized the knots in the wood, all solid and full of character as knotty pine could be. It was quiet on the other side of the doors. What did he expect? People are supposed to sleep here! Taking a big breath, Darren told himself all he had to do was go through the doors and find Jason, and watch his back.

Once inside, Darren noticed to his left a sunken lounge area to sit and drink one's coffee or maybe meet a party and fellowship for a while there. Each chair or couch was an invitation to sink one's self in the over-comfy, over-sized big chairs. The sectional was what one might find in someone's recreational room in front of an over-sized TV screen. Over-sized was such a good word for all of it! He laughed to himself. Even the fireplace was oversized! Looked good to him!

He would love to sink in one of those chairs and leave his problems behind. Walking a bit further, to his right was a couple of clerks with noses in their computers—every once in a while whirling around to grab a key out of a nook type shelf to hand to some customer. Keys, huh? That had to be part of the ambiance they were trying to create from some old times long ago. Cute.

The further Darren walked, the truth of the quietness seemed to fade as loud and boisterous people's voices were heard as they tipped their beers and whatever else they found to tip. He knew Jason would be found in that room.

"Keep your back to the wall, Darren." Darren would rehearse in his mind the old but true safety tactic. It didn't look like that was going to be very easy to pull off. Darren entered the salon of clamor and peered through the smoke and haze. Off to his right a man jerked his head up looking in a particular direction, and Darren followed that gaze right to Jason.

Jason caught Darren's entry to the lounge and all of a sudden acted like Darren's best friend. He held up a stout and waved

Darren in with it. He smiled from ear to ear and pursued Darren until Darren's feet finally moved.

~℘~

Somewhere up in the hills of what used to be Issaquah, and now Tall Pines, drove a young woman with two children; missing one dog, and going totally on survival instincts imbedded in her DNA. But even *that* was useless without the nudging and obedience to the Holy Spirit Krista leaned on, and she knew it.

Tall Pines still resembled the Swiss Alps as its multi-layered hills led to the Snoqualmie Pass mountain area. There were old logging roads seemingly as numerous as rabbit trails that led in many directions. Wildlife had repopulated through the centuries but there weren't as many men to abate them. The trees could hush any movement or wake it up, and in their expansive arms Krista took refuge.

~ Chapter Six ~

THE CITY OF God. No one could describe it accurately, nor would each story be exactly the same as another's. The beauty was non-parallel to any grandeur that had ever been on the earth before the millennium. Las Vegas tried, but was plain and quite ordinary in comparison; the equivalent of particles of sand when compared to the City of God. The City of God was two-thirds the size of the United States, times twelve levels, but was located where Israel once was. It hovered in the air, yet connected to the earth through ostentatious stairwells, escalators, and elevators that gleamed and shone.

The escalators alone ever rolled toward the treasure house of His kingdom around the city leading up to the entrances where His most beloved family lived. They were liquid silver with rainbows of colors electrified in glowing particles throughout. The streets inside the city were translucent gold, yet glittered in places from reflections as the light of God would hit a lively lake or sea at just the right angle. Flowers, trees, mansions, and various blue skies also reflected in the golden streets on each of the multi-colored levels. Each stage of divided floors all caught the light of God's glory and His magnificence differently, as each level had its own beauty and splendor different from the other. The jeweled walls that decorated the outside of this city penetrated the air, releasing particles that gave extraordinary life and depth wherever one looked.

Walking into the City of God made one's status of royalty an understatement. Here, the King of kings resided, and His Father's glory rested. Around the City of God was God's throne; it resided in the top seven levels and could only be seen by believers. How something so real could not be seen by those who dwelt on the earth was one of God's many mysteries. Each believer had access to the throne of God, but only timed access to enter the brilliance of which no human words could ever describe its radiance and glory.

Planes directed by jet streams around the city kept the earth's flying crafts away from it. Many people who flew could see the City of God as high as airplanes went, but they could not gaze into the area of God's holy throne. They believed the throne to be a myth.

In the stunning light of God's glory and opulence were chambers the size of mammoth coliseums that dwarfed the pre-millennium's stadiums and coliseums. Scores of these coliseums held movie screens as large as house, and they revealed real life images. The rows of screens would disclose what was happening at any given place. These screens would be twenty feet apart from the other and each one took up at least one hundred square feet. The walls within these chambers would carry at least five of these screens high, winding around two-thirds of the room, and then at the bidding of Father's word, one or more angels would step right into the very scene taking place anywhere in the world. Four different levels of crystal glass flooring held rows of people and angels to view whatever level they were on. Myriads of angels were seen everywhere throughout the entire room.

Other chambers that existed reviewed the past history of God's creation, where a human could walk into any era or any point of history to review, learn, or rejoice over how God put the beginning together with the last. Angels also could go in and out of the history screens; although many were there teaching and sharing alongside many of the saints who wanted to go in and out of those screens during those times while observing more closely. It was one of the multitudes of blessings God reserved for those who faithfully served Him before they died.

Standing by, in each chamber of present time, were warring angels and blessing angels, as well as those who protected, intervened, or were just answers to prayer to minister in any way the Master bid. Often, when one observed the activity of angels flitting in and out of the scene, it was like a part of God's glory went with the angel. A trail of light would appear then disappear as fast as it had appeared. It was a mesmerizing site to behold no matter how many times someone watched. Every awe or remarkable feeling that was experienced in heaven never seemed to dull the next awing moment. The awe never quit.

~ Chapter Seven ~

D ARE, MY MAN! Pull up a chair! I have a beer waiting here for you."

"Aahh, that's all right, Jason, I really don't drink."

"No problem, Dare; I figured that, so I had them serve up an ice-cold virgin beer just for you!" Jason winked at the bartender who pretended to be preoccupied but glanced up just in time. "It's great! You'll love it! Have you had one of these before?" Jason slid the mug, slightly slopping over the rim, right in front of Darren.

Darren took a deep breath. *"How can I not look paranoid right here?"* "Sure, this is fine." Darren managed a grin while he stared at his fake beer, hoping it would disappear on its own. To be polite, he wrapped his thick worn hand around the long ridged handle to show a hint of respect and the promise of a drink he was to take.

"Hey, let's go over here." With that, Jason put a convincing pull on Darren's left arm as to escort him elsewhere.

Darren let some drink spill over the edges while they walked toward a table.

"Drink up, Dare. It's good for ya." Jason cackled out a good laugh, and they sat down near an exit of the noisy pub.

"Jason, what's this about my family?" He put the beer up to his lips, but kept his mouth closed as much as possible. Looks meant everything.

Squirming in his seat just slightly, Jason recovered with his best grin and seemed pleased Darren had taken a swig, "Dare, I hate to be the one to break this to you, but your kid brother has run away from home and headed out here. He found the headquarters of the base camp and the boss thought you should know. We need you to get him back home and, ah, out of the way...ya know, somewhere safe, where he belongs. He's just too young to be here with this gang. Ya know? This just isn't the place for him. Maybe in a couple of years..." Jason trailed off as though he was planning for someone's future.

Darren tried to take it all in. His kid brother? It wasn't like Kyle to rebel or chase around for any reason. Time for a Holy Spirit check. However unsettling it was, Darren took the bait for a moment.

Snohomish County was a good hour's drive to where headquarters was, but he would certainly high-tail it out of there if there was any truth behind Jason's speech.

Jason could see Darren wasn't buying this but was prepared for that. "Hey, Dare, I didn't want to believe it myself. But these days, things are crazy. Haven't you noticed that?" Before Darren could answer, he continued, "Kyle says he has something important for you to know, and that he didn't really run away, but had to find you."

That eased Darren a little bit; still, he had to listen to the Lord on this. "Hey, Jason, I need to head out and think on this. Sure, I believe you, but I need to get out of here to prepare to pick him up. So, the office is still open?"

"Nah, the boss left his address for you to meet your brother on the east side of Lake Sammamish up in the hills." Jason reached in his inside pocket and pulled out a map and address and handed it to Darren. "You can get him there, bud." Jason slapped Darren on the back which caused a red flag warning bell that bolted through Darren's spirit. "We're here for ya, Dare. But hey, drink up!"

Not to show he was shaken, he put his mouth up to the rim again and put it down, letting it purposely slosh out. Darren acted like he appreciated Jason. "Thanks, man." He grabbed the paper and got up from the table to make his way to the front door. He needed to find Brent, and if this was going to happen, he wanted reinforcement.

Once outside, Darren started to look around for Brent, but much to his surprise Hank was leaning up against the Inn in a cloud of cigarette smoke. Thinking he could ignore him, Darren started a quick pace in the opposite direction when Hank practically jumped out at him.

"Hey, Darren! The boss told me to give you a lift to his place tonight. Guess he wants to see both of us. It's his idea, and I didn't argue. My truck is right over here." Hank pointed to a blasé brown vehicle.

Darren's right eye-brow arched in "all right" reaction as he slowly walked, yet felt propelled to go with Hank, toward the vehicle.

Hank was right behind him, slapped him on the back and said, "How ya feelin', bud?"

Darren just waved him off as he went around the front of the cab to get in.

Hank tried to catch a good look without being seen to see if Darren was sober. Hank figured it was just a matter of time.

Hank took the less traveled way to Sammamish via Preston and Hi-way 202.

"Hey, man, isn't it shorter to take 405?" Darren was throwing sharp glances all around him.

"Nah,". He looked dark and troubled and lost in his crazed little world. Every once in a while he would check out his rear-view mirror.

Nothing odd with that, Darren thought. But seeing Hank tapping his wheel whenever he did, now that was interesting. *"Lord, what do You want me to do?"*

Twenty minutes or more into the drive, Hank pulled over in the depth of the forest. "Hey, man, sorry, but I've got to acquaint myself with nature out there."

"Sure, man," said a wary Darren.

Flashes of light came as quickly as lightning, and it wasn't clear just what it was. Darren reeled his head around to see, but couldn't turn his body around in the seat until after he took off his seat-belt. He couldn't see anything moving out there, but he knew he had seen something past where Hank had disappeared to. *"What was it?"*

He hadn't even watched carefully where Hank had gone; it wasn't polite. *"Sheesh, what a dummy I am! I'm more concerned about being polite than my own safety! Get a grip, Darren!"* Darren figured his reaction of self-degradation was just another distraction, so he tried to focus.

"Agh! Hey!" Bam! Branches broke—snapped—and it was done. Suddenly, a body scrambled out of the woods right toward Darren.

"Get out of the car, Darren! Get out!" Brent was racing toward him stumbling and groping to stay upright.

Darren grappled in shock for the doorknob, wherever it was. This time he forgot about his bulging eyes.

As Darren stepped out of the truck, Brent grabbed him—out of breath and gasping for the next. "Darren, follow me!" The two went clambering to another vehicle hidden behind thick boughs.

Darren looked back toward Hank. There was a faint schism of light blues and reds fanning up like an arch, vibrating and almost resounding. *"Why would the presence of God be there?"*

Stumbling into the car, the two gave a quick glance at each other. Almost afraid to grin, one slightly crept on their faces anyway. They didn't dare feel safe yet. Then Darren's mind shook out of its ambient fog, "What about my brother? I need to get to my brother!"

"I know, I know," panted Brent. It was all he could get out at the time.

Darren was fidgeting like a cornered varmint.

Brent recouped as fast as he could for Darren's sake. "Look, man, I overheard a conversation that could have killed me instantly had they known." Taking a long breath to encourage his recovery, "You were set up. Mal and some lynch guys had it all planned out for you to take the sting of Hank's death. They figured with all of the heckling they'd given you lately, you'd be a likely subject to get back at one of them."

Darren was still balancing his anxiety over his brother with this new-found report. He was about to open his mouth when Brent kicked right in with the rest of the story.

Brent had the truck in drive now heading down the road. "Your brother didn't run away. It was a fabricated story to gain control of you." Brent looked carefully at Darren with the help of the dash-board lights. "Are you feeling all right? Aren't you sleepy, groggy, or weak, or anything?"

"No, man. They—I mean Jason—tried to put a beer down me. It must've been potent, whatever they put in that "virgin beer." I pretended to take a big swig, and Jason seemed pleased with that, watching to see me keel over or something. I think that was supposed to happen in the truck, actually, on the way to the boss's place. Does he live on the east side of Lake Sammamish in the hills?"

"I don't know, Dare. I only went to headquarters in Snohomish somewhere when I got out here. This is all pretty new to me. Had I not heard their route for you tonight, you may have been a goner even if you were sober. You are sober, aren't you?"

"Well, yeah, I didn't drink anything." After taking a few more moments to catch his breath, he said, "So now what, Brent? And hey! What did you do to Hank? I heard some awful yelling, but it sure didn't last long. What did ya do?"

"Me? I didn't do a thing!" Brent was grabbing the wheel as though it was holding him up.

"I'm tellin' ya, I didn't do anything. I saw two big thugs whomp on Hank's head and gut before he hit the ground. I turned my back to it behind this huge tree, see..." Brent trailed off thinking on something that hadn't occurred to him. "Hey, maybe their clubs or wood slabs are still back there. Maybe we should go back."

"No way, Brent! Going back where we just came from feels really wrong, and leaving there feels really right. Just keep going."

Brent was lost in his thoughts while his SUV made it to the highway. Tonight, they would be sleeping under the stars.

~φ~

Out in the woods in a bloody pool of death, Hank lingered, his breathing labored with a heart clearly broken. *"Call on the name of Jesus."* Isn't that what Brent said earlier? Fighting to be coherent, Hank remembered that talk with God he had after he left Brent earlier that night in a huff. No one knew but him the turmoil and grappling with life he and his wife had gone through the past few years and especially recently. Her parents had died just days ago. They had always talked about the God of the universe. His wife wasn't acting nuts since their death. She had some crazy peace that really was perplexing him. He had his own searching going on that had been festering in his confused heart the past five years since his own sister died. Jesus was all his sis could talk about; now his wife.

Broken and lifeless, desperation found no protocol, nor worthy arguments. In a fitful whisper, with tears wetting the sides of his bruised and bloodied face, Hank moaned and pleaded, "Jesus. If you're real, rescue me." And that was all he needed to give as his last breath wafted into the night air.

～ℓ∂～

Those in the glory throne room of God applauded with the angels. They could get used to this! As an angel stepped out of that picture, the screen closed and was replaced with another location for another angel positioned to intervene and minister. All over God's realm, around His beloved city, screens closed and opened. Some of God's children remembered in awe how they once thought three-dimensional movies in IMAX theatres were exalting! What a silly thought it seemed to them now as those theatres and screens of long ago were no comparison to this. They gazed upon God's very presence on every screen as angelic hosts moved and disappeared in a twinkling of an eye into screens with rich and deep dimensions, drawing onlookers in as though they were virtually there.

~ Chapter Eight ~

KRISTA AND THE children had found a nice cove type refuge far up into the hills the night before to snuggle into and catch some sleep. Checking for the witness of the Spirit within her for peace and stability, she took advantage of this place to rest. It would be awhile before she would get back to her house, but at least she was always prepared with blankets, drinks, and some easy energy food packed away in the car. She knew very shortly they would need more than that, or hopefully find Grandpa and Grandma soon. She really missed Misty.

Children always look like angels when they are sound asleep, Krista thought. Morning was upon them, and Krista took this time to commune with God and get a sense as to what lay ahead for the day. Some days were easier to navigate than others. They were told in the City of God that angels would frequently appear to them for guidance. Krista wished this would be one of those times.

About forty-five minutes later, while Krista was in worship, she could hear little moans and sweet murmurings. She knew that the children were stirring awake. Krista was ready to clean them up and plan out their adventure for the day.

After their tasty, simplified breakfast, Krista nuzzled her back to a tree, sat down, gathered each child next to her, and invited them to pray with her. The children were all smiles; they pranced their little legs and clapped their hands as they enjoyed His presence! Krista was getting used to this constant humbling feeling as fresh tears filled her eyes. How much more God the Father must be touched when his adult children were excited to worship and commune with Him. That was a thought she figured she would build on later. She knew in her heart she was always glad and eager to spend specified times with the Father. She hadn't pranced, however!

Thirty minutes later, all filled in his little spirit, Rusty announced, "I'm hungry!"

"You can't be Rusty! You just had something to eat!" Krista responded with perplexity.

"But I am." His voice slid up in little more than a hushed tone. "Mommy told me that I get extra hungry when I go through growth spurts. I think I am growing, Krista." He threw his arms around her neck and smiled ever so gently right in her face.

Krista took it all in. No one ever told her that her heart could melt over a child, especially one that wasn't hers! She smiled and glanced over to Sissy who nodded her head in agreement. She wasn't hungry, but she sure was her brother's best pal.

"Okay, kids, let's get all of our stuff together and get into the car! If it is food we need, Tall Pines it is!" They probably had no idea where the place was or what it was, but it sounded promising, and they trusted Krista completely. She sounded happy, and they could barely keep from bursting with joy.

One thing was for sure, it was a simple answer to prayer for direction. Krista knew lots of *to-go* food shops and stores with special bakeries and delis that would satisfy even a king. Their path was set, and they made ready to go.

Piling into the comfy and cozy, red zoom-zoom, Sissy wheeled around right before she got in. She looked beyond the trees, and her gaze went up onto a little knoll.

"What, Sissy?" asked Krista. *"Another angel? More light showings?"* Krista wondered.

"I heard something, Kissta." At that, Rusty leaned out of the car door for a moment. They all listened carefully. Several moments went by, and there was nothing.

"Seatbelts on!" commanded general Krista as all settled in; she put the car in low gear. The car crawled its way down the narrow grassy road with a little bump here and a little bump there as though it had to wake itself up.

"Missy! Missy! Missy!" yelled Sissy, as she had not yet put her belt on and was on her knees staring out the back window.

"I'm sorry, honey, but Misty got lost last night," Krista tried to sooth the cries.

"Missy! Missy! Missy's here, Kissta!"

By this time, Rusty was up on his knees too and joined in the yelling, "She's here! She's here!"

Krista put on the brakes, and without warning, hers eyes blurred up as she pushed the door open to look where the children were staring. She couldn't see anything.

"Oh no, are they just imagining this because they wish it so hard?" Krista scanned every inch of ground.

"Rark rark!" Out of the low-lying brush ran a silky black, and ever so blissful, dog. Bounding across the little ground left to get to Krista, Misty flew into Krista's arms and licked her face rapidly and reassuringly. Everyone was out of the car, and the kids did their giddy dances as they enjoyed having Misty back safe and sound.

"She's all right, Krista! Look at her!" Rusty exclaimed with wide eyes and disbelief.

Sure enough, there wasn't one scratch on Misty and she was as beautiful as ever. Krista and the kids took time to thank the Lord with all of their might. It was a blissful time.

With one more thing to buy at their destination that would appease a loving dog, the now foursome high-tailed it out of the dense, deep emerald forest to Tall Pines Village. There was a lot of rejoicing going on. Oh, what a happy day!

~ꝑ~

"Rrrmm!" Going at a good clip, a red sports car passed Brent and Darren. "That was close, Brent! Someone should take out a few trees here for a better view of that road."

"Yeah," said Brent slowly. His eyes followed the car with a strange feeling in his heart. *"Do I know that car or those people?"* He didn't know exactly why, but he felt like he should know them. *"Just another one of those mysteries that keeps popping up ever since the Millennium passed, and what would a red car like that be doing up here anyway?"*

"Did you see a dog's face hanging out the window?"

"Huh? Oh, uh, yeah, I did!" Brent snapped out of his fog. "Probably just some campers. Let's head into town for some food before we head back to Zipper. I'm glad I left him with the trailer's maintenance gal. He must be wondering about me!"

~?~

In the meantime, the joyous four were making their plans for a meaningful breakfast.

"I want hotcakes, Krista! Sissy and I haven't had those for a long time. Could we have bacon too?"

As always, Misty looked at Krista as though she understood the whole conversation with eyebrows arched and questioning eyes.

"*Oh, I've missed that,*" mused Krista. "Yep! That sounds like a terrific plan, kids! I know just the place. It's going to be lots of fun."

Bear Pa's was a relic in its own right. Each plate of food for one was more like a platter for four. Stuffed animals and historical objects decorated the outside as well as the inside of this fabulous eatery.

Owner, Blake Adams, and his family survived in the mountains during the wrath of God and throughout all of the many centuries.

Flowing artesian wells were not very well known near the desert lands in the southern regions of Colorado where the headwaters of the Rio Grande were located. But Blake's family was tough—a survival minded people. They hid out in desolate areas in the high hills and found those wells. It seemed then like a supernatural supply, and indeed it was for those left behind. There the family remained until they could re-establish themselves again.

The mountains became their friend. Apparently, they weren't alone. Others thought this was a good hiding place; many Christians and non-Christians alike settled there whether from the leading of the Lord or what others thought to be common sense in an ever-increasing evil government.

As Blake told it, his family didn't believe in all that religious stuff. Their area was inundated with Christians from all over. Thankfully, as Blake revealed, so many people shared with his family about the Lord, His rapture, the wrath of God, and so much more, that when the rapture actually took place—and they disappeared just as they said they would—the Adamses became quick believers.

With horror-filled seasons and many deaths amongst his clan those many years ago, the Adams family became a formidable, "daring to live" folk that had many offspring to show for it. Without the luxury of plenteous doctors in their myriad of fields of exper-tise, all of life struggled to survive for decades to come. But God, in all of His glory and eagerness to bring yet more to His eternal plan of life and not death, knew everyone who had survived and where they were planted.

After the days of the rapture, the years were filled with moun-tains collapsing, borders realigning, the sky falling, and numbers beyond counting ending up dead. All of the considerably strange phenomena that had taken place seemed to last forever. People in different regions throughout the world had their own stories, never the same as someone else's. But with Blake's family's stories, there were some whoppers about the grizzly bears and how the Adams crew found themselves protected and regularly fed by these grand critters.

One of the many stories one could hear after having sat down for a while in this vast and enormous restaurant was when Great-Great-Great-Great-Great...Grandpa Nathaniel went for a walk one particular day out of the cave that his family had been hiding out in. There were caves that had long channels of pathways going to other places; but with several people helping, easy barricades were erected so others could have some form of privacy. A lot of home stuff, such as cushions, tables, linens, dishes, and anything else that was able to make the journey up over the rough terrain, had been brought up to the caves in order that living might have some con-temporary feel about it—with a good imagination.

The Adamses, by now, had become solid if not astute believers in the Lord, and carefully followed what was written in the beloved but worn pages of the Bibles the believers had left behind.

Already miracles had manifested to the Adams family and the groups around them. Eventually, the whole community of them, about fifty persons in all, had come to believe. Their unity was just the right recipe to see God unfold His amazing and almighty hand toward them.

The night before that particular day that Grandpa Nathaniel walked out of the cave in desperation, the families had a group gathering to pray for food and for God's wisdom on how they might come upon such a necessity. Food had been scarce and light volcanic ash covered the autumn berries. Before dawn the next morning, Nathaniel stirred himself awake from an odd dream about thick fur, smells of barbeque, and a gnawing stomach pain. With nothing to comfort his thoughts or belly, he set out to pray and walk outside. He was drawn to walk toward the main stream about a half mile away. A couple of tributaries flowed closer to their caves where they drew water from. The water was clear and pure, and they continually thanked God for the remarkable blessing.

Nathaniel headed out along the cliffs to the small natural plateau leading to the main stream. They named the stream LeTort after some famous stream in Pennsylvania known for its brown trout that always kept the fly-fisherman challenged and for its baby streams that kept major flooding in control for the main stream. It was a haven and a headache all in one. The fish were not easy to catch and seemed smart. No one had fishing rods, and no crafty plan of catching the tasty morsels had succeeded. Nevertheless, Nathaniel neared the site to hear from God; besides, he felt compelled to be there.

Frighteningly, some twigs snapped upwind from Nathaniel. It was like a slow motion snap, carefully, though heavily. Nathaniel mentally thanked the Lord he was not downwind from that, and froze in place.

Had he paid attention to his journey? Had he been clambering his way through the paths not heeding precautions about the presence of wildlife?

His blood chilled, and nausea tapped his empty stomach. His

eyes immediately blurred from the fear and he tried oh so hard to see down through the thickets of brush and bramble to wherever that sound came from.

"Don't move, don't move," came the thoughts. Nathaniel was in agreement with that, but still fought to see why. Many moments passed that seemed forever.

At last a hint—no—it was obvious; a growling grunt came from what could be nothing else but a grizzly. That is the last thing Nathaniel wanted. Obeying that small voice that had told to him to hold still, he watched as his eyes slowly cleared up, and dawn broke over the trees.

The grizzly stretched upward to stand on his hind legs, methodically sniffing the air. He cast his gaze from the left to the right, seemingly to nod while distinguishing various scents.

Nathaniel knew nothing about how good or bad eyesight was for grizzlies, but he knew if he didn't move, there would be nothing to catch the grizzly's attention. He hoped.

The grizzly went back to being on all fours and headed toward the stream.

"Were there other grizzlies in the area?" Nathan couldn't quiet the fearful thoughts coming until he purposely silenced them with a choice to believe that Jesus was standing right there with him. He gave out a little sigh resigning to greater peace, but still had a ways to go. Then, as the grizzly looked up stream, opposite of Nathaniel's hold, Nathaniel felt free to duck down behind a thicker bush to his right, nearer the stream. He somehow needed to keep an eye on this furry beast.

Furry! His dream shot back in his thoughts, and without any reason, a smile came over his face. A new perspective entered his mind, which gave him new peace and determination to watch what the grizzly would do. *"I think I am in God's will,"* thought Nathaniel.

On all fours himself now, Nathaniel quietly crept toward the edge of the stream and hid behind one of the many boulders lining the shores. He spotted the massive creature slowly maneuver his way out to a place of advantage. Maybe God had Nathaniel there to learn how to catch the fish in the stream. Could he learn from a bear? Wasn't there something in the Bible to learn from animals or something? Right then and there Nathaniel named the bear Ben because of some TV show he had watched decades earlier, and this made Nathaniel relax even more. He now felt his outing was more of a lesson than terrifying act, and he was going to stick to that story for the time being.

Ben, the reddish, thick furry brown bear waded out into the stream, eyeing fish flipping around as if they were shooting for some invisible star in the air, only to land deep into the stream with a current a human would rather avoid. The weight of the bear seemed unaltered by the current as he hoisted himself half way up to swat at the elusive fish flicking and diving—just out of reach. This didn't seem to work for Ben as he needed better balance and control. Ben had been there before.

Looking around again, Ben felt unchallenged as he stepped over to a slight rise in the middle of the stream. Maybe his position would cast more fish his way. Jagged boulders, some more smooth than others, had remembered footholds for Ben. Ben nodded his head around to take inventory of his circumstances like he was part desperate, or wise. Only the bear knew. Then all of a sudden, up jumped a fish and out went a swat! The fish went hurling back onto the shore, flopping on uncomfortable ground. Swat! Another fish went hurling and landed by the other.

Now this is a very tall tale Nathaniel thought to himself. No one, but no one, would believe what he was seeing.

Swat after swat, fish landed on shore, and the bear would grunt or growl in pure pleasure. This went on for over five minutes before Ben seized a beauty between his teeth and headed back to land.

Nathaniel was perplexed. He had no idea that bear did this. "*This wasn't his imagination was it?*" He slapped himself and decided that was just about as silly, so he waited another ten minutes before venturing from his hiding place. How many other bears would be around for fishing he could only wonder.

"*Get the fish,*" Nathaniel heard.

"*Whoa,*" Nathan mumbled to himself. He had just stood up, but he sat back down for that. "Get the fish" was the same voice that told him to not to move earlier, so he wanted to make sure he had that straight in his spirit and mind before taking the risk. He carefully stood back up again, slowly looking for any sign of movement anywhere. He was still upwind from the site where the fish lay silently. He couldn't quite see where they all landed, but figured he would be able to smell them when he got closer.

"*That's right, you don't smell fish if they're healthy and fresh,*" Nathaniel reminded himself. He knew a little about cooking when he had had loads of money way back when.

He figured he was about fifteen feet away from the fish when he saw them wriggling and snapping around. Their scales sparkled in the morning light like flecks of the rainbow. It was a great sight to see.

All of a sudden, another snap of brush or something came crashing in Nathaniel's ears. This was too close for comfort. "*What, God? What do I do?*" Frozen on the spot, Nathaniel was too frightened to turn around. Again, he didn't want to move, but God didn't tell him that this time.

Maybe it was just God's timing for Nathaniel to go home now after that beautiful show that had just been given him. Nathaniel braced himself and chose to die in peace and thanksgiving.

"Nate! Nate! Is that you, man?"

"*Huh? An angel beckoning him to go home?*"

"Nate! Tell me that's you!" called out Levi, one of the guys living in one of the chambers of the cave.

Fear on hold for the moment, Nate turned around and saw Levi walking toward him crunching the ground below.

"Shh! There are bears around!" answered a frantic Nathaniel in a loud whisper. Geesh, he didn't need this. Nathaniel looked everywhere for any sign of bears. Thankfully, none were visible.

Levi stood beside Nathaniel looking down at the fish. "How did you get these, Nate?"

"I—uh, well, I was watching this bear, and here are these fish."

Nathaniel didn't feel like he was going to explain it all now, and he certainly didn't want to take the time to.

"Levi, let's put these fish in our shirts and head back to our homes. I think God just did a miracle here. But don't ask me about it now, let's just get these and run out of here!"

Still not sure if the bear was setting him up or not, Nathaniel mentally leaned more toward God having done a miracle, so they walloped the fish and carried them in their big T-shirts and rejoiced, oh so happily, yet oh so quietly, back to their homes. From that day forward, miracles of food came in all kinds of ways, and Nathaniel had other unusual encounters with Ben. But that's another story.

Blake never tired of that story. He had more fun watching people's eyes bug out and bodies fidget in their seats while telling it. Somehow, some way, Blake managed to point to a couple of bear hides, heads attached and all, on his walls and bring them into his story about Ben. By the time he was at that point in his story, most people had forgotten that Nathaniel and his clan were probably not taxidermists, nor could the animal have stayed as well preserved over all those years in the technology of the early 2000s. People may hear a story from the past, but they usually carry today's culture and technology in their heads while listening. That's part of the art of good story telling.

~ɛƒ~

Krista pulled into Bear Pa's to enjoy the oversized servings at one tremendous good deal, hoping for lots of leftovers for their impending journey. She knew the children were going to have the time of their lives seeing all of the artifacts and trophies of other stories that flew around in that restaurant. Krista smiled as she piled out of the car with the cute twosome while Misty waited knowingly and happily, as her tail could reveal, for she would have to wait to get her first taste of chow—bacon, sausage, and biscuits with gravy—out in the car.

"Krista! Look at that bear standing up next to the door! Is it real?"

Krista rolled her eyes realizing that perhaps she had gotten into more than she bargained. But perhaps that would be part of the fun.

~උ~

"Brent, I don't know about you, but I'm starving. We got paid yesterday, and I'm feeling mighty rich. What do you say we head to Bear Pa's? I've waited two weeks to try that place. I feel like I could eat a bear!"

Brent laughed. "I had the same thought. You talked me into it, Dare! I'm draining fast and could use a great meal right now. I say we do it!"

"Yes!" exclaimed Darren with a shout. This was going to be a good day, he just knew it! The tension of the last night had drained away with the good night's sleep and with the thought of steak and eggs dancing in his head. He got lost in his appetite with the hope of pure deliciousness.

~ Chapter Nine ~

ITH HAPPY TUMMIES and clean bodies, as much as was possible in the restrooms, the fierce threesome went out to the car to get the fourth one of the pack. "*What now, God?*" It just seemed so apparent to stay in town and take the dog for a walk. Krista just knew that all would be ready for a long trek to some seaside dwelling where hopefully a couple of grandparents were eager to receive the precious cargo.

"Okay! We're going to pass some shops and head toward a park. Maybe there is something we can buy to make our trip more interesting?" Krista just threw that out for reaction with hopes of more inspiration.

"I've got my sling-shot, Krista. I don't think I need anything." Rusty was simple and knew "what was what" as far as he was concerned. That sling shot stayed in his back pocket wherever he went. What more could an adventurous nine year old boy want anyway?

His little sister Sissy was a new five-year-old, but already thought that clothes had importance.

"Kissta, can we buy me some new shoes?" Krista looked down at Sissy's shoes and remembered a thought she had last night when she took them off. She was ready to respond to this.

"You got it little one. I know just the place for you." Krista had the immediate urge to pick her up and carry her. This just felt so good.

While the little tribe went shopping, Brent and Darren walked out of the sumptuous eatery. With a big yawn and stretch Brent declared, "I think the big meal and last night is catching up to me. I wouldn't mind a nap. Where can I drop you off, Darren?"

"I'm up for a long nap myself. I felt so energetic when we got here! Just take me back to my place, and I'll catch up with ya later," he said with a slap on Brent's arm.

49

"Good enough." replied Brent.

Walking out to the truck, Brent noticed the red sports car along the back side of the parking lot next to the trees.

"Hmmm, hey, Darren, did you see that red sports car when you got out of the truck when we first got here?"

Darren followed Brent's gaze.

"Nope. Is that the same car that went careening past us up in the hills?"

"Yeah, I think so. That's funny," replied Brent, subconsciously scratching his head. "I keep thinking I know that car or something. How about you?"

Darren was already looking to get into the truck and had to refocus on Brent's train of thought.

"Umm, I don't think so. Why don't you take a look at it?"

Brent paused, "Hmm, Nah….I just keep looking at it, that's all."

"Maybe 'cuz it's red?" Darren scratched his head and headed into the SUV.

The guys took off to relax, but they also wanted to work through the night before. They agreed to gather the next day for church and pray together for the day. They believed God would show them something. It was time to take a closer look at this venture they were on.

~ℓ᠈~

Trumpets sounded. All of the buildings throughout the Great City of God could not mistake the reverberation. Every head turned toward the center of whatever room they were in.

Deep in the belly of the earth, fault lines groaned and ground against each other. Angels were in key positions holding ridges of rock and sediment together, while others kept lids on fiery, red molten lava dancing within itself, looking for opportunities to erupt and liberate its fury. From continent to continent, through the depths of the pits in the shining seas all over the world, the earth's crust and rims were boasting to each other which of them was the most powerful and which would cause the most damage.

Yet creation in its arrogance knew only One who could release the power they were designed to manifest. They waited for their trumpet sound. Each angelic figure held on as they recognized that this trumpet sound was not their command. Yet, they knew...

All of creation waited for a special hour, a special day.

In the meantime, satan, the old rascally devil, hung around a ripe suspect who was hungry for power. Insecurity bred her fears, and fears bred her cunning and chronic lies. Beyond any human's understanding, this deceptively proud woman gave off the most aromatic display of humility that men fell for. They mistook her show of humility as vulnerability, which was like a magnet, an intoxicating perfume to the proud and cocky. Men simply wanted to strengthen her, feel needed, and show her how important they were to her. The fact that Durdana was beautiful to behold was the frosting on the cake. She had magnetism in the supernatural realm. Many targets were aligned for her manipulation, and particular leaders were about to have a transfer of deep and grave darkness.

Although these leaders were spread throughout the four quarters of the earth, each of them represented Gog and Magog, the enemies of God. Durdana had been raised from the one who ruled these leaders—her dad. His influence over them and all of their endeavors together was like dripping gold. Her dad was Emuel Abd-Al-Aziz and was raised from generations of technology moguls and controlling marketers from the Middle East. His family's wealth was undeniable with great forces in the greedy world emerging for final conquer. The City of God was the final and ultimate conquest, and it was in for a big surprise. Emuel and his leaders had mapped out a plan to siege the Beloved City, regardless of its superior technology to emulate something spectacular and foreboding. After all, technology was just a tool of great illusions; and he and his team of leaders had come up with a worthy scheme that would knock God off His Throne, once and for all.

Emuel had studied ancient wars and strategies all his life. When other children were reading fictional fairy stories at bedtime, his dad would read to him about wars and battles with his exaggerated animations and sounds that only stirred Emuel to come up with his own stratagems before entering slumber. Recess at school and summer vacations were periods of testing out these battle plans formed in Emuel's over-active mind.

There was a map or series of maps Emuel and his family, as well as generations before, had searched for increasingly. Emuel believed that the maps revealed a route that the City of God had been hovering above for over a thousand years now. He only knew that the maps revealed a place that had been captured by satellite for years before the wrath of God. Since satan had been thrown into the pit for a thousand years, God had formed a City over Jerusalem's grounds, and satellites had not come back into existence. That was a sore spot for the devil, not being able to have satellite control. He was sure that was all about to change as he gained back control.

The maps were a secret that Emuel was convinced would outdo God and His believers, who were unfortunately popping up all over the world. His informers would report to him all new converts like a well-oiled machine.

It seemed impossible to tell the difference between the believers who survived all of these years and the ones who came from the City of God. Maybe there would be a clue on this hidden and seemingly veiled map that revealed more than just a route under the city.

He just knew there was important information and keys to overcome God and His massive presence in the Middle East. There was only one plan for Emuel, and that was to gain control of this area once again for his people and their fathers before them.

Durdana had the taste for power like her dad. He groomed her in the area of politics. What he didn't realize was what he had taught her from a distance while she observed him. She found that he lied and coerced people with great finesse. She walked in his footsteps. The icing for her cake was that she was well aware of the attraction she had on men, and she used it. She also knew that power hungry men were attracted to her because of her dad, causing them to want her even more. It was hard to know which gave her the upper edge with men: her relentless beauty or being her father's daughter.

The deception of the nations had to come to an end soon, for satan was impatient with his plans. He stewed and planned and re-planned every detail during those one thousand years he was chained in the pit. He did not want to wait any longer.

He had two objectives. One was to build a massive army so great that the City of God would have to spend days just cutting back the numbers while satan's generals maneuvered their way into the heart of the city. The second goal was to stir Emuel up to retrieve the maps that, when put together, made up one large map that gave routes hidden from the eye. He could hardly tolerate thinking about it. His concern was just to obtain it, and then work with it. It angered him furiously that he didn't know everything. Yet, he was confident that the maps were the key to overcome God and His followers once and for all.

The devil knew he could destroy God with his surprise blow within just a matter of months, or weeks if the maps were found soon enough. His impatience was getting the better of him, and he was about to explode with frustration. However, he had to make sure this plan worked.

His hatred for God Almighty kept him busy fuming and figuring, planning and demising. It's what he did, and he liked it. Whatever he did, he had to let man know and believe fervently that all power was really his, and that he would overcome God's show of power. It was easy for him in the centuries before to cause man to believe that God's power was not genuine, and in the latter days, satan hid behind the innovation of technology to convince humankind, in its selfishness, that God's power wasn't real. The devil knew he could use technology to dismiss God's grandeur as pompous and misleading yet again. Man hadn't changed, not really.

All the while he was manacled, he formed plans that he had successfully used before to easily deceive man. He had outsmarted God once before and tore the kingdom down from a third its size; he could finish the job in just eight weeks and destroy Him if everything went right. He threw away his three year plan for a three month plan, and now an eight week plan, feeling more arrogant and conceited by the hour. So much was fitting into place so quickly. He was going to pull out every stop he could to bring the fullness of deceit to the nations and into attacking the Great City of God. His demons were scattered everywhere with a lot of confusion and disruption at every turn. Even though satan had to pull rank and reorganize his hideous dark forces, his motivation was to keep each person away from God in every detestable way imaginable.

Naturally, he wanted to entrench extreme hatred in every soul against God and His selfish city reserved only for His believers. That was easy. All the non-believers already felt some hatred, but they had to become organized and fit into the scheme that had not only been plotted and drooled over during the past millennia, but had been formed centuries before that imprisonment. Every soul God didn't have was satan's aim, and any of God's souls roaming about the earth were practically equal targets. He just wanted ever-lasting revenge and was convinced that he had found a way. He caused serious casualties to God before, and maybe suffered some surprise losses at the end, but this time he would not fail and would embrace much greater success. It was a number's game for the devil; more people for him, less people for God. That was his simple focus and driving force until he lay down his final plan of takeover.

~ℓ𝒹~

The trumpets silenced; the majestic screens near the top of the ceilings opened with skies of remarkable blue and wispy clouds moving and changing shapes while God's messengers directed everyone's attention to what God had to say.

~ Chapter Ten ~

COUNTING DAYS ON the calendar isn't what happened at the City of God. There were calendars, but it was a calendar of seasons and projects, of things to prepare for and things to come. At one time, a calendar page would have, "Salvation Invasion" written across the top, while another heading for a different page would be, "Miracles, Signs, and Wonders". Oh, yes, there were days and events very precious to God with feasts He still held dear to His heart. He also knew days that were precious to the hearts of His people and would surprise them in many ways. It wouldn't be unusual to have someone's spiritual or physical birthday celebrated. After all, God oversaw every birth and released each person into the world to glorify Him. He had purpose over every day, but out of His extraordinary kindnesses, He knew how to highlight various days, seasons, and celebratory moments keen to each individual. Sometimes there would be a day during a season when many people with the same type of celebration would celebrate all at the same time, or at times a person would be singled out where he or she lived. You never knew with God, for He kept surprising and blessing.

Everything God's people did throughout the Great City was in sync with the theme that was going on. Days didn't have earthly value, but were heavenly valued and heavenly minded. There would be moments and days of heavy bustling, and then days of admiration solely set aside to worship the King of kings and the Ancient of Days. That was everyone's favorite day. Fellowship days, worship days, feast days, surprise days, preparing days, teaching days, observation days; the list went endlessly on.

Were there prayer days in the City of God? Everything was perfect all around them, this is true. But when satan was loosed and roamed around the earth after his thousand years were up, people came and went from the City of God bringing prayer concerns with them. People who watched in the coliseums of viewing screens also prayed while watching a "live" situation. Prayer was once again instituted, but it wasn't the pleading that took place on earth. Prayers were thanking God for His Word. They sang prayer requests, they spoke prayer requests, but it was all in a form of worship with His holy Word that kept every saint free and full of joy.

Worship and adoration was a given at every turn, but when the colossal gathering of millions gathered before the throne, it was beyond any awesome and grandeur time of splendor, past all comprehension from when anyone was on Earth dreaming and imagining the glory of God.

Angels would often join in the praise and worship times. On earth there was a time in the Twenty-first Century referred to as "star sightings," which meant that if a movie star or someone famous came into town, the local news people or bystanders with their phones that took pictures would snap a photo of these people, then share it on the news for everyone else to see. Here in the City of God "star sightings" were constant. It was a regular happening to see such great men and women of faith seen standing next to you, such as Daniel, David, Moses, Peter, Esther, Hannah, Paul, Jacob and so many more. Not only would they be standing next to you, but after the worship time and other gatherings, you could strike up a conversation with them, and they might escort you to one of the screens in one of the many coliseums of history. Nothing like hearing Joseph's commentary on what he was thinking and feeling after his brothers betrayed him and sold him into slavery.

God's throne that was to the south as well as round about His city was high and lifted up—*and the train of His Glory filled the temple.*

Each floor of the City of God had its own uniqueness and beauty. Many floors showcased majestic mountains and oceans. Valleys and rolling hills with plenty of flatland and not so flat pastures existed everywhere. Flowers were always in abundance with colors and hues one could not dream about before the city came into existence. Everything exuded the life of God. Nothing died, and everything consumed was instantly replaced. The City of God was heaven brought down. Roads were lined with trees much of the time. Many of the trees were covered in leaves that danced and reflected God's light of glory in glittering colors. Other trees had ample fruit on them, so you could pick what you wanted, and eat when you wanted. The juiciness of each mammoth sized fruit disappeared on your face as fast as it appeared. There was no striving to make anything comfortable for it was all as it should be. It was heaven in a city; it was God's City.

Just like God's Word said in Revelation 22:5, the city was lit from God's own light. Even though God is omnipresent—being anywhere and everywhere at any time; He still sits on the throne. He is the same yesterday, today, and forever!

Because no depression or anxiety existed within the Great City, joy was over the top for everyone all of the time, yet it was deep seated from within. Business was always the order if one looked at the city from a distance, but times of refreshing and relaxing were in abundance. Everyone was different, and each of these people wanted to be doing something in God's Glory. There was structure in the midst of liberal freedom. If it was natural, then men on Earth could wrap their minds around it and try to duplicate it. But that was impossible, for this was supernatural. Minds were not supposed to obtain all of the understanding that only God had.

When God released an announcement, it would usher in a new season. Sometimes seasons were only days long, while others were months long. God, right now, just announced a new season, and the name of this one was, "Marvels and Suddenlies." There was a buzz of excitement that seemed higher than normal. Marvels and suddenlies meant God was going to be glorified a lot in the earth.

However far away the manifestation of God's throne was, while observing it from within the city, you could look toward the throne of God and feel like you could touch the Father. Space and distance didn't follow the same binding rules as on Earth. Here in the City of God, everything was so...heavenly.

A pure river of the water of life, clear as crystal, flowed out of the throne of God.

From God's expansive throne high above and beyond the city proceeded the mightiest and most glorious river that rolled right into the city and branched into three main tributaries. The first tributary flowed into the twelfth floor—God's highest level of the city. Each floor was approximately the size of the western half of the US, give or take a mile. The city was as tall as it was wide. It was like a magnificent Rubik's cube of colors that was made up of precious stones such as sapphire, topaz, emerald, and beryl. Each level was specifically designed with a specific stone of God's choice.

The second tributary flowed into the eighth floor and the third spilled into the fourth level. This living water of God would make massive waterfalls for the levels in-between, and not one level missed out on this river, which seemed never ending, expanding throughout its landscape. The living river of God meandered like a maze from time to time, winding around God's majestic land-scape so different from one level to the next. Each floor was a mar-velous landscape of indescribable and unique beauty. Because the river was clear as crystal, it would take on myriads of hues from that level's stone of architecture. With the twelfth level being ame-thyst, deep purples and light lavenders with flecks of pure gold and flaked diamond dust danced in the river and reflected God's light and glory. You could walk into the river, and the flecks would go right through you.

There was no end to the exuberating experiences God designed for His children.

If someone wanted to see all of the waterfalls, which were plenty, he could take an all day excursion using one super-natural trans-port after another. If a group wanted to see them together, they would simply agree on the level and waterfall they wanted to start at, think of it, and instantly they were there. It took both thought and desire to actually be whisked away to the place you wanted. One was free to think on any of God's blessings and places in the city, but to purposely want to be there at the same time, at any given moment, was the catalyst to show up there in that moment.

Many times, when people discovered how much stunning beauty was around these waterfalls, they would plan longer excursions to discover and explore all the surrounding beauty. There was so much delight over the thought of that, because it was yet another thing to do that would take years! And they had all of eternity to do it.

The pure, crystal, living water of the River of God was ever pulsating, like resonating music or breath from God Himself, that when first timers came, having been brought from Earth after death, they were awe struck because of the beauty and energy flowing through it. There were no words to describe its life.

A group of people in tattered clothing stood at the river's edge on the bottom level. Angels had escorted them from Earth. There was no other way for the new arrivers—the redeemed of the Lord—to enter the City of God but by passing through its river. Today was the most special day for each worn out traveler. One in particular—Hank. Hank stepped into the river of God, into the depths of true life, and came up cleansed on the other side, remembering his sins no more. He and the others would then pick of the tree of life, which grew on either side of the river, and then new life surged through them, and they were no longer the same.

~ Chapter Eleven ~

BRENT WAS REFRESHED after the weekend of ups and downs. He and Darren had hours of praying, reading, and ignitable fellowship the day before. They heard from God. Brent took one last look at the semi-fog filled valley, which had left large dew-drops that sparkled every color of the rainbow, from the edge of the forest where he was working. It was like a glimpse of the City of God he had heard about. He felt the presence fill him up and charge him like a super powered battery, but now Brent was off to fulfill his day of work and see what God had planned.

With his axe over his shoulder, and Zipper at his side, Brent walked on to meet up with Darren who would drive the two of them to the south quarter of Douglas Firs.

Brent loved his mighty axe. Yep, that's what he called it, "his mighty axe." Chuckling to himself, Brent thought about his favorite bed-time story as a child. Pure Paul Bunyan was he! He wanted to be just like him. Of course, Brent could not complete the picture and dream without the best ax made on the face of the earth. It wasn't just any axe. It had been his dad's and his dad's dad, and so forth, back through many generations. There were a few stories that went back to the survival days of God's wrath connected to his axe. Stories he would faithfully pass down to his children or whomever he felt he needed or wanted to share them with. He certainly wasn't going to leave out the fictional story of Paul Bunyan with the real family stories. No sir, not him.

This axe was especially honed out of silver hickory wood, which was a rare wood from before the millennium. Technology was so great in the mid twenty-first century that with biocidal silver, not only would Brent's axe handle last for centuries, it contained a silver gleam and sparkle-like glow that no one else ever possessed, not before or since, to Brent's knowledge. Of course, what made it even more special was that his dad had cleverly put real solid silver in it to refortify it and give it added weight and beauty. Brent had laid down that axe a few times, forgetting exactly where it was. But on nearly any day, the light from the sky would always draw out the shine as though heaven itself was illuminating it. It simply could not get lost.

Axe heads were usually made up of good carbon steel because, with a good sharpening, it would last many years before it had to be replaced. Brent's dad, Allen, had put a new head on it before he died. "There is a secret to this axe, son." Allen would say. "We'll have a special talk over a dinner, and I'll tell you all about it." Weeks had passed before both of their schedules complimented the other so they made a date they could keep for some savory barbeque, all-you–could-eat, dining experience. For years he and his Dad would try to get together every three months for a dad and son dining fellowship. They could talk about anything and everything. He and his dad weren't afraid of a good debate, but most of the time they pretty much agreed on everything. They both loved the Lord and enjoyed their discussions with each other that often provided fresh insight. His dad and mom had that every day of their marriage. Brent could only hope for a relationship like that for himself at this stage of his life. It was a plan, a goal; when he was ready for that, he was confident he would know. He would probably find a different career than logging, which kept him in the forests for weeks on end. He would had to hear from his heavenly Father for all of those details when the time came.

The set date to meet with his dad was fast approaching and Brent's mouth already started salivating whenever he thought about it. They had picked a place they had gone to the year before that served the meatiest baby-back ribs that dripped in a saturated, semi-sweet smoky barbeque sauce that had years of awards to show for its excellence and popularity. This particular meeting time was when Brent lived and worked out of Oregon, and his Dad lived in southern Idaho. The trek to meet his dad in Idaho was not a long trip at the time, and they talked about it for a couple of weeks on the phone. His dad wanted to get together more often since Brent's Mom passed away a few years before that, but they did what they could do. Sis, Brienna, had a few children that Dad would drive or fly out to see in Wisconsin, and that seemed to suit everyone well. They knew Dad was a social being, so in between visits with kids, he was busy with his church and their activities.

The dinner was set for a Saturday night when both of them felt fresh and in need of a good meal. His dad gave him an impromptu phone call Friday morning affirming the dinner date and all was well.

Mid-morning, Brent started to feel a nagging oppression come on him that he couldn't shake. He tried praying during work, but nothing was coming out to relieve him. That lunch hour was taken with a group meeting for the coming Monday's new logging location for another couple of weeks. He had been at his camp and just showered and was ready for a good pray when his sis Brie called with the news of Dad dying in a car accident. It hit Brent head-on for the unexpectancy of it all. Brent knew he shouldn't feel so lost and empty because he knew he would see his dad at the City of God with his mom someday, but still, it was so unexpected! Their dinners wouldn't be anymore. His best friend would not be there at the other end of the phone. Dad's dog Gatlin would miss him terribly as well. Sure, it was wonderful his dad was at the city, but there were so many reasons it wouldn't be the same. Brent just liked having him nearby. He missed him.

Sis took the dog Gatlin, and she and her husband Doug took care of most of the estate settlings. They kept the house in its beautiful rural scenery, and Brent and Brie made it their vacation home to gather together. It was just Brie and Brent now, and they cherished their visits together.

Every once in a while, it would distress Brent that he never found out what it was that his dad was going to share about the axe. A new head was on, and other than that, he couldn't tell the difference. His dad loved a good story, and Brent couldn't get enough of them.

Brent just had to pray and trust God to find out answers that only God could reveal. God was good at telling Brent all kinds of things when he least expected it.

"You know, Zipper? We just may have to head to Idaho and kick back for a few days. What do you think of that, buddy of mine? Hmm?"

By this time, Brent was at Darren's camp, and Darren was standing outside holding a large mug of coffee, sipping and smiling as he watched Brent and Zipper jabber while making their way toward him.

"Hello, Brent and Zip! How are you guys this morning?" Darren always seemed so light-hearted. "What were you guys jabbering about on the way here?"

Brent just laughed. "I think Zipper and I are going to head out to Dad's place in a few weeks. You should join us, Darren! Trees surround the place except for the golf course type lawn Dad cleared out in front of the lake. It's worth a hundred vacations just to get there for a few days. What do you say?"

"What? A vacation with my new found friend? I might go with, Zipper!" Darren teased.

"What a strange sense of humor," Brent thought. But it felt good to feel so light and goofy, even if it was a Monday.

"I talked with my sis yesterday, and she and the family will be there for a week before that. She promised she would stock the refrigerator and plump the beds if I wanted to stay there for a while. If I keep thinking about it, I'll never get any work done here today."

"Hmm, does sound pretty good, Brent." With a twinkle in his eye, Darren said, "Can I get back to you on that? I want to make sure I've cleared the calendar from all my dates. I've got girls lined up all over the place!" He loved keeping up his façade until he could tell Brent he was from the city.

"Yeah, yeah, yeah. So many girls, huh? You crack me up, Dare, you really do."

They swung their equipment into the back of the truck, and Zipper joined the guys in the front.

"I'll say one thing, Brent, today is going to be very interesting on the job. I can't say as I'm looking forward to seeing Mal. But like we said yesterday, we will act like nothing happened and all is well. If we keep our peace in God's presence we will know exactly what to do when we need to. I'm sure glad God fights for us. We asked God to keep us together as a team to work, and that is something I'm very grateful for. God confirmed in us both that He would keep it that way for the time being. What do people do without the Lord, Brent?" Darren just seemed to trail off in his thoughts when Brent piped up.

"I think they walk in fear and make more problems for themselves." With that, Brent looked out the window in a trail of thoughts of his own. Today would be interesting.

~ℓ~

Krista felt that somehow the excitement of last week had lifted, but was also cautious that apathy could be a trap for her. Right now she needed to gage how fast she really needed to get to those grandparents. Did they know their grandchildren had suffered trauma?

All of a sudden it occurred to Krista that she hadn't found out how the kids got to the woods. In all of the excitement, survival was the number one focus and keeping the children calm was her heart. Now she had some unanswered questions that needed to be answered.

As Krista assessed the surroundings and her circumstances, she felt like what she imagined Moses must have felt when the Lord went before them as a pillar of fire at night and a pillar of cloud by day. The Israelites did not move forward unless the pillar moved forward. When it rested, they rested. It felt like the presence of God had rested for part of the day, but late afternoon, God's urging was to have them go and find a different city, then wait for His direction. Regardless of how often Krista had been challenged, she knew there was only one safety route, and that was the will of God—staying in His presence.

The fearsome foursome gathered back into the car; and with

spirits high, they headed south to get to the ocean. What was once a narrow passage called Puget Sound that ran west of Seattle was now a large gulf of water with tiny islands between the island of Seattle and the main coast in Bellevue. Violent storms had taken place along with severe earthquakes that caused large sections all up and down the West Coast of America to disappear. Washington had the Olympic Mountains to guard it's peninsula that was on the west side of Puget Sound. About fifteen to thirty miles were lost to Washington's coast inland, which wasn't bad compared to California and parts of Oregon.

Krista had to drive down to Centralia before she could head west to get to the ocean. Olympia barely existed for many years except for its higher hills like Seattle. It eventually moved its boundaries farther south where many people had hidden in the dense woods and sparse population of the times. The drive from Olympia to Centralia was now only about four miles, for Centralia had become the new capital of Washington and had moved east into the hills. North of Seattle had suffered a lot more than the coast due to tectonic earthquakes in the Strait of Juan de Fuca and the Strait of Georgia, all north of Puget Sound. Puget Sound had been Seattle's port and glory. Its northern neighbors had received towering tsunamis that went inland and wiped out close to thirty miles of beautiful pasture lands, as well as the cities that ran here and there all the way up to Canada. If it weren't for the fact that Seattle included seven hills, it would be non-existent. Bridges to get to Bellevue were destroyed, and flatlands to get to Seattle had been wiped away.

Nothing in the geography of the entire Earth was the same, with few exceptions around some mountain ranges. Billions of people had lost their lives because of the assorted catastrophes during the wrath of God. If earthquakes didn't kill them, tsunamis did. If fire didn't destroy the people, floods and the stench filled water with disease did. Meteors as well as satellites fell from the skies. Volcanic ash was many times worse than anything that had been recorded in history up to that time. Nothing was the same. Some mountains blew up; others just melted and caved in. Hailstones weighing one hundred pounds would fall from the sky, and fire accompanied their onslaught of death. It was all too horrifying for the non-believers left behind. Many of those non-believers became believers because of the message of God's gospel that had gotten out so strongly before all of this happened. They saw the proof of what was preached and prophesied. Then there were the ones who surrendered to the mark of the beast, and all they could do was continually rebel and blame everything on anyone or anything they could think of. They begged for death, but it would not come to them. Many of them knew it was God's wrath and shook their fists at Him, but their fates were sealed. God had spoken, and His will would always be done.

For many years the earth grew cold and little could be done about it for the sun was only two-thirds of what it used to be. This infuriated the non-believers, but never so much so as when the City of God appeared and there was a place of light and warmth for the believers, and only them.

The believers had no desire to ever leave the city for centuries. It wasn't until the past couple hundred years that God sent forth a plan that incorporated plans for various people who had been trained to go out and strengthen the other believers on the earth. God had a plan.

Now that the devil had been released back into the earth, everything seemed to fast-forward. There were believers meeting underground who had to prompt specific things to happen for God's timing to be performed.

Krista was a part of this group; and like everyone else, they had to walk through everyday situations as God helped them make things look normal and undetectable to the enemy's watchful eyes. She never imagined that a part of her assignment would be dealing with children and grandparents. She liked it though, a lot, and was smiling while cruising down the highway.

Easing into the conversation of how she found them to begin with, Krista started asking about their grandparents. "How old are your grandparents, kids?"

"Old," chimed in Rusty. "I think they are fifty something. They once said they had lived over a half of a century, and they told me what a century was, and then what a half century was. But that was a couple of years ago." Rusty's musing, while looking at the scenery outside with Misty on his lap, occupied him.

Sissy was laid out in the backseat resting or sleeping, Krista wasn't sure. She figured that the grandparents were probably near their sixties. She carefully asked the next question. "How old are your parents, Rusty?"

"They're in their thirties. Dad is thirty-five years old and Mom is thirty-three years old...I miss them Krista." With that, Rusty held onto Misty with a cuddly squeeze against his chest and acted like he wouldn't let go. Tears filled his eyes as he watched the landscape glide by.

"Where are they Rusty? Where do you think they are?"

Silence filled the car for what seemed like a long time to Krista while Rusty tried to process what he had seen and heard.

"The angel said we would see them again. I'm going to see my mom and dad again..."

Before Krista could get the next question out about their faith, Rusty added, "We all love Jesus, Krista. The angel told us to keep loving Jesus, and we would see our parents again. I will always love Jesus, Krista." Rusty looked at Krista with pain in his eyes, but an uncommon strength shined behind those eyes for such a young boy. Then he quickly looked away and back to the trees and various houses he could see from the road.

Krista thought of King David for a quick moment. She knew he had red hair, but wondered if he had freckles like Rusty when he was a child. She smiled inside of herself thinking of the joy it would be to ask David when she went to the City of God. That gave her something to look forward to. Now she just wanted to comfort Rusty and learn what happened.

"Can you tell me what happened to your parents, Rusty?" Krista found herself starting to hold her breath, but recouped and concentrated on Rusty while staying in the Spirit.

"Some bad men came into our house, Krista! Dad and them were yelling. Mom was with us in the backroom and told us to run to Aunt Becca's house. She moved over a wall that let us downstairs to get into the cellar that opened up on the other side of the yard. She didn't hug us, but she threw kisses at us. She was in an awful hurry, Krista. She closed the wall behind us, and I heard her voice go away. She was scared."

Krista thought about that for a moment. "Did your Aunt Becca live far away? Did you get to her house?"

Rusty let go of his tight hold on Misty, and his arms became animated telling the rest of his story. "Sissy isn't a very fast runner. We could barely see, but the full moon was out, and she acted all scared, but I got her there. I told Sissy I could run that path blindfolded. You see, we go to Aunt Becca's all of the time. Mom and she would have coffee in the mornings a lot."

Krista just kept silent to let Rusty unleash all that he had been carrying the past several days.

He was breathing quickly now, "Aunt Becca didn't act scared like Mom. Uncle Luke wasn't there, so Aunt Becca took us to another neighbor's house that lived a long ways away. Sissy started to cry, so Aunt Becca had to carry her. I was okay. We had to go through the woods."

Krista would catch him reflecting like he was far away.

"What happened at the neighbor's, Rusty? Were they nice people?"

Rusty broke out of his pensiveness and said, "Oh, yeah! She is really nice! She is one of the ones who came over to our house for prayer meetings."

"Where do all of you live, Rusty?"

"We live in Preston, Krista. We live in Preston. We got to ride in Mrs. McCauley's truck! It goes really fast! She got us not too far from where you found us. She got out of the truck and told us to run down the path as far as we could go and hide under bushes, and that she would come after us. She said she would pray for us and not to worry, for we would see Mommy and Daddy again, and that God would send His angels to watch out for us. We didn't know where we were going, Krista! We were scared! Well, Sissy was really scared. We would see light flash ahead of us, and we kept going in that direction. Mrs. McCauley never came back for us though.

We waited a long time, Krista." Rusty went back to looking out the window, staring at nothing very far away.

"How did you know where to stop and hide? Did anyone chase after you? Did you hear any noises?" Then Krista realized she was asking too many questions all at once, but Rusty didn't seem to mind.

"My dad always told me to call on the name of Jesus anytime anything happened whether I was happy or sad. I called on the name of Jesus. We ran until we felt something all pillowy. We just ran into it! It felt really, really good. So we stopped. I kept whispering Jesus' name, and so did Sissy. After a while, an angel that was so beautiful came in front of us, and his wings were really big!" At that, Rusty spread out his arms as far as he could.

"That is when he told us you would come with your little doggy!" Rusty had the silliest grin on his face, the, "*I told you so*" kind. He was so sure of himself.

Krista felt this confidence was a good strength for him to have at this time. Did she dare ask what happened to his parents again? No, that wouldn't help at this point.

"By the way, Rusty, what is Sissy's real name?" Krista smiled sweetly, knowing she was back on safe ground for Rusty.

"Evie. Evie Suzanne Bastian. Sometimes I call her Evvs. I'm Rusty Bastian! Rusty Arthur Bastian. My dad's name is Arthur. Grandma says it is an important name. I think so."

"Is Rusty what your parents always call you, honey?"

"Nope! When Mom gets angry with me, she calls me Ryan or Ryan Arthur. I'm in real trouble when she calls me Ryan Arthur. Ryan is my real name, but I like to be called Rusty. Almost everyone calls me Rusty."

With that, he smiled with his beautiful blue eyes right into Krista's. She hadn't noticed until then how long his eyelashes were, but they had gotten wet when he teared up, and it was like his eyes glistened.

"Well, Rusty, I'm glad to call you by that name. Now how about you tell me more about where your grandparents live. I need to know if they live near the ocean or in the woods, or in the city. What do you know about their place?"

"Grandma and Grandpa are really cool, Krista." All of the tension had run out of Rusty now, and he talked on about his grandparents with great joy and chattiness. After he talked about what they looked like and things they liked to do, which included reading stories to him and Sissy and taking walks on the beach looking for shells and crabs, he got around to their house and other buildings on the property.

"Is their house near the ocean?" Krista was hoping for more specifics now because she didn't know quite where to go yet but to the ocean!

"Grandpa always said he loved looking at the mountains in his backyard. But they aren't really in his backyard, Krista. He just says that cuz they seem so close and big! We went there a couple of times with Grandpa and Grandma on picnics! I love picnics. Do you know what they are, Krista?"

"Oh yes, I do! I love picnics also. Maybe we could talk your grandpa and grandma into taking us on one when we get there!" Krista realized she had gotten caught up in Rusty's love of where they were going and thought she probably was offering too much of a promise. She had no idea where all of this was going. Would they all be in danger there? But the angel did tell the kids that she was to take them to their grandparents. Surely there must be a good reason, and she would soon find out.

The presence was very strong in the car. Krista had no doubt of their path being just right.

One thing was for certain, Krista's path would be to head north instead of south along the coast. The Olympic Peninsula had taken on some of its own changes, but from the history Krista had read about that region, it seemed almost unaltered after all these years.

Although the tsunamis and storms had taken away a lot of the coast, landslides had been dramatic, and years later, that dirt was hauled to the coast to help in gaining back some land and territory. No one built on that for many years, but after a hundred years or so, things were more stabilized and creativity was in full swing throughout the whole Earth. People were looking for places to hide from the anti-Christ movement and just trying to stay out of the way. There was a long road ahead of them, but people did what they could and trusted the Lord.

"Rusty, did you have to walk far to the ocean to see shells, or did your grandparents drive you there?"

"Oh, we could walk there, Krista. After Grandpa and Grandma sang a few songs, we were there! Sissy likes to sing. I like to find crabs!"

The two started giggling, and before they knew it, Krista was well on her way to somewhere—even though she didn't know exactly where—and a confidence started to overtake her; she felt the Spirit leading more strongly by the moment. Oh, how she loved God! They would sleep well in some little town tonight. Perhaps in Centralia.

~ Chapter Twelve ~

Hey, Brent, do you think it is true that people who die here to go be with God really get to take whatever it is they have in their hand with them, as long as it isn't a living being?"

Brent looked over at Darren on the other end of the saw with a look that said, "*What? Where did that come from?*" Smiling, he went back to his sawing on the fir they were about to bring down, keeping steady attention on it. "Let's finish taking this tree, and then I'll answer you." Brent checked once again on the direction of the wind and did a quick study on the other side of the tree they prepared before finishing off this opposite side. Just a few...more...grinds, and away she went! "Timber!" yelled Brent and Dare at the same time. Big grins and hearty arm movements of victory gave finality to yet another tree closer to their quota. They glanced back at Zipper who joined in with a couple of barks, and they moved ten feet over to the next tall timber they would take on.

How Brent loved his job. Remembering Darren's odd question, Brent turned to him and said, "I was told some awe-inspiring stories once from someone who was from the City of God. He claimed God had some special surprises and had made changes since the earlier days. Yes, I heard that several people had gone to the City of God with something that meant a lot to them in life. This one story I particularly liked was about a woman named Gabby. Apparently she loved horses and had a horse that was like a best friend to her; she had named him Gabriel. Both names are the same, you see, and they mean, 'God is my strength.'"

Darren nearly broke out in laughter, but nodded on to encourage Brent's story.

"Her family was in equestrian equipment, you know, horse tack and riding apparel. Her great-grandpa had made saddles, and his son after him took on the trade. One particular saddle had been passed down to her grandpa, and he made one just like it for her; years later she inherited the older saddle as well.

"One day a terrible storm hit her city, and trees managed their way to the ground all over her neighborhood. Right before she moved out of the way, she saw a tree come crashing down on her barn right where her horse Gabriel was penned. One of the branches from this old oak tree brazed her head while slamming onto her shoulder and chest. She knew her horse was gone and she fell on top of her precious saddle she had been carrying. With her right hand she grabbed it and sent out a prayer to God about her horse. Next thing she knew, she was standing at the Living River of God. She didn't have her saddle with her, but still sensed it in her hand. After she walked through the river, she was met on the other side by an angel and her horse with her saddle on it. Her horse whinnied and pranced in place to see her. He was just as excited as she was. She mounted Gabriel, draped over his neck, and cried tears of joy. When she lifted her head to grab the reins, right next to her was Jesus on His horse.

"She cried and worshipped Him. Quickly He comforted her and challenged her to a brisk ride through the streets of gold. With boldness that could only be gifted, she took Jesus' challenge and they went riding away with each other. Now that's just plain cool, Darren."

"Huh, I'd think she would want the old saddle handed down, but I suppose it was too old or something?" Darren scratched his head with a puzzled look on his face.

Brent burst out loud laughing because of Darren's funny reaction. He was such a funny man!

All of the sudden Brent's eyes popped wide open for he just remembered something he meant to say. "Oh! I forgot! The man told me that the next day she saw different members of her family and right there was her grand-dad on his horse with the old saddle he had left to her when he passed away. It became a strong family tie to them even in the Great City. God never ceases to amaze me. It isn't just a part of heaven come to Earth; it's all of the details God keeps in mind over each one of us. That's just beyond me, Darren. Really beyond me."

Darren was thrilled that Brent had learned of some things to come; he wanted to keep him focused on the good things of God yet to come for him. How that other saddle got in heaven was yet a mystery, but neither spoke of it. Darren had been visited by an angel through the night telling him about the trouble brewing and some strategies to consider. It was going to get tougher before they could see their way out of it.

"You know, Brent, we should each have a horse of our own up here in these hills. Wouldn't that be great? Trucks can't follow so well, if you know what I mean."

"Hmm, you may have a point there, sonny boy; let's pray about that! That story always makes me feel warm and fuzzy towards animals. Hey, Zip! You gonna be in heaven with me?" Brent slapped his leg a couple of times for Zipper to come over, and with that, Zipper leapt up with a bark and happily panted in Brent's face as only a good dog could do. Animals were often prayed into heaven, and Brent had asked God a time or two for Zip to be there and was very confident he would see him there someday.

Every once in a while, Brent or Darren would look over his shoulder just to see what he might see. They weren't nervous, but thought it good to be cautious. They couldn't ignore Friday night and believed that anytime now they would see Mal or Jason fuming his way over to them. The presence of God was always present as long as Brent kept trusting the Lord to keep him and protect him. He couldn't afford to start doubting now. *"Why open a door to the enemy when your faith has it slammed closed,"* he would often say to himself.

They got all their trees felled and felt really good about the day. Darren took them back to his place where they sharpened their tools and had more prayer time. The more they prayed, the more angels God sent to them. The more they prayed, the more they sensed victory in anything that would head their way. They could feel something was up but couldn't put a finger on it yet. After a meal shared, Brent and Zipper took off down the road to their camp. It hadn't started getting dark yet, but it would soon, and Brent had a letter he wanted to get off to his sister. He would send a few needles off some tree he worked with or had seen that day and stick them in the envelope for his niece and nephew to guess what kind of tree they came from. It was a way that kept them close and bonded.

Even though he and Darren had pleaded the blood over each other and all that pertained to them, Brent had an inkling to do it again. He started to quote the Word out loud until he witnessed in his spirit all was taken care of. They were in battle mode now in the spirit. Battle mode meant extra prayer, extra Word time, and extra proclamation of God's Word over whatever it was they were coming against or was coming against them.

That night Brent entered into a fitful night of sleep. He tossed and turned and sometimes woke up from a nightmare all broken out in a sweat. Sometimes Zipper would come up and lick his face. Brent would fall asleep again praying. In one dream, he was wrestling with a couple of dark black wolves. He kept seeing their fangs, and with one on top of him, he tried to roll over the other one yelling, "The blood of Jesus! The blood of Jesus!" Finally it would break off of him, and he would wake with a start. He would remind himself that the enemy couldn't take him unless he gave him permission out of fear or doubt. Since that wasn't an option ever, Brent kept praying and praising the Lord. At last, sweet sleep came to him, and he slept on through the last few hours until his alarm went off in the morning. He got up amazingly refreshed!

"Who says there is no God?" Brent voiced hotly within himself. The presence was strong and Brent went on with his day after some good worship time.

Not so high above Brent and Darren's camps were angelic forces moving on their behalf when they were allowed to. God always had a bigger picture moving in His sovereignty, and the angels never questioned it. They always saw and knew God as perfect, and strengthened themselves to aggressively act on His behalf as they always had done and always would do, forever. This was a time they were allowed to be very aggressive, which they all noticed amongst themselves was getting to be more regular and common everywhere throughout the earth.

Once in a while, the angels of darkness, called demons, would get word out of their victories, but more often, their attempts were foiled. This morning, they were too ashamed to share their defeat over Brent. Besides, they told themselves they had done a good job and did just what they were supposed to do. They convinced themselves of having worn Brent down. He had to be worn out after the thrashing they gave him last night. Who would debate that? Their leader, whom they reported to, was a proud demonic force of his own and knew how well his imps could wear anyone down. That was their job, and they were good at it. Deception ran rampant between all the demons. These particular ones were sent against Darren and Brent that very night and for a while longer yet.

Brent once again gathered up all of his stuff, and with doggy close by his side, headed back to Darren's. He wondered if Darren had any visitations through the night. Sometimes Darren's eyes had a special subtle glow to them that would make Brent look twice. He couldn't figure Darren out. Interestingly though, he remembered that man who visited him from the City of God had the same glow but much stronger.

Brent and Zipper got to Darren's cabin, but Darren wasn't out and about drinking his coffee like usual. Brent hoped he hadn't slept in. Electricity couldn't be used up in these hills. Most everything was solar, gas, fuel, or battery operated, and not always dependable. Sounds could carry well through the woods that were not too heavily thicketed by trees and brush. So, Brent decided not to yell from a distance. He waited until he got up close to Darren's place.

Brent knocked on Darren's door, but there was no answer. *"Ah, must be shaving or something,"* Brent figured. Brent knocked again, but it was strangely quiet. Brent checked his peace and couldn't tell what he felt. He looked in a couple of windows and tried both doors. The back door wasn't closed tightly, so he and Zip walked right in.

"Darren! Where are ya, man? Darren!" Zipper added his bark to the silence.

"Darren!" From room to room Brent began to look frantically. In the back room on the floor where Darren does laundry were boxes tipped over and some blood on the floor. Brent wanted to get frantic. "*This couldn't be! How could it be?* Darren! Where are ya', man?"

Zipper was now over at the back door barking. Brent ran over to see if he had found Darren.

"Hey, Brent! How are ya?" Darren called out, wearing his usual sheepish grin as he walked toward the back door.

"How am I? How are you?" Brent just looked on dumbfounded.

"Fine! Just had to handle a raccoon that got in by accident. I cornered him in the back room and things got a little messy." There was a bloody cloth around his hand, and Brent wondered if he would have to take Darren to the nearest clinic for shots.

"Hey, we need to get that hand looked at. Did you get your shots in the past five years?"

"Yup. Sure did. I'm fine, man, don't worry about me. I've had a run-in with these critters before, but this one was a little nasty. I'll be fine. Give me a few minutes, and I'll be ready to head out with you." Darren took a good look at Brent and said, "Really, I'm fine. No big deal." With that, Darren kept his smile going and everything seemed fine.

Brent was thinking he should wait to tell Darren about his nightmares later on, maybe during lunch. They had enough excitement for the moment.

They took off and were only minutes late. Normally that would not create a fuss, and hopefully wouldn't this time. Each team had their own area to clear or handle with their particular duty, so they were pretty much their own bosses. Sometimes there would be a swarm of them, which happened when the cleared areas met up with each other. Logs had to be taken off the hills and some branch clearing had to take place.

Lunch came and went, and Brent started to feel like his dreams were silly now. He didn't mention anything to Darren. If there was a time to, he would.

"Brent! Grab your axe next to the cedar and get over here!" demanded Mal.

Oh, swell, Mal was back around, and Brent tried hard not to roll his eyes. Why did Mal care about his axe anyway?

"Yes, sir, what's up?"

Mal raised his eyebrows at Brent and said, "Nothin's up, Brent; I just wanted to see your axe for a moment."

Brent was nonplussed. Nevertheless, he held on tightly to his axe before he knew just exactly what Mal wanted with it.

"Hey there, you don't have to feel threatened; I'm just curious as to why you have such a fancy axe way up here in these hills. It's kind of pretty don't you think?"

That bristled Brent. He didn't like hearing it said like that, but decided to get into nonchalant mode about the whole thing and was embarrassed he acted fearful. "It's a beautiful axe, Mal, not pretty." Shoot! He was acting defensive again! *"Come on, Brent, you can do better than this."* "Why, do you want one like it?"

Mal didn't realize that Brent was serious. "Oh, sure, a pretty axe is just what I wanted." Mal shook his head but continued, "Where did you get that anyway?"

"My dad made this for me. That's why it is so special. This handle is designed to last for years and years, way beyond my life and my children's."

"He must have treated it with biocidal silver and then put some real silver on that thing. Had your dad had the axe long?"

Brent felt like clamming up immediately. It was none of Mal's business, and he was going to keep it that way. "I really don't know how long he had it, Mal. He's dead now, so I can't ask him."

"Did he go to the City of God, Brent?"

Brent just played dumb. "He's dead, Mal. Can I go back to work now?"

Mal just waved while turning around and walked away from Brent. "Yeah, go back to work. Take care of that pretty axe of yours." Then he trailed out of sight.

Darren tried to listen as best he could. It was a bit noisy around him, but he got the gist of it all. Brent approached him, and Darren whispered as loud as he could to be heard, "What was that all about?"

Brent now rolled his eyes and shook his head, "He was snooping about my axe. Why he would want to do that is beyond me." Brent held up his axe and eyed it thoughtfully for a moment. He sure wished his dad had been able to tell him about the axe.

"Well, I'd keep a good eye on it from now on if I were you. I don't trust that guy at all. He gives me the creeps." With that, Darren made his way over to their work area, and Brent considered following him.

Just for fun and out of sheer curiosity, Brent shook the axe to see if he could hear anything. "Ha!" He let out a big laugh and this time rolled his eyes at himself. Did he *ever* get caught up in a made up mystery in just a matter of seconds. "*Where your mind will take you,*" he started the thought to himself. As if to clear his head, he shook it back and forth out of silliness and turned to go toward Zipper. He hadn't seen him for a while and thought he'd just love on him a bit before he hacked at another tall timber.

"Ya know, Zip, it seems like the enemy is really trying to rattle me. He almost had me for a second there." Brent's gaze drifted over the valley for a moment while rubbing Zipper's head aggressively in love. "Well boy, let's go get a treat, and you drink up some of your water, then I'll get back to work. We'll play some catch tonight. You like that, Zip? Huh? You like that?" With that, Brent and Zip ran over to Darren's truck for the snack, and afterward Brent directed himself to the next timber.

It was time to share with Darren what happened in his dreams last night. The day proved to be getting too weird, and he knew they needed to do some more praying together. God's Word says one can chase a thousand, but two can chase ten thousand. Brent just hoped that the two of them would be enough. Something was brewing, that was for sure. Maybe they needed to stay at the same camp together. Now that was a thought.

~ Chapter Thirteen ~

THE NEXT DAY, Krista and her troop got a good start. They had yummy cereal bars and leather fruit with juice. Krista also had bags of crisp vegetables for snacking along the way, plus other healthy drinks she was sure they would all enjoy. And yes, she had goodies for Misty as well.

The driving went quickly, and they had covered quite a bit of territory, when all of a sudden Sissy yelled out, "Cotton candy! Cotton candy!" Both Krista and Rusty jumped in their seats with a start, but Misty just lifted her head. "Cotton candy, Kissta! Cotton candy!"

"Where, Sissy? Where do I get Cotton candy?" Krista was feeling pretty good about this clue which told her this road was familiar with the children. They had driven for over an hour heading north to the west side of the Olympic Mountains. *I wonder what this all used to look like way back when,* Krista thought to herself. She would have to wait to see it through one of the many history stadiums at the city.

"Ah, Sissy, it's not for a while." Rusty looked up at Krista and with a slight prod, said, "The cotton candy is good, Krista."

With a twinkle in her eye, Krista said, "Well, if it's cotton candy you want, it's cotton candy you get."

"Yay!" shouted Rusty and Sissy.

"So Rusty, do you think we are close to this place? Is the cotton candy in a restaurant or on the beach, or where is it?"

"There are a bunch of stores around there, Krista. You go to one store, and then you go to another store. Grandma calls it window shopping, but we always get something."

Rusty would never cease to amaze Krista. "OK, then do we have to head toward the ocean or stay on this road? Do you know, Rusty?"

"Umm, I think we come to a stop light somewhere and turn that way." With a wave of Rusty's left hand, Krista knew she would have to head toward the ocean. Sounded good to her!

"That would be to the left then, Rusty. Good job!"

Rusty put on his grin and felt satisfied that he was helping with directions. Misty was getting a lot of pets, and everyone was in a good mood.

It wasn't long, maybe fifteen minutes, when the road actually came to some intricate lane maze where stop lights lit the air and signs were galore. "Help me out here, Lord." Krista found herself praying out loud, but didn't mind at all. She was grasping.

"Go that way Krista, go that way!" Rusty tried to help, but it wasn't just going that way, it was *how to go that way.*

"Okay, Rusty, I think I got it." Krista made a calculated guess as to which ocean front she wanted to go toward and just went for it. Had she known a few miles ago, she could have studied the signs along the way, but she did have the Holy Spirit, and she was truly grateful.

"Okay scouts, do I turn off this road at any time?"

"Yup, you sure do! In a little while you will go that way, Krista."

Krista glanced over at Rusty, and he was now pointing to the right. She told him the direction and thanked him. She felt they must be really getting close, to the cotton candy anyway.

One more turn after they had driven a good distance, and urban life came into view. However little it was, it had that urban feel with strip malls, apartments, and houses scattered everywhere.

"Over there, Kissta! Over there!"

Krista noticed how much the kids repeated themselves when they were very excited, but why not; they had gone through so much, it was probably healing to release joy in a double portion. Krista picked up on the direction which made perfect sense, and drove past several little shops in the strip mall. The atmosphere was adorned with a beachy feel that was consistent with the entire town, not just the shops of the strip mall. She could tell that a couple of blocks west of her was a high, mound-like barrier that ran as far south and north as she could see. The ocean had to be on the other side. It was time to roll down that window and smell the ocean air.

"There it is! The cotton candy shop!" Rusty exclaimed with such matter-of-factness and joy at the same time that everyone felt electrified and victorious having hit the target after such a long journey.

Krista found a great parking spot, and after everyone had piled out of the car, they decided Misty should go for a walk. They agreed that cotton candy would be a great reward for taking care of Misty first, and besides, they were all relieved to stretch their legs. Soon they wandered back toward the parking lot, and Krista put Misty back into the car. Grabbing each child by the hand, they forged toward the Sweet Shop to retrieve their prize.

Entering the little store was an experience of colors and smells all too yummy to keep one's mind focused on the original plan. All except Sissy. Cotton candy was all she could see. They walked around anyway before everyone's mind was made up, and they all ended up with cotton candy and just a little bit more to keep those, "I wish I had of" thoughts away.

The threesome now equipped for some serious window-shopping gladly marched out to the sidewalk for their journey. Several minutes ticked by and one store led to another when Krista had a thought; that should they actually find Grandpa and Grandma, it would be nice to take a present to them, and maybe some food for the three extra guests.

Down the sidewalk, about eight people away, a woman suddenly got very fidgety and nervous. She ducked out of sight only to appear a couple of moments later with a man by her side. She ran in the opposite direction as the man went back into the store to eye Krista and the children walking their way.

Just a couple of minutes later, yet another woman came out of a store hasting her way toward Krista. When she got close to Krista, she slipped a piece of paper in Krista's hand. Krista was standing in front of one of the windows pulling the last of the cotton candy into her eager mouth when the woman approached.

Krista turned fully to face the person, but she had already gotten out sight.

"Who was that, Krista?"

"Not sure, honey, but it's all right. Here, hold this for a minute, will you?" She handed the empty paper cone to Rusty and smiled reassuringly.

Krista read the note and thought hard and fast. She was to meet someone, whom she did not know at a turn-out near the levee. Instructions were there, but she was quite hesitant. Who was after her, or worse yet, after the kids? *"Lord, what should I do?"*

While she was pondering, another person stood in the shadows watching all of this take place.

Krista was struggling to get use to these suddenlies, but that was what she was bred for, handling things quickly—stealthily—in the most unexpected circumstances. *"Okay, okay, I'm not going to do this."* But as soon as she got that thought formed strongly and decisively, she didn't have a peace about not doing it. She tried it again. Still no peace.

"Guess what, kids! We're going to find a way to the ocean! Let's go!"

They easily got caught up with Krista's enthusiasm like all of the other times, so they trekked back to the car to an eager Misty awaiting them.

Misty barked when she saw them and seemed quite happy. Krista was trying to read that reaction, and decided she was getting too weird about it all and just needed to get going.

Krista followed the directions and when she got near the place by the levee, she saw a van pulled in the same turn-about. Krista didn't want to park too closely, so she decided to move very slowly, and decided to not pull the brake.

While she reached for her seat-belt, Rusty peered more closely out the front window, squinting to recognize something.

At that same moment, two people, a man and a woman, got out of the van and made their way toward Krista's car.

Deafening cries blasted Krista's ears as Rusty groped for the door handle, and Sissy started to climb over them all.

"Grandpa! Grandma!"

The mad dash of the century ensued as tears hit everyone and the hugs lasted forever. They went around once and then again. Each grandparent ended up with one of their grandchildren in a hold as if to be clinging to life itself. It was easy for Grandpa and Grandma to realize that Krista was not an evil force against them, but a messenger of great things, namely their grandchildren. Excitement went down just a level or two, but still stayed high on the charts.

"Hello, my name is Gordon, and this is my wife Jan. We're the children's grandparents."

More hugs and giggles and wipes of wet faces.

"Hi there. My name is Krista, and I must say you have the most wonderful grandchildren I have ever met. They are pure joy."

"They certainly are," Grandpa concurred, and hugs started afresh as two little faces beamed while looking up into their grandparent's faces. Grandma scooped up Sissy into her arms, and Sissy wrapped her little arms around Grandma's neck. What a happy day, and what a happy reunion.

Grandma lovingly urged, "Please come with us, for we have a lot to talk about. We have dinner simmering in a slow-cooker that is sure to fill up everyone's little tummies." She jiggled little Sissy while looking at her with twinkling eyes.

Krista agreed to go along and went back to the car where she found Misty licking her own face and the outside of her mouth over and over. Krista looked at the car a little closer and recognized pink melted sugar on the seats, but the paper cones they were on were clean. Misty looked at her with her "*what?*" expression.

Krista laughed and said, "Good doggy, Misty. Good doggy." She could get a steamy hot wash-cloth to clean the sugar right out once at the grandparents'.

Down the street, far away enough as to not be detected, was the same onlooker as at the strip mall. He was speaking something into his digital voice piece with a seemingly evil smile.

~ Chapter Fourteen ~

E MUEL'S DAUGHTER DURDANA was having such a sweet
dream. Men were walking up to her handing her silky bags
of diamonds, emeralds, and rubies—the most precious jewels
known to man. They would bow before her and hail her queen of
the lands.

Then one particular man walked up to her carrying nothing in
his hands for her. He was suave, debonair, and took her breath away.
As soon as he got close enough to make a locking connection with
her eyes, he walked away with a hidden smirk. He knew she would
follow him.

Durdana looked about the room and saw nothing of interest to
capture her above the mysterious man, so she followed him, but
maintained a controlled distance. She too wanted to play a game of
not interested. Someone would have to give, and it wouldn't be her.

The covert man was as smooth and slick as his several thousand
dollar suit that hung with a life of its own—loosely but weighted,
complimenting muscles acquainted with weight lifting, and lean-
ness that showcased his discipline. As Durdana was to women's
beauty, this stranger was to men's.

"*What a nice couple we would make,*" purred Durdana to herself
while checking to see what direction he went. "*I wonder how powerful he is.*"

All of a sudden the hairs on Durdana's neck stood up while chills
ran through her body. He stood oh so closely behind her, breathing
on her bare neck and shoulder in resolutely slow, deep breaths. Her
first reaction was to whirl around and slap his face, but she, too,
was disciplined and wanted to flaunt it. She stood her ground.

His breathing shortened and breaths came more quickly.

She got caught up in the excitement, and her body wanted to
throb in reaction, for she was tantalized and overwhelmingly

enticed over this control he possessed. Deep feelings of arousal were forming and building. She had been taken by surprise. She wasn't used to this. Durdana wanted to speak, but all of a sudden could not. *What was this? Why couldn't she speak?* For the first time since she was seven-years-old, when an uncle visited her in the privacy of her bedroom, she became terrified. She didn't know why she was frightened now and tried to compensate for it by fighting for control; but she had lost all control, all resistance. She loved it, but hated it. She felt like running, but had to have more.

She had more.

Surreptitiously, satan slipped out of her dream as easily as he had slipped in and was satisfied with his conquer. Now all she had to do was become "one" with about four special, hand-picked generals for satan to complete this stage of takeover.

He had already set up the plan.

Lying in a pool of sweat, Durdana felt herself all over to see if she was really awake. What had happened to her she wasn't sure, but she felt certain it was real. No, on second thought, she knew what had happened to her, but she didn't know *who* it was. Would she see him again in real life? Was he a real person? It felt horribly so that he was, and that she had gone through a terrifying, yet exhilarating, experience. She lay there for hours playing it over and over again trying to figure it out, and she planned to gain control if it ever happened to her again. Even so, there was no mistaking that there was something supernatural about the whole dream. She was overtaken and stunned—literally. She had to find a way to gain back total power. She never played second to anyone, except that one time from her uncle. With her uncle it was repulsion, but with this mystery man it was mixed feelings, and she couldn't get a strong handle on it, and that bothered her a lot. She had told her dad everything about her uncle, including the threats; he had blood chillingly threatened her and her family if she ever whispered a hint as to what had happened. Her uncle just didn't know who he was trying to take advantage of. It was just a few days later that everyone, from commoners to those in the social clubs, was reading his obituary in the papers.

Emuel sat in his conference room with three men, waiting for the fourth to arrive. He wished he could regard any one of them highly with sincere respect. Had they not come to their positions through cunning and unscrupulous manners such as Emuel himself, he would respect them. No man would ever seem to gain his true respect, for they were all liars with selfish ambitions to gain only for themselves and not the common good of others. On the other hand, it gave Emuel such great satisfaction that it made it easier for him to control them. All he needed to know was what vein of selfishness controlled each person so he could play into that darkness and reel them in. Greed usually worked. The love of money seemed to have no end, which kept it an ongoing ploy.

It didn't hurt any that Emuel had a beautiful daughter that was searching for her own power and supremacy. So many pawns on the table of life. It was constantly amusing and stimulating at the same time for Emuel. During the night, Emuel had gotten a surge of diabolical energy as though he had been visited by something or someone very sinister. Plans he had contemplated and drawn up for years seemed to be clearer and falling into place. He saw the bigger picture of takeover of the Great City as crystal clear as the River of God. It was as if he could make it all happen in a matter of days. All morning it was all he could do to stop from giggling and digging into darker avenues of destruction and horror. He felt better than ever. The devil had been deliciously busy through the night.

Aram was not a man to be late or flustered, ever. He ruled his eastern corner of the world with a finesse that would put most notable men to shame. He moved with the agility of a roe deer in business matters, and with the delicacy of a feather and rose petal amongst women. This noon time of day he had made an extraordinary conquest that he earnestly believed no other man was able to reel in. He had been captivatingly intimate with Durdana while promising her a great position in his kingdom. He sought her out to reign by his side. This would give him the power over the other three rulers that were just now about to meet with Emuel. Aram had just about thirty seconds left to make his entrance without breaking his impeccable record of punctuality.

"Composure, Aram, composure. You are the best, and you just had the best." With those words floating over his tongue in his sealed mouth, Aram entered the conference room at the top of his confidence level, ready to make the plans he knew would make history and a name for himself—and his sons, and his son's sons—for generations to come. He was about to shine, and nothing at this moment could remove the smirk off his face.

"Come on in, Aram! Glad you could join us. You look a little flushed. We hope your lunch went well for you." Emuel always loved to dig if he could. Just keeping the edge on everything abetted his strength.

Aram dare not weaken at this moment, but was extremely perplexed that Emuel had asked such a question. Aram thought he had recouped, but did Emuel know something? "I apologize for being detained. I hope I wasn't late." He hit his statement with a full smile and didn't budge an inch.

"No, no. You are on time as always." As though Aram had just been a courteous thought, Emuel quickly looked around the group and went right to the heart of the matter.

"Gentlemen, as you know, we've been working on a plan to infiltrate the City of God and bring down His false illusions to the world. We've had many ideas float around far too long, and have forever prepared armies into the millions and hundreds of millions for such a covert plot; but I have recently come across some vital information that will crystalize our decades of dreams and culminate them into what I believe to be our final hour of victory."

Aram and his fellow colleagues, Sabtah, Omar, and Jerahmeel, sat forward in their luxurious soft leather chairs to hear what they hoped would be the unraveling of their long sought for scheme. Their fathers before them and their fathers before them for centuries had despised the Great City and never ceased to accept defeat. Vision held these men together through the years, and now at last, this generation could sense they were on the precipice of victory. They listened.

"The key to this city is a series of maps; when put together, they reveal what was only seen before a great part of the earth was destroyed and when satellites existed to take pictures from the heavenlies. In fact, gentlemen, these maps are pictures taken from a satellite a millennium ago. These maps reveal the territory under the City of God which will give us our advantage over their said God. We will be able to go underground and rise up to destroy the very foundation of the city, which will open up the doors for us to infiltrate and overtake it once and for all."

The four men sat with wide-eyed expressions and ears that hungered for this long awaited knowledge. They were flushed with excitement and dared not move for fear of upsetting a presence they hoped to be real. Slobbering demons standing behind each general showed an array of fang-like teeth as they smiled and rubbed their hands together in great anticipation. Muted black, green, and grey vapors traveled through the room, unknowingly to the generals, wrapping them in a totally submitted hold. Their fearful silence was just what Emuel was hoping for. He continued.

"The City of God has kept us from putting up satellites all of these eons, not because of a lack of technology, of which you know we have, but because of the height and vastness of the city and other things we cannot control. It has been a thorn in our side all of these generations to keep us from having ultimate control as we once had a thousand years ago. Those days were cut short because of the natural disasters that fell upon this globe, but now we can proceed to regain our dream, our vision, and our sovereignty that will last for many millennia."

Emuel bent down to retrieve his attaché case and produced a map.

All four gentlemen rose out of their seats to gaze upon this treasure that seemed too good to be true. But there it was—a map.

Emuel watched each one's reaction with a sense of pride and superiority. Drool felt like forming in his mouth. He kept in full control as this was the cinch of all plans and campaigns that would keep him on the top forever. At this moment he felt invincible.

"Gentlemen, I cannot tell you how we retrieved this map, but I can tell you that there are two more out there quite similar to this one. Notice the odd shape to this map. We copied this shape and tried to fit it together. We made a few more copies and this is what we finally came up with. It's amazing, really. One of the copies seems to make up a third of some shape, but obviously leaves room for one particular map that goes in the middle. That would be the fourth map.

Emuel placed three identical shapes on the table that would reveal anything but a square with a perfect circle in the middle once they were put down touching each other. It was unmistakable.

"Three in one," whispered Omar.

"What was that?" a troubled Emuel retorted.

Omar wasn't the least bit frightened to say it. He was in too much awe at the present. "Three in one."

The others looked on and saw what he saw. You could tell by their faces. They fought to keep horror from showing, to keep up a façade in front of Emuel.

Emuel saw it exploded. "Blast it!" To keep power he demanded, "I want you to forget about that! Put it out of your mind! It's nonsense!"

They tried.

"I cannot stress enough to you; or let me say it to you this way, I cannot *press* you enough—and believe me, I will—that these three other maps must be found and be found instantly. The center circular piece may or may not be a map, but it is vital at this point. The faster we move, the more upset we make those in the believer's realm, and the more we upset them, the better likelihood that they will make a mistake. Am I understood?"

"Jerahmeel was the first to speak up. "This looks like the border of my kingdom, Emuel. May I obtain a copy of this?"

"I have a copy for each of you in my briefcase. Get back to me in three days with a plan to subdue these maps, and we will meet here, say, three o'clock in the afternoon on Thursday. Shall we?" With that, Emuel motioned to the door for them to exit. He had totally regained composure and a sense of victory wafted in his nose.

"Thursday it is," they said as they took their copies, their adrenaline in high gear.

The sly fox satan was pleased, and Emuel's grin reflected his master's.

~ Chapter Fifteen ~

D EAR, OH, DEAR, what a time you have had of it, sweety. I am so sorry to hear what you had to go through to get here." Grandma was lamenting over the grandchildren, which doubled her agony, for she did not know yet what happened to her own daughter and son-in-law, Madeleine and Arthur. Times seemed so frantic and confusing. Yet Grandma and Grandpa had a way of throwing their cares on the Lord and were always comforted. She just had to get out of the room and be alone for a short while to work it all through and hear the Lord on this. She knew well of His faithfulness through the years. She knew His presence. She and God were no strangers.

The children were all snuggled in their bunk beds in a room designed just for them. Each wall had a painting of ocean waves and shells. Blues and greens blended into one another with foamy whites spraying over different waves crashing in to the shores on the walls. One wall had more little crabs playing in the sand and around the rocks that Rusty particularly enjoyed. Sissy just loved the shells. On top of her dresser drawers were a few of her found shell treasures. Some of the big shells kept her necklaces and a couple of smaller ones held a few of her bracelets. If it weren't for the ionizer that dusted the room automatically, Grandma wouldn't have allowed it. But such things weren't a problem for this era.

A couple of big chairs that molded to the body were in the room with a couple of little tables for them to play on. This was a large bedroom, which was able to hold a couple of double beds if wanted. The closets held toys from the strip mall, Rusty's favorite stick from beachcombing (Sissy had one too), and some precious gifts from the grandparents, Mom and Dad, and friends of the family. The kids always loved this refuge and could happily stay there for long periods of times.

Grandpa excused himself from the threesome discussion and headed through the kitchen out to the back porch. It was an expansive back porch for cook overs and neighborhood get-togethers. Plenty of lawn was easily manageable, and the neighbors around had slight acreage. It was a great neighborhood. Barbequing was a regular thing that aided in acquainting people as well as helping get Grandma out of the kitchen. She loved his barbequing. She couldn't help but throw together a good potato salad or greens to go with the meat. As far as Grandpa and Grandma were concerned, they were two peas in a pod. They were a team.

Out of his pocket came a little mirror that if held just right and from a proper light source for reflection, could send messages to some other neighbors for long distances.

"Gordon?" asked Krista as she came out to the porch. "Are you all right with me being here?"

Gordon had the mirror pretty secluded already, so he didn't feel his cover was blown. At least she didn't look in the direction of his hands. "Krista, not only is it all right for you to be here, but it is a pleasure and treat to have you with us. The children have really grown close to you, and you can stay here as long as you would like. Please, don't be in a hurry to go back."

"Thanks, Gordon. I really appreciate that. You are right about the children. I've grown very fond of them also. They are the cutest kids, and full of surprises." A twinkle came to her eyes just thinking of them. "I have a few stories you will enjoy hearing. It's just that I'm all talked out right now. I think I'm going to bond with that bed tonight, and soon."

"Anytime, Krista. Have Jan show you the ropes for breakfast in the morning in case you are up before us. Grandma, I mean Jan, has a good breakfast menu and could fix you anything your heart desires. The kids, well, they love her pancakes. She fixes a mean syrup that melts in your mouth and turns the whole hotcake experience into something heavenly. If you aren't shy of cream, you'll do fine with her cooking. However," a smile crinkled around his eyes, "I've never heard anyone complain yet."

Krista's mouth automatically started to salivate. "Hey, I've never turned down a hotcake yet. I don't think I'll start now. What time should I expect breakfast?"

"We're pretty slow around here. I'd say about 8:30 while the sun shines through our east window. She says cooking in God's sunbeams is like having the favor of the Lord. So, that's where she will be, and the kids are usually wound up a good long time before that. But feel free to sleep in and take it easy. No expectations here." He smiled wide at her, which gave her the sense that she, too, was home, and she loved the feeling.

She thought he was going to say 7:00 a.m. or something. She let out a sigh of relief under her breath when he quoted her the time, and she felt comfortable with it all. Normally she was a "night-owl" and slept in later than 8:30 if given the opportunity, but this was more than wonderful to her. It was about eleven p.m. now, and she wanted that bed.

"I'll see you in the morning then Gordon. Again, thank you for everything. This means a lot to me. It will be fun to see Rusty and Sissy in the morning without having to figure out the next moment and the next." She turned to go and spoke, "Good night!" With a large smile of her own that was full of gratitude, she went back through the kitchen into the living room where Misty was by the low-lit gas fireplace sprawled out like it was the beach of Florida on a hot summer day. Krista sighed happily with the thought of no car rides, for a couple of days anyway; that would suit the two of them just fine!

Grandma was reclining, watching Misty sleep, while she murmured her thoughts and prayers to the Lord. Grandma was one grand intercessor—like a wall of cement plowing through the enemy's camp. The enemy would love to get rid of her and had someone keeping an eye on her all of the time throughout the day. They thought they would find a weak spot or moment of fault with her so that they could close off her life and get her sent to the City, out of their way. They kept waiting... and waiting.

"Good night, Jan! How I loved meeting you and Gordon. Your

grandchildren are like little angels to me. They are the cutest and most adorable little people I've ever known. They are like little journeys all on their own." Krista laughed and Jan joined in nodding her head in agreement. Misty looked up from her nap and blinked her eyelids in one accord. Jan saw that too, and they both had a good laugh out of that. What next!?

"I'm going to head to bed now. If I don't roll out of bed at a decent hour, just ignore me. I feel like I could sleep for a couple of days at least!"

"Good night, honey. You go right ahead and sleep those couple of days if you want to. Our home is your home. Thank you for taking care of our little darlins. Now sweet dreams to you and be sure to rest in Jesus' arms. They are always there for you, you know, honey."

"Oh yes, that is exactly what I do. All day long in fact! I am looking forward to getting to know the two of you better while I'm here. I have a few questions I'd like to ask, but just too pooped now to even think of them. Until tomorrow morning then?"

"Yes, yes, of course, honey. Until tomorrow." Jan gazed sweetly down at the dog. "It's all right if Misty stays out here. Just to let you know."

"Thank you. I'll have to think about that. I don't want her to be in your way. For now I'll just have her mosey in with me, but you never know! Tomorrow is a new day!" With a wink to Jan, Krista called Misty and she quickly went and followed her to the guest bedroom. Bed and rest was just a few yards away. "Goodnight, Jan!"

"Goodnight, honey!" With a wave of her hand, Jan wished her well and went out to the kitchen to check on ol' Gordon.

Sometimes she and Gordon would rock on the porch on their special swing, capable of holding the two of them comfortably as they rocked away the day's events. Their swing conveniently held cups of delicious drinks and perhaps a bag of yummies in the middle pocket that served as a mini storage for books or notepads. Late at night they could talk their little hearts out, which offered a peaceful bonding time before sleep would be upon them. They were usually lulled by the sound of ocean waves and gentle breezes that blew. Except, the swing was on the west side of the house facing the ocean and Gordon was on the east side this balmy night. She wondered what he was up to.

It was well past their swing time, and past their falling asleep time, but the day pretty much wound everyone up. Because of the day's excitement, it just hit Jan how tired she really was. She found Gordon and slipped her arm underneath his. He immediately tightened the grip and turned to smile at her.

"How are you holding up, honey?" He loved her tenderly always, for he cherished her commitment to him and her bravery toward the seasons of turmoil they'd had to endure through the years, but this season was to rival all seasons they had yet endured.

"I'm doing well, honey. I'm getting sleepy though. I was just wondering what you were doing out here. Did you get the message out?"

Gordon, feeling pensive and unclear about things, answered back the best he could without bringing too much alarm. But she had to know; after all, she was his prayer partner as well. They made a formidable team, and he was not about to break that up now. "Not yet, hon. I'm listening."

Jan knew well what that meant. He was trying to hear the Holy Spirit for his next move. She did not know what was going on, however, and was about to gently prod him when he offered her what she needed to know.

"I saw him again today. He certainly suspects us of something or we wouldn't have the honor of him spying on us. I'm just making sure the air is clear of him and others. I haven't detected him at night yet, but I don't know how much longer that will last. I wonder if Krista is a point of interest to them. We have a lot to talk to her about tomorrow or the next day. My gut is telling me that she is safe here, and we should keep her here as long as possible. What do you think, darlin'?"

"I'm hearing the same thing, babe. I know she is safe with us, and we are safe with her. I'm not sure how long she should be here though. I keep wondering about Madeleine and Arthur."

"I know, honey. Me too. God will show us when He is ready. He knows all the details and what is best for us and the children. We can trust Him for that. I have been thanking Him for that." Gordon stared away for a short moment. Then as if he got a revelation, he whispered softly but urgently to Jan, "Just got a clear signal. I'll meet you inside."

Jan rushed to her tip toes and planted a quick kiss on his face, whispering back, "Okay, honey." She quietly went through the kitchen and moved her way down the hallway to the bedrooms. She snuck into the grandchildren's room and saw they were sound asleep. It sure felt good to have them back. She didn't know how, but just had a reassurance that her daughter Madeleine knew the children were all right. "Oh, thank You, Father for showing me that. What a wonderful gift You just gave me, Father. Thank You for telling me." Tears ran easily down her face and she decided to stay in the room for a while and pray and praise softly, and usher in the presence of God yet more.

~ Chapter Sixteen ~

THE WEEK WENT by, rolling into the next with the usual tension that had been lingering in the air for a few weeks now. The days went by quickly, and the promise of summer was heating the air. It would be another few months in the high grounds for Brent and Darren before lower elevations would be necessary. The Northwest used to have mild winters before the Millennium, but God used jet streams to change all of that.

God made a lot of changes during the season of His holy wrath, and everything became just as it should be. Knowledge had, once again, come against the obstacles of division and destruction that had gained ground the first decades of desolation. God preserved many wise and witty men, though many of them had been scattered during the constant disasters. Pockets of people wondered if they were the only ones who had survived, but in time realized they were not alone. Some underground phone services still existed, but with gaping holes in their service. Most phone towers had been demolished, but one could find some scattered here and there. Still, due to the fact that satellites no longer existed, towers were of no use. Ground lines worked better than wireless anything. Life had become slow again, and just finding other survivors took decades upon decades for networking to really gain ground.

According to Blake, who loved telling stories in his restaurant, Bear Pa's, his family, and entire cave dwelling community, didn't find another pocket of people for well over a year. Their group was so thankful to have each other, and was preoccupied with finding food and rummaging towns to find anything of value to add to the comforts of their homes; they did not venture far from their familiar valley and hills. But one day, on an extended excursion to explore other valleys and sites, seven brave and hopeful men observed human activity north of their encampments, about a three day's journey away. Grandpa Nathaniel and Levi were part of this team of explorers. God had been speaking to the prayer groups for weeks now that there would be an expedition coming that would bring a connection, which in turn would bring another connection, and so on and so forth. God would go with them.

Ash was not falling as much as it used to, and the rains of the winter and spring helped wash it into the ground, which hungrily absorbed most of it. The clearings around them were abundant in rich soil and things grew easily. Nathaniel's wife Candis was a great cook, as many of the women in their cave compound were. It was more fun to cook and prepare food than it used to be, for they had more time to do so and made it a social activity since most of the women were not running their children around for activities, nor just having come home from being at a job. They would share their ideas and expertise of recipes that came down through their own generations, and everyone learned from everyone. They found that time passed quickly during such good fellowship. They told stories to one another, and the children picked up some of those stories when they were around.

Barbeques were one thing they especially treasured and made sure were part of their belongings when they moved everything up to the hills. Unfortunately, most of the cave dwellings had no outlet for the heat or smoke, so they had to be creative with who used theirs and when. Everyone shared everything. Many men took on the role of barbequing because they had always done it before, and no one really minded who did what. They all loved to eat and were incredibly thankful to the Lord for the bounty He provided daily for them.

As a result of the exploration, the two compounds decided to close the gap and do what they could to start building and moving closer together. They had to consider many things in protecting themselves while wandering far away from their own compound. Wildlife proved to be a challenge at times, and no one knew how many people who survived were greedy and power hungry. Those were natural enemies they always had to be wary of.

Nathaniel found that many Christians existed in the second compound, but they had others among them who still did not believe. This caused mistrust and guardedness from time to time. People would always be people no matter what they went through, but at this point, most of them clung to one another and sought to live peaceably. It just didn't pay to make enemies. Someone might just need something another had, whether it was food, clothing, or a trade. Besides, it was a strong, unspoken understanding that they had all gone through enough already. They were tired and sometimes confused. It was a struggle to come to terms with all that had taken place, and many were dealing with guilt over their disbelief—for ignoring what the Christians had tried to tell them. They had been forewarned about all they had gone through. At the same time, they were grateful in words they could barely express, that God had spared their lives and that for some reason, they had never accepted the mark of the beast. The non-believers had mental and emotional baggage to deal with that caused many to become believers, or to finally wander away from the Christians to make their own camps and life somewhere else.

For believers, life was pretty much an everyday walking and trusting in God, for they could not wrap their understanding around His grace and mercies. But that was okay, too, because God told them in His Word that *the just walk by faith*, not by understanding. As soon as they stepped into faith, His grace met them to get through whatever they had to, whether they understood or not. God always met them.

Nathaniel's party of seven became five after a couple of days, for two of the men journeyed back to their home compound to deliver news with a few items that compound number two shared with them. Likewise, as a foresight, Nathaniel's party had come with some essentials they thought might be good to share as a gift to anyone they thought they would encounter. Sugar was one of those treasures. It turned out that compound two was in disbelief to see so much sugar brought to them! They listened eagerly to hear how such a find was available, for they had run out of sugar quite a while back, with no hope of getting anymore ever!

"It seems that God has seasons of 'marvels and suddenlies,'" Blake would say.

One story of marvel Grandpa Nathaniel told about compound two was that a special day a year before; most of the families were rummaging through an area of flattened city that was nearly fifteen miles from camp. Before the rummaging started, a picnic, one that would rival any picnic before the wrath, took place and made this outing a distinctive day. They tried to do this every couple of months with the families, just so they could get out and teach their children about how things were and could be again. Besides, the more the merrier, and children had a way of finding things that adults did not. Children weren't always methodical, which was a great advantage to the outing.

Once, on one of those outings near the flattened city, three little children were holding hands (a rule if they wandered very far away from Mom and Dad, even though they were required to stay in sight) while roaming around singing their songs and playing their games. Piles of lumber and sheet rock had been loosely organized in many spots and made great play areas for children to peak under and imagine what they once knew or pretended to know. The three little pumpkins went by a very large pile of debris and giggled as they played an "I dare you" game, each pretending to fall into the huge pile. It seemed all innocent and actually was, but one of the little girls on the end slipped out of her buddy's hand and fell backward onto a loose pile. Just then the pile sank about five feet as other debris around it gave way. This got the people around the area curious, and those closest by went running to find the little girl. The other two lost their balance and fell back just short of the newly formed pit. They were screaming and horribly frightened because of the danger their friend was in and because of the guilt they felt over it. Two men got there first and almost jumped into the pit to grab her. One of the guys grabbed the other's arm just before he was going to drop in after her and yelled, "Wait! You don't know if this is deeper than what we can see. Let's get something to pull her out with—something she can grab."

The little girl's eyes were open as big as saucers as she lay there very still and too scared to speak. She thought if she made a noise, she would sink further. She could hear the groaning of the wood underneath her and before the men got back, with other's looking on now, she felt a slight dropping movement like it all wanted to give way.

Reassurances were spoken to her when a woman took off her coat and yelled, "She can grab my coat!" The two men ran back as they instructed the girl to put one of her arms in the sleeve while they held onto the rest of the coat to pull her up.

The little girl looked up at all of them and whispered in a frightened and most tense voice, "I'm sinking."

Several of the people got on their stomachs and also took off a piece of clothing to use if they had to. The thick coat was let down, and one of the women said, "Honey, just hold on to the sleeve and you won't go anywhere but up; I promise you." The others gently affirmed this direction given her and had the girl put her arm in one of the sleeves slowly while holding onto the furry collar of the coat. As slow as it seemed and as carefully as they managed, they actually moved rapidly and quickly pulled her up. No telling what could happen at any second. Everyone could now hear crackling of the wood and debris as it seemed to sink further and further.

Once everyone was far away from the big pile, they came up with a plan to see just how deep the hole was. Was it wider than what they could observe?

People had come closer to see, for they were all curious as to what happened. Many had been praying throughout the duration and now sought God for direction on this probing new development.

Then some of the men yelled to everyone to get far away. One by one they quickly backed off, feeling that something big was about to go down. As they all watched from afar, they could hear sounds coming from the area; they were getting louder and louder. The ground moaned and grumbled as the little pile that had sunk now started to pull parts of the bigger pile down more and more. It was like watching a show from afar. Then, off to the side, some yards away, the ground that had no rubble on top started to cave in. It just got scarier. No one knew what to think. Still, they had a peace during this awe and marvelous thing that was happening right before their eyes.

Some said they felt an earthquake, others said it was the sinking of the mound of debris. But a big thud ended the whole show. Dust from the cave-in rose high and spread everywhere in chalky billows. Out of wisdom, they all decided go back to their temporary camps less than a half a mile away and check this out in a couple of days once everything was settled, if it was truly settled. They would find out soon enough. It isn't like they had ever seen anyone else around this area, for it was always exactly the way they found it before each time. Sometimes some of the older kids would come down and look around just for fun in hopes of being a hero who found something wonderful for the compound; but other than that, this place had been a no visit zone from any outsiders as far as they could tell.

Eagerly, a couple of days later, several men went out and brought along their teenage sons who could run quickly back in case of an emergency. They were a type of search party to discover the truth of the sink hole. What could be down there was anyone's guess. It was time to find out.

Men checked the ground for sturdiness as they approached the site. It looked like everything had certainly settled, but they didn't want to be stupid. They kept one ear in tune to the Holy Spirit, and the other on what they heard around them.

As they advanced toward the edge of where the sink took place, they pretty much just saw more debris below. They inched their way to the odd cave-in area where no debris had been; they looked around and there was a ramp! A ramp? They decided to form a hiking group with ropes attaching each other as one by one they would walk down the ramp.

They anchored the end of the rope at a secure place so they could pull themselves back up when they were going to leave. It wasn't a steep slope, but they wanted to make sure they could get back out. They had prepared well for this search. However, what they found, they were not prepared for. It was nothing less than a wonder and a true marvel.

Just in sight of all who got down to the bottom was what appeared to have once been a grocery store that had sunk in the ground. There was a bit of a problem to that theory, however, for places where debris had not toppled over, there were shelves still intact. On further investigation, it seemed that a level existed underneath half of the store for storage, and the ramp was a special loading dock. Trying to make sense of it all, someone suggested that maybe it had once been an ancient bomb shelter turned storage for the store built in its place. It was all quite confusing, but they all loved a mystery, and there were plenty of those to solve; they did not lack running into new ones on a monthly basis for quite some time.

They stood there in awe realizing what had happened was nothing short of a miracle. Suddenly, a couple of days ago, a little girl fell, and a marvel was there in the waiting for all to glorify God. Had the girl weighed more than sixty pounds, the debris would not have sustained her in the short distance she went. God thinks of everything.

Sugar was there along with many other goods that did not get ruined. There was certainly plenty of it. The compound now had sugar in abundance, hence, a perfect gift to take to the new discovery of compound number two or any others if they found them. It turned out to be a perfect find that became the perfect gift.

~ Chapter Seventeen ~

BRENT HAD A fabulous morning watching the sunrise and beholding things he had not ever seen before. He was eager to get to Darren and compare notes with him. They were both seeing spectacular sights and experiencing the unexpected suddenly, out of nowhere. One day, Darren thought he was about to have another run in with a raccoon when all of a sudden it got up on its hind legs, shook its right front leg at Darren as if to mock a handshake, then took off running back in the other direction away from the house.

On another day a storm came upon the guys when, all of a sudden, after Darren and Brent ushered a quick prayer of agreement and authority over it, the sun broke through like a veil had been whipped off of it, the rain disappeared, and the wind literally and most abruptly quit.

Yet another time they were in the town of Tall Pines when a truck came right for them having crossed the line and jerked back at the last millisecond to keep from crashing into them. Before them had been a burst of electric light, blue flashes of light, and a prism of colors that seemed pancaked between the two vehicles and spread out several feet in all directions. That wasn't just a marvel, Darren said; it was a marvelous suddenly and a sudden marvel! The guys could laugh at this because they knew from their personal quiet times with the Lord that manifestations ordered by the Father would take place all over the earth.

Throughout the skies and the woods flashes of lights of different colors could be seen as if they were at times exploding. The guys often wondered what they would see if they were in the spot where the lights came from. Was it an angelic war taking place right there in Washington? What could be so important there that the heavenlies would find a cause to clash here?

"Darren, did you see anything toward the east during sunrise this morning that seemed odd to you? Perhaps even a phenomenon?"

"A phenomenon, Brent? What do you mean?" Darren could goad Brent in the most amusing ways when Brent least wanted it. But they always had fun and never took either too seriously when they smelled a tease coming on.

Brent just rolled his eyes. "Come on, Darren, what about that singing tree you were telling me about last week? Now that was a marvel!"

"Well, it happened suddenly if you ask me."

"No, it was a marvel. And don't tell me it was a sudden marvel, because it was *just* a marvel!"

"Well, don't all marvels happen suddenly?" asked Darren, goading more.

"All right, all right." Not to be taken the better of, Brent came right back at Darren and said, "Well, since wonders and marvels never happen to you, I will once again tell you what happened to me, and it was this very morning!"

Darren's eyes just flickered smilingly in the fun of it all.

"I was sitting out with my orange juice and ol' Zipper, out at the ledge where you know I like to go and talk with God, when all of a sudden—"

"Stop! You said, 'all of a sudden,' Brent! I heard you! You said, 'all of a sudden!' See? Marvels happen suddenly!" Darren just took off howling his head off so hard, for he was so pleased with himself that he "got" Brent, who always argued over marvels and suddenlies. This was too much!

Brent held up his hand in surrender and said, "Okay, okay, Dare! It's not going to happen again though! You'll see." He too was laughing at the silliness of it all. Darren really got him that time. After the laugh, Brent was eager to share what he had seen. He was just about to when Darren spoke up.

"Let me tell you something, Brent. I'll tell you something phenomenal. Something phenomenal is when you see angels, like cirrus clouds, holding babies in their arms, filling the skies, and music filling your ears with sounds of worship that seem to escort you into the very throne room of God."

Brent stood there with his mouth gaping in awe since that was exactly what he was going to tell Darren!

"Why you little stink! You took the words right out of my mouth!" At that, what had been a silent Zipper up to this point, was now a barking advocate for his master, Brent. Both guys now were howling up a storm with laughter to the point they had to hold on to their stomachs as they bent over in hilarity. Zipper came up to the both of them rubbing his head on their pant legs still barking, but not constantly now. The guys rubbed his head and neck and just kept on laughing. It was a special love time for Zipper and a great release for the guys from the oppressive attacks the enemy had been bombarding them with half the time at work through Mal and Jason.

While heading toward their next site of clearing in Darren's truck, Brent spoke up, "There must be a lot of people getting saved, Darren. I don't think it's just here around us this phenomenon is taking place, I think it is everywhere. What do you think?"

"Uh-huh, I think you're right. I keep getting the word *showdown*. Are you hearing anything like that?"

"No, I get the words, 'face off.'"

Darren wheeled around to look at Brent like, *duh*, when Brent slugged him in the arm.

"Gotcha!"

"No! You did not 'get' me! You are a goof! That's what you are! A pure goof, goof, goof!"

Well, this went on most of the day. Friendly bantering felt good, and sometimes they pretended the other was Mal or Jason. It was just one of those days.

When they got back to Darren's camp site that evening, the air felt altered. They agreed to have dinner together and spend some serious time praising and praying together before the evening ended. They didn't want to miss God, and they needed to focus on the protection He gave to them as long as they were in His will. It was a good way to end the day.

~ᴔ~

"Missy! Missy! Where are you, girl? Missy!" Little Sissy and Misty were playing hide-and-go-seek out in Grandpa and Grandma's backyard. Unbeknown to her, Krista was going to have to leave them all, for the Spirit was leading her back toward home. Krista would leave right before lunch to get a good start on the day for her long trip back.

Grandma had packed a couple of grocery bags full of food and snuck a couple of other goodies in there for Krista. One of the goodies happened to be a book that Jan's great-grandma had written. It was on the history of Jan's family that had been passed down through the generations on to her. A few centuries were covered in the book, but other than that, Jan couldn't remember what all was in the book; but that God wanted Krista to have one was all she needed to know. Jan had several copies and made sure that one of them was going home with Krista. The idea had come to her in the night after she had been awakened by the Holy Spirit to pray and intercede for Krista. Jan had forgotten all about the book, which was in the attic with all of the others. While in the attic, the pen holder that she and Gordon had talked about a few nights earlier caught her eye. It was made of beautiful onyx marble that had come from either old Russia or Turkey. Jan knew why it was there in the attic, and she slipped it in her apron pocket to remember to speak to Gordon about it. She knew that, too, was going with Krista.

It was time. Krista looked around her bedroom that had wrapped her in love each night she had crawled into bed. She especially loved the windows on the south and east walls adorned with long flowing sheers that floated out to her when the breezes were up, and they usually were. The blues and whites in the room kept her mind clear and peaceful all at the same time. Rich dark woods that hued of red tones warmed her at every glance, and she felt she could have stayed there a lifetime. But it was time to go.

The night before, Grandpa sat the kids on his lap and shared a story with them about when it was a good time to let go and when it was a good time to keep something. Then he ended the story in a way that sent the children giggling, because he also taught them that there was a time to say adieu. After he taught them what the word meant, he would poke one of them and say, "Adieu to you!" Then he would poke the other one and say it again. Pretty soon the children caught the sense of it being like a game and started poking Grandpa, saying, "Adieu to you!" Then they all started poking each other saying the phrase over and over. Then the chair got poked, then before long, Rusty and Sissy were all over the room poking everything in sight saying, "Adieu to you!"

The giggles and game went on for a while when Grandma interrupted it with a fresh plate of cookies. Everyone was delighted at the sight and scrambled to sit down; they were having such a good time. Grandpa and Grandma were grounded people and didn't believe that children should have to go through so much drama over common every day happenstances. They tried to give the children a good outlook and strength on being able to say good-bye to Krista and Misty. There was still no word of the kid's parents, so Grandpa and Grandma felt the children had enough disappointments. These were tough times, and wisdom called for loving kindness in every way possible. What was so wonderful is that Grandpa and Grandma were always like this.

Krista walked in the front door with a couple of bags in her arms and smelled the freshly baked peanut-butter cookies. "Oh, Jan, those are my favorite! I hope you made a lot!"

"I did, dear, and plenty more for tomorrow." Grandma didn't want to say anything more and was glad she stopped her words right there. The children didn't know Krista was leaving yet, and she didn't want to be the one with the crushing news. For not saying all that her mind was thinking, under her breath, Grandma whispered, "Thank You, Jesus."

Krista smiled at Jan and went into the bedroom to sort what she had bought. Some of it was for her travel, some of it was for her house when she got home, and a few items were for the kids, Jan, and Gordon. It was going to be difficult to say goodbye, but the three adults were in one accord on this decision. They had several discussions about what God was revealing to them as well as others they were in fellowship with. Visions and dreams were building throughout the Christian communities as God spoke to them, preparing them for events about to unfold.

"We can see the calling on your life, Krista." Grandma looked as though she could see right through Krista. It made Krista feel really good to have such deep affirmation. She missed her parents. Gordon and Jan filled a great nurturing void in Krista's life, and the three of them agreed on staying closely knit until God called them all to the City of God.

Krista's stay had been a time of observing marvels and suddenlies that she had never experienced before, but only read about. It seemed to her that God had different seasons in life, seasons with different purposes and plans to be performed and accomplished. This was a fun season. She wasn't sure how long it would last, for she knew it was only a lull in the storm.

One night before it was time to watch the sunset, the group took off to go to the sandy beach, all bundled up like little Eskimos. It was a late spring evening, and on the coast, things could get very nippy in Washington, for the evenings got brisk very fast. But the kids had to go to the beach and play in the sand and just be out. Mugs of warm tea would be in the adult's hands as they sprawled out on their lounge chairs.

They stayed much longer than planned and watched the sun go down. The sunset was particularly spectacular this evening. The sun was close to the horizon of the water's edge as the sky seemed golden with blue tones fighting to stay in the background. The water reflected the gold ball of the sun and made it look like a melting pot of true gold that sparkled and danced on the ocean. Suddenly drops of this molten gold started pouring from the sun onto the ocean as it would land and bounce back up through the sky like fireworks. As those fireworks spread out and fell back into the ocean, more of the droplets from that landing would bounce back up in multiple smaller droplets—sometimes as flashes of emerald green gems; but much closer to the surface. It was like the whole picture was a scene of explosions and glimmer.

Grandpa looked at his wife and said, "God still sits on the throne." Tears came to all.

The children were frozen in their places.

It was a marvel.

There were many other memories Krista could draw from, she thought, as she closed her bag to take out of the room after she told the children that morning. She could not put off telling the children about her having to leave anymore. She would be leaving within the hour. There would be two of them leaving, which made it all the harder. But she and Gordon had planned well for this event to make it as light as possible for everyone. If you leave them with hope, you only leave a part of you, for hope leaves them with something to hold onto, and that was their plan.

Grandma called everyone into the living room for milk and left-over cookies from the day before. They tasted even better the next day.

From down the hallway, the family could hear Krista call out, "Where are those cookies, Jan? Here I come!"

The kids giggled some more, and everyone was all in smiles.

"They're right here, honey. They've been waiting for you!" With a song-sing voice, Grandma always knew how to make people feel comfortable.

Krista picked up two cookies and looked at the kids. She raised her eyebrows smiling, "One for each hand! Krista has it all!"

"Krista has it all!" yelled back Rusty! He ran over to the plate of cookies, and he too grabbed two of them. He put one in each hand and mimicked his beloved friend. "Rusty has it all! Rusty has it all!"

Well, now, Sissy couldn't be left behind, and she did the same thing; everyone was in high spirits.

Grandma's eyes teared up slightly because she knew what was coming up next. But she let them have their fun and even encouraged them with her laughs and claps of her hands.

Everyone chatted and talked about casual things and still acted goofy.

"Kissta! Let's go to the beach tomorrow!" yelled out Sissy. She was talking more and more since they had gotten to their grandparents. She was a regular little chatter box now.

"That's a good idea, Sissy. But guess what? I have something to tell you!" Krista kept the positive and cheery voice going and slapped her legs to invite the children to come over and sit with her.

"What, Kissta? What are you going to tell me?"

Krista looked up at Gordon and Jan for final strength and started right in. "I'm going to tell you something very important."

Maintaining her cheerfulness still, she continued, "I have to take a journey that will lead me back to my house. Just think! I will get to see my house again!"

That last sentence threw the kids for a moment. It allowed them to realize that Krista had a need, and this was all part of sharing the news the best way she knew how. She smiled at them, gaging her next words, when Rusty shook his head trying to process the news and took charge. "Do you have to see your house now? When do you have to see your house?"

Krista was so relieved just having gotten it all out at last that she jumped right in with great confidence and reassurance for each of the children.

"You see, I have a lot of things that need to be done at the house, things that have been waiting for me. But I wanted to stay here a long time, as much as I could. I love you so much, and I love being with you all of the time. But you have to understand something, I have a job that is waiting for me, and you want me to do my job don't you?"

Rusty was still processing and automatically started to agree when little Sissy broke in. In such a small thread of an inquisitive and dreading voice, she said, "Does Missy have to go to a job too?"

Oh, boy, Krista didn't anticipate this one. But out of faith, she started to open her mouth to satisfy her sweetheart little friend.

"Misty's job is to take care of Krista, Sissy," Grandpa offered just in time. "Don't you think that is a wonderful job to have?"

Again, the children had something more to think about. Even with all of the wisdom in handling this news, sad expressions were on their faces.

"I have some good news, kids," Krista said, hoping this would make the turn they all planned on. I get to see you again! We can plan a picnic together and make some real fun plans as to when we will see each other again, so I won't be gone too long! How do you like that? So instead of saying goodbye today, how about we just all say, 'Adieu to you, Krista, Adieu to you!'" Krista gently shook the children and kept her end of the cheerfulness going.

It took but an instant until the kids said, "Adieu to you!" Smiles returned, and the game of adieu started all over again. Misty got involved with her precious little bark, and everyone was happy. *Lord, let this joy last, please!* Krista pleaded lightly with God and stayed in the joy of the moment.

~ Chapter Eighteen ~

DARK FORCES AROSE in the Far East as clusters of demonic activity gathered—gaining ground. Flashes of light were rarely seen as the lair of satan built momentum. Westerly and northerly winds blew in massive dark clouds seemingly layered upon layer until the sun was ultimately blocked out.

Ruling spirits—high ranking demons—hissed and blew ominous vapors of crimson reds, browns, and blacks. The red vapors wafted every time they thought of spilling blood. Fangs hanging out of their mouths were measured by victory. The greater the victories, the longer the fangs. They grew so slowly that if lower ranking demons saw really long ones, they knew undoubtedly that warrior was a high ranking captain or general. With many victories under the belt, the wings also grew, but faster than the teeth. Some spreads could cover large areas of cities. When the wings were furled in, demons were always drawn to look at the fangs first.

The demons in charge had a way of tapping one of their fangs with their sword as a warning. Spirits of anger and lust were often so out of control, they needed the reminder often. The fangs were like a coffee stained enamel in color, each having serrated notches from the top on down, like an upside down Christmas tree, so it would tear its victim unmercifully as the it came out. There was just no way the smaller demons wanted to encounter them. They tried to get their rewards of growth through every victory.

With so many leaders and their hordes cloistered in the same sphere, battles would spring up and contests of supremacy ensued among the lesser demons. *Deceitful* imps buddied up with *division* imps and would throw a tizzy in *jealousy's* camp. Normally they didn't have to be cramped together while swarms of *hate* and *torment* rubbed on each other. Things were bound to get out of hand.

On the ground, millions of soldiers under the four generals' rule were forming together for what they thought was some sort of drill. They didn't want another drill, they wanted bloodshed and vengeance. They wanted war. Whenever they would get a reprieve from their barracks, various individuals or groups would wander around "checking out" their so called rivals of equal standing.

The *lust of the flesh manifesting in a soldier* couldn't resist the taste of whiskey—round after round after round. After that, all the whispers and thoughts the dark spirits had told the drunken soldiers repeatedly throughout their lives began to take form oh so very easily.

"Hey, you!"

One somewhat inebriated soldier sitting at the bar wheeled around, nearly knocking himself off the stool, to eye the soldier who sounded threatening.

"Your Momma says you are too young to sit in here and your girly legs ought to walk you out of here!"

The drunken soldier stared at the bully who was grinning in an over-confident manner. At first, his comrades didn't know if he heard the threat. Slowly and deliberately the drunken soldier lifted his chin but his eyes never left his point of glare. The spirits of *impatience* and *hate* tantalized the spirit of *anger* hovering over him as old familiar spirits within shouted, "Revenge, Revenge!" Soldiers had been taught restraint. Drunkenness never got the message. After the soldier had sized up his opponent, he slowly rose up out of his stool trying to be in absolute control wanting to give his own message to his challenger.

"What's the matter little girl, cat got your tongue?" The challenger was confident with his comrades standing behind him. Besides, in his experience, no drunken man could fight well.

The tipsy soldier put his hand over his mouth as he let out a slight cough for distraction as he shot up his leg in lightning speed into the soldier's gut and another blow into the guy's face as he bowed over from the gut hit. That knocked out the soldier, but his friends came in to cover him. This soldier however was a fifth level blackbelt and moved instinctively. He started to teeter after the second blow he gave his challenger when his comrades also stepped in to thwart off the opposition. Like a match that had been ignited, the fight broke out trashing the entire room. No one could stop them. The fire had to burn out, at least until higher ranking officials heard about it and came to bring control back.

Above the commotion, in the unseen world, demons were seen rubbing their hands together as they watched many of their peers fight and slash at one another through many of the soldiers they controlled.

~୧ᢣ~

Across the world in the Northwest, another fight ensued.

"Darren, have you seen Zipper?"

"No, man, I thought he was up by the trucks. He was there the last time I saw him."

Zipper was missing.

~ Chapter Nineteen ~

D URDANA STEPPED OFF the elevator wiping her hands down her scalloped cut, black velvet dress adorned with half karat sized blood red rubies that sparkled randomly in a triangular pattern across her left side from her shoulder down her sternum to cut below her chest to under her arm. It was stunning to look upon. She had her long black hair pulled off her left side to sweep behind her neck which cascaded down several inches on her right side. It was all part of the look to keep the rubies in center stage. A black widow spider could not have been more garlanded. She didn't miss a beat.

She continued out of the five star hotel, down the steps, to be met by a taxi that only took her four blocks. She then got out of that to enter a popular clothing store a few stories high that had two entrances to dart in and out of. She made her way into the clothing store on the east side of the building and exited out the north side of the building where her driver was awaiting. She did her best to keep from being detected and monitored. She was in control.

She had just finished her fourth and final conquest of the four generals by having sexual contact with General Omar, who, like the rest of the generals, promised her land and leadership if she would be by his side in every way. That would be interesting, for three of the generals were married, but yet again, had more than one wife. It really didn't matter to her anyway, because she expected to take her daddy's place and rule over them all. Her mission was to bond so tightly with each of them that they would be putty in her hands at the right moment for the right cause for the right reason. Her plan was moving steadily closer to utter overthrow and no one suspected a thing. It felt good to be slithery.

Thursday had come quickly for the generals. Each hated the idea that they had so much to do when all they really wanted was to spend every waking (and sleeping) moment with Durdana. None of them had the slightest idea that she had snaked her way into the other's life. They would get this Thursday behind them with Emuel and start delegating as quickly as possible so they could turn their time toward Durdana and give her a taste of real power so that she would submit her life unto theirs. What a dream, to be one of the most powerful men on Earth with the most powerful woman on Earth. They couldn't wait.

Emuel was sitting at his usual conference table that was made of wood and gold swirls that ground into each other in waves of glitter and masculinity. He had always had the best of everything, and nothing cost too much for him. He hired men to get him good deals because he felt all the more in control. Why be in control of only half of the things in your life when you could be in control of everything in your life.

Even though he was a power monger, he considered himself to be a patient man. He had to teach many how to craft their skill so he could give them a level of trust in that one area. He was always at work to attain the ultimate. When he wasn't with the four generals, he often surrounded himself with his pawns, instructing and giving orders, or being constantly served in some way.

Omar, Sabtah, Jerahmeel, and Aram had their own entourage, but would leave them behind when coming to meet with Emuel. Each man arrived at nearly the same time for the meeting today, and each had Durdana out of their mind. It was like being an athlete. Certain things took too much energy, and there was a time and place for everything. If they couldn't please Emuel with their plans for the retrieving of the maps to overtake the city at last, there would be no hope of Durdana. That reasoning made it easier to concentrate on the task at hand.

The men got along with one another, and often, when they knew they had a meeting with Emuel, two or more of them would meet for a meal beforehand. It was another business expense to see how the world was running and pick up ideas from the other to gain better control and handle any type of situation. A few of them shared borders in the world, and there was always something to talk about. They knew they were stuck together anyway because Emuel had hand-picked them years ago from a secret society type of organization. They had a lot in common, like greed and pride. They were evil men in every way and didn't seem to mind. After all, they had the power, unlike the imps they called governors, mayors, and police security that served below them. They stayed within their geographical borders while parading voracity and fear in their kingdom to keep their rulers below them subservient and in total submission.

Those menial rulers below them had their own sense of control in the world. Ideas of staying out of other men's business were encouraged amongst many corporations that had trouble reining in trouble makers. Heads of these corporations operated with the kind of power that treated many employees as slaves.

Christians and non-Christians could amazingly work side-by-side. The past many weeks, however, scrutinizing and painful persecution kicked into over-drive. A lot of people not in the "ruling" mode but in the middle ground were confused and never knew quite where to stand on conflicting issues.

The season of marvels and suddenlies doubly confused them and many turned their lives over to Christendom as a result of what they believed was God manifesting Himself. News headlines were picking up the strange phenomena and satan's camp was getting a brutal beating. The devil was about to turn that around, however; it was all he could stand of this. All the more he slithered his way through Emuel and his daughter Durdana, who both had the four Generals hopping. The devil knew he was going to get his way; he just had to let God think He was getting His way.

The generals were seated, and Emuel rose to start the meeting. "Gentlemen! The Plan!"

Each general took approximately half an hour to present his plan—concerning everything from his captains and their men under them to marketing ideas, advertising, and great schemes of espionage—to uncover the map if it was anywhere to be found. And of course, it was, because Emuel demanded so.

Emuel tweaked each man's plan, but was actually pleased at how ingenious each proposal was. It was as though they had each slipped into Emuel's own dark alley of deception and power. They spent the rest of the day sharing details of their programs with one another and Emuel. They would start with their chain of commands to persecute the people and rally in all of their law enforcement facilities to bring on the pressure to the people. Emuel had a few plans and demises of his own to add to theirs, so by the end of the day, satan was again pleased with himself, and so was Emuel. Yes, this would all come together wonderfully.

Now it was time to find those maps! Emuel had sent hundreds of thousands of soldiers to the Far East in the western and southern regions to make a few days' journey to the northern tip of the Middle East region where the northern most part of the City of God started. He wanted to be ready at a moment's notice to move the army forward in order to bring forth his surprise attack. He was about to send the rest of them there in a few days. He had thought of everything.

～ Chapter Twenty ～

BRENT COULDN'T UNDERSTAND where his dog could be. He and Darren had driven all around and walked many paths hoping to get some clue. After they had trampled down a path of about two miles, flashes of light could be seen in the far distance, so they decided to walk in that direction. They were a long way from their cabins and felt despondent.

"Let's stop and pray, Brent." Darren was gentle as he spoke to his friend. They knelt on the soft ground below them under the forgiving boughs of the evergreens. "Father, show us the way to Zipper. Don't let him be far away. Bring peace to Zip and reveal to us Your plan here, God. We ask these things and thank You now for the answer, in Jesus' name, amen." Darren patted his friend kneeling beside him on the back a couple of times and gave him a reassuring smile. "I know we'll find him, Brent. I got a peace from the Lord."

"I feel better too, Darren. Thanks. Let's seek out those lights."

Zipper had been with them that morning and most of the afternoon. Jason had stopped by to pester them about their quota, of which they were never short. Nevertheless, Jason harassed them and took off. The guys never saw Jason back toward the trucks waving a doggy treat like a proverbial carrot that dangles in front of the racing dogs to keep them sprinting forward. Zipper innocently followed the hopeful rewarding jester until he found himself inside a jeep where another treat was there to add to the one Jason finally gave him. Jason took off to who knows where. He was following another one of Mal's orders.

Brent and Darren walked down a hillside over a valley about a half mile wide when they thought they heard a yip coming from the direction in front of them up on the next hill. They heard another yip and saw a flash of blues and oranges. The guys glanced at each other and knew some battle had to be taking place up there. They immediately took off running.

"Zip! I'm coming for ya, pal! Zip! I'm coming!" Brent yelled as loud as he could to let Zipper know they were there. The guys were in good shape but found trudging up the hill was a challenge. Yet, they didn't count it as anything as they could hear Zipper's yips getting stronger and louder. "Why isn't he fully barking, Darren?"

"Maybe he's muzzled. We'll find out soon." Darren was starting to pant now and so was Brent.

Brent kept reassuring Zipper that he was getting closer until they found a shack with old boards that had slits between them from the decades of harsh weather. Darren tried the locked doors, but Brent pulled out his axe and started chopping at the old boards. Once inside, Zipper was laying on the ground in a cage with a chain holding him in. Sure enough, he was muzzled. Brent took one whack at the chain connected to the wall and figured he would take off the collar later, back at his cabin with other tools he had. The first thing they had done was take off the muzzle and look for a container to hold some water the guys had packed with them. Zipper was so happy that he pressed and pressed into Brent's side and wouldn't let him out of his touch. They looked around to scope out the small dwelling. It was filthy and held odd objects like chains and lots of rope. Mal and Jason had to know about this place. It made the guys sick to their stomachs, but they decided to quickly get out of there while there was some light left in the menacing air.

Towards the middle of the valley where there was more brush amongst the trees, the guys stopped and knelt down and thanked God for leading them to Zipper. They took only a few moments to worship the Deliverer, but made it count in their hearts. As fast as they could they headed back to their camps. God would show them what to do and how to handle this. It didn't feel right to confront Mal and Jason, as wisdom dictated, at the time, it would only stir up more strife and trouble. It was difficult to restrain themselves, so they prayed a lot and cast their cares on the One who cared for them.

~ එ ~

Krista had gotten home unscathed and unchallenged. She had made a few stops for Misty's sake, but other than that, it was smooth sailing.

She unpacked her bags and found a couple of things she didn't remember she had packed. Instantly she knew Jan had slipped them in, and Krista smiled at the warmth of her love all over again. She was planning on going back to the ocean very soon to be with her new found family.

Thoughts had formulated in Krista's mind a lot on the drive home. She was seeing things a bit more clearly concerning her mission to protect a map that she knew nothing about. Her talks with Gordon and Jan had been informative and eye opening about the trouble with the maps. Gordon alluded to her unpacking when she got home but very clear about calling Blake right away.

From what Gordon shared one day on the back porch, there was an organization that existed made up of early survivors who protected particular things that had not been destroyed during the wrath. Some of these things were revealed by Jesus Himself in visions, dreams, and visitations. A lot of the information was to remain hidden until a very special day that was far in the future. Krista knew that they were in the "far in the future" season of the world, and she only hoped she could do her part. She didn't feel any actual rush, but she did feel the pressure of having to get it done.

She decided she would take care of some business of her own for a couple of days then swing on into Tall Pines for a visit. Blake knew Gordon, as their fathers had known each other, and shared in this secret organization of hush-hush. Krista was intrigued. Come to think of it, she never asked Gordon if he was in it. It was all about the generations that came before him and their special mission. Hmm, now that was something to think about.

Misty was delighted to be back home and romped all around the yard and pastures. She hid behind trees and jumped out to frighten away squirrels and chipmunks. She could take care of herself and have one good time doing it. Krista enjoyed looking out the sliding glass door at her. Someday, life would be carefree for all of the believers like that. What a promise to hold onto.

Krista took the car into a shop that knew her well and was run by believers. They plugged some wires and clamps into a place inside her car that told them everything they needed to know about it. They gave her car a tune-up and all the goodies that go with that; then washed it for her and sent her on her way. While she waited for her car, she reflected on her stay at the ocean. Gordon had announced that suddenly the man that had been spying on them was gone. Just suddenly! She liked that kind of suddenly. The thought warmed her and made her smile.

Early Friday morning, Krista got a head start for the day to get all of the other little things done. Krista was mindful to shop for fresh supplies to stock her car with as well as her house. As the day moved on, she started to get agitated like there was something she was supposed to be doing. That perplexed her, so she stopped somewhere and listened to the Holy Spirit. When she heard Him, she knew she was on track except for one thing. Her vacation was over. She hoped to have the four days just to hang out, but it was time to move and move now. First thing Saturday morning she would head to Tall Pines instead of putting it off for a couple of days as originally planned. Something was up and timing was everything.

~ℓᶚ~

Brent and Darren were planning on going to southern Idaho for the weekend, but each got a check in their spirit that Friday afternoon. They were going to stay back and pray. Brent would call Brie and let her know. Something was up, and they were supposed to do more than pray, but that was where they were going to begin.

~ℓᶚ~

Friday night Emuel and his daughter Durdana sat down for an unusual dinner together. It was a small casual dinner for them with only six courses served. Emuel kept to having just one Cognac after dinner, and he knew it would have to last him the entire evening.

A great leader knew when to drink and when not to drink. Battle mode was not the time to drink, and Emuel felt like he was in battle. Plans to recover the maps yesterday seemed so simple, yet it would take complexity to carry them out. He was confident it would be very soon. He could practically taste the victory, and at that time, he would have more than one or two brandies. He was a large man and could handle a lot of liquor before he got a true buzz going, but still, this was not that time. He wanted to keep his senses intact and sharp.

Durdana purred every time a man looked her way. If men only knew the attention and victory it gave a woman when he succumbed to having to notice her for some reason. It kept her in control on a low level, but it didn't matter. Control was still control, and she wanted it everywhere.

She was careful to ask her dad questions about the invasion he and his ancestors had planned for so long. He seemed sharper and lighter, and yet more intense the past week, and she wondered why. She opened up with a bit of news she had been holding onto, hoping it would cut his tongue free to share with her some secrets of his own. They were good at one upping the other subconsciously. It was such a habit with them they hardly thought about it. It was a way of life to them. Each of them always made sure they didn't tell everything to keep ahead of the other. Somehow, they would often find out as time went by what the other knew. They would frown at one another for having kept it from the other. It was a game and nothing more or less than that; just a sick and evil, manipulating, conniving, power-play game.

"Dad, I saw Omar earlier this week. We had lunch together. He is quite a nice man. I hope you don't disapprove." With that she smiled demurely thinking that would be cute to him which he normally reacted favorably towards when he was in a "spoil-my-little-daughter" mode. This dinner felt like that to her.

"Well, that depends, honey. What was the lunch for?" He sat forward just slightly with his elbows now propped on the table, fork in his hands clutching each other in front of his mouth. He sat there chewing and gazing at her with his becoming smirk that she well understood.

"Oh, I believe it was all innocent enough, but he told me some things about, 'some law that was ripe for the harvest,' and that it was time to implement it. Of course, I asked him what that law was, and he said it was to gain back control over the Christians. Too many people have become Christians lately, and it seemed to concern him."

After a short little pause, with eyes piercing into hers, Emuel raised his eyebrows with curiosity in his tone, "And this does not concern you, my sweets?"

"Well, Dad, does it really need to? What is power for if it isn't to subdue one's enemy? Our numbers are big, and we own a lot of important people in high places. Do you think clamping down on Christians is a necessary cause here?" She knew the answer to this, but she loved hearing it. She just sat there looking her dad right back into his dark eyes for his millennium-old-answer that she could not get enough of.

With a bit of fire running through his blood now, but not in a wrathful sort of way, Emuel told her what he had shared with thousands and thousands of people for decades.

"Durdana, it's as simple as this: Christians are our enemy. They take over like rats, they run and hide like cock-roaches, and they mouth off fantasy notions, like His presumed Throne somewhere, leading many to believe in the God of illusions," he said with a roll of his eyes, "and they get in the way of plans to take back what is rightfully ours, which makes them thieves and varmints!"

"Varmints? That is a new one, Dad. How did you come up with that?"

"Because varmints, my dear, are undesirable animals looking for prey. My whole kingdom has been robbed of too many of my followers because of these varmints! It will simply stop."

"Easy there, Dad. Have another sip of that Cognac." Durdana's eyes twinkled in pure pleasure of seeing him upset with the foe.

She couldn't stand them either, and it felt good to get this boost of hatred.

"Durdana, Omar is right in what he says to you. In fact, we had a meeting yesterday to implement plans to put a mighty squeeze on the Christians. I think they will be begging us soon to take over the land in the Middle East. None will like it here anymore, and we will promise them anything they want to hear to get what we want. All of the people who are wavering on the fence with their beliefs will be pressured as well. We can't just be thinking of the Christians for mass take-over. We need to get all of the weak-minded to be a wall of antagonism toward the Christians so they have no more people to bring in to their maze of delusion. We must create a flood of dismay and defeat to the Christians, Durdana. This is our time and our battle to finish once and for all. He stopped to smile at her with a sense of victory again. "Now I'll take that drink."

Neither one shared much that the other didn't already know, but it sure kept them on the same page. They continued sharing with one another while a dark and hazy ribbon of hatred and revulsion wove its way in and out of them crossing over their hearts and breezing past their ears and eyes. It lingered like bad perfume, but it was intoxicating to the ones already sold out and unified with the devil.

The next week was going to change the whole earth, well, all of it except that city satan absolutely despised. But it was in line for a doosey on the right day just around the corner. The devil had learned from his mistakes and there was no mistaking his plan would succeed this time.

It was time to stir things up everywhere, but especially in Tall Pines. He was placing spies and a lot more agent guards to be there, for he couldn't shake the fact that something of value was there from the reports he was getting from various legions of demons. It would be just a short stop in order to make a few corrections. He picked Monday to initiate the beginning of the end everywhere, but he was going to give personal attention to Tall Pines.

~ Chapter Twenty-one ~

BRENT SPENT SOME special time with God this Saturday morning like he usually did, but Saturdays were given more time with Him, for intimacy with the Lord was all of life to Brent as a believer. The mornings were getting warmer as summer approached, but he still loved to stir the fire from the night before to bring some instant warmth to his cabin. After a few more logs and a cup of coffee, he waited for Darren to come over so they could take in a hearty breakfast at Bear Pa's.

Darren had been transported to the City of God earlier that morning. He had kept up his cover, that he was born here, rather than being on mission from the Great City, pretty well, but Brent would find out soon enough. Even if it was not until all the believers were gathered there for the ushering in of the new times after all of the judgments took place. Darren shuddered when he thought of judgment day. What a sad day for millions as well as the Lord himself to have to see so much of creation that rejected Him. Talk about finality of so many things.

Darren had heard about devastating plans the enemy was planning for the earth and God's people. Of course, God was not surprised by anything and knew from the beginning of days how this was all going to end. He had a plan.

Brent was putting out the fire when Darren came knocking on his door. Zipper was already outside and found his nuzzling spot under Darren's hand and against his waist when Darren offered a whispered thanksgiving to the Lord, "Thanks, God, for giving me the joy of this dog while I'm here. Your unconditional love is everywhere."

"Hey there, Darren!" Brent was all smiles when he swung open the door and stepped outside, locking the door behind him. "I'm famished, how about you?" He gave Darren a good pat on the arm and the two of them turned to get into the SUV.

"I'm pretty hungry. Is Zipper going with us?"

"Yup. I think he and I need more time together, so he will be our side-kick for the weekend. Good with you?"

"Perfect! I was hoping he would come along. He reminds me of my loyal dog I once had. I miss that old critter. He was smarter than a troop of soldiers."

The guys laughed, and Brent got out a, "Yeah, yeah.

"Brent, there's something I've been meaning to tell you."

Brent poised to hear the next jab come forth, but Darren paused which got to Brent a little. Brent looked at Darren quickly to see if this guy had gotten serious all of a sudden.

"Yeah, what's up, man? What do you want to share with me?"

"Remember when we saw the angels across the valley last week standing there with their swords crossed?"

"Yes, I remember."

"Well, Brent," he paused for affect, "that was a suddenly."

"Ah, come on, Darren!"

Darren exploded in laughter.

"What is it, exactly, you put in your coffee every morning? Are you all right?" Brent started shoving Darren with his right hand while his left hand steered the vehicle. "What is with you, man? You're goofy I tell ya! Pure goofy!"

That started the trip, and it didn't calm down until food was in their forks at Bear Pa's. There was no mistaking that Brent and Darren had bonded into true friends and rarely got offended with one another. They knew each other too well at this point.

From another direction heading to Bear Pa's was a beautiful young woman in her sporty car with a much smaller, but very intelligent, comrade. Krista was on a mission. She had a map to locate to piece some mysteries together that had come to her attention for some time now. She could get part of it together without the map, but at this point, she still had too many questions. "Dear God," she pleaded, "please have Blake give me answers I've been needing. Thank You, God. Thank You always! In Jesus' name, amen."

~ℓ}~

Krista had done her warfare earlier that morning, walking around her property and speaking with the Lord. She imagined her property as the garden of the Lord and went there to be strengthened all of the time. Just stepping outside brought strength to her. It wasn't just because of the beautiful green grass and flowers, nor the evergreens planted everywhere that were at least twenty to forty feet tall; it was just because it was her land. God had given it to her and His life poured through it. She knew by His Presence she would have to enter into battle in her spirit more often. That was all right with her; she had been there before. Although she could tell this was different, she was confident in whom God said He was and is. That was good enough for her. She had even pondered having more fellowship with people her age this morning. She thought she had been doing well up to this point with the groups she was involved with, but she needed a few people closer to her. Grandpa Gordon and Grandma Jan filled that niche perfectly regardless of their age. This weekend had high priority though. It was what she was called for. She had to remain unassuming to fulfill her mission. Even though that was a challenge, it was fun for her. Anointing was like that; it brought joy and took out the struggle when she knew she was in His will.

~ℓ}~

Blake was distant this morning. He felt the sullenness with what he witnessed last night, but threw that care on the Lord. "God, if You have changed, let me know. But Your Word says You don't change, so I'm not going to quit believing You have everything under control." He continued to do some warfare and pleaded the blood of Jesus over everything. He found himself doing more and more of that.

Blake noticed from the talk of several of his customers, as well as his own observation, that there were more angelic manifestations everywhere. They weren't necessarily big sightings, but sparks of light about the size of the back of a kitchen chair or often smaller. Colors of reds and blues, yellows, greens, and purples were the transparent displays being seen all over the place. It wasn't just at night; it was during the day as well! Sometimes the air seemed so thick with tension the past week, Blake noticed he wasn't sharing his stories as often because he was preoccupied with piecing events together. Some of his part-time employees were working more hours as Blake had other things to do and places to go. He kept reminding himself, that the outcome was in God's hands. *"But, God! But, God!"* It was his continual thought.

Blake had gotten a call from a gal named Krista who was due to arrive any moment now. That was fine with him, because an old pal from long ago had called him a week ago about her. Blake was looking forward to meeting with her. He could feel everything was about to change from the frantic chaos that was taking place the past few weeks to serious pandemonium. Last night was a good sign of it.

Poor, Mrs. Gunther. She was elderly and had just received the Lord as her Savior a couple of weeks ago. Her older brother had died a few days before that. He had inherited everything from their father who had died many years before. Now everything was left to her because her brother never had the children their dad figured he would have. She was thankful to receive everything, but was sad her brother was not with her anymore. Her brother was proud and very worldly. He had fought his dad secretly, but in front of him pretended to please him and did the "Yes, sir" with everything that was spoken. His dad had been deceived but had great hope in his own son before he died.

Boxes of items were still unopened by her brother from the things he had inherited. Mrs. Gunther was moving the boxes to her house and had hired out help to carry them and get them to her house. She noticed a box marked "Open Now!" that was in her dad's handwriting. She could hardly wait to get that home, for it was still taped closed. She knew her brother had no intention on opening it ever. She would pick up where he left off.

Saturday morning the news had gotten around that she was found dead in her brother's house in a room filled with boxes. They figured she had a heart attack trying to do too much. No one did an autopsy, and no one found the "Open Now!" box.

When Blake heard about her death, he wasn't surprised. An unusual amount of police cars had been parked outside the brother's house early evening and shouting was heard throughout the whole neighborhood. How could there be such uproar over an old lady dying from old age with no autopsy ordered? Something sure was screwy, and Blake needed to find out what it was.

Blake's dad had known Mrs. Gunther's dad. Blake had even seen him in his much younger days. Back then, men of the secret organization that protected certain objects against the enemy, used to meet regularly. But those meetings had been stopped, for it was getting impossible to hide as a group. They started communicating in other ways, unseen by the public, and harder for a trained policeman or detective to discover.

Undercover agents of some sort or another weren't dumb. They had ideas and theories as to who had what, but were never sure what they were looking for or who to track down. It wasn't until Friday that they had a memo from the top leader of their region explaining just exactly what the "what" was. Now they knew what they were looking for. It was time to put the theories into practice.

~ℓ⅃~

Krista drove into the parking lot of Bear Pa's and kept the windows down enough for Misty to get good air. Water was available on the floor in the back seat, so Krista got out of her car to march into the restaurant.

A low "woof" was heard, and she looked at Misty to see if her voice had changed! That was funny she thought. It couldn't have been Misty. "Woof." It came again, but this time it was easy to hear where it was coming from. She reeled around to find a happy, large golden retriever wagging his tail in the back of a SUV parked next to her, acting like he wanted to be friends. She took a couple of steps to get closer to this friendly dog, and Misty followed to the back of her car to get a better look.

"Hi there, fella." Krista smiled and pretended to pet the dog through the window.

Zipper stood there with his big smile on his face and wagged his tail.

Misty let out a couple of barks to say hello, and Zipper woofed right back.

Krista got a kick out of that and felt oddly relieved. Probably because she knew Misty would not get bored now. Krista sensed freedom to spend the time of her visit without Misty being in the back of her mind, so she headed on in at a light pace. She remembered the cinnamon roll from last time she was there with the kids, and her mouth started watering. The thought of the kids made her home-sick for them, but a warm smile met her lips.

"Hi, my name is Krista, and I'm here to see Blake Adams. Is he in?"

"Yes, just one minute, Krista, and I will go get him. Please make yourself comfortable; I will be back shortly." The receptionist was full of smiles and kindness, and Krista felt totally at ease.

Barely a few moments had passed when out walked a man of great stature and build. He looked a little rough around the edges, but all in all pleasant to look at. He did a quick look around his restaurant and walked up to Krista with a hearty smile on his face.

"Hi there, young lady; you must be Krista."

"And you must be Blake!" Krista liked him already. "Thank you for letting me come to see you. I've been here before, and I love your food. In fact, it wasn't that long ago that I was here with two small children."

Blake held out his arm and moved it toward the heart of his restaurant to welcome her in. "Won't you please follow me, and we will sit out here for a minute. What can I get you? Coffee? Soda? How about some bacon and eggs?"

"Oh, no, that won't be necessary, Blake. I plan on having a cinnamon roll before I leave though." She wanted him to know that she was willing to be a paying guest.

"Nonsense, Krista, let me get you one for right now. You can whittle away at it while we talk. Do you mind?" He said it so heartily and warmly, she couldn't refuse.

"If that is really all right with you, I'd love one now! My stomach is growling just a little bit." She was excited and just remembered that she'd be thirsty, "Oh, yes, and may I have a glass of milk with that? It's too early for me to have coffee just yet, but I love milk with breakfast."

Blake got a good laugh over that. He hadn't heard of someone who liked coffee, but not in the morning. That was a first for him, and believe him, there were few of those.

"Excuse me for just a minute, Krista, then I promise to be a better host. I'm just going to take care of that and be right back. Is there anything else you would like? Some orange juice maybe?"

"Oh, no, Blake, that is more than plenty for me. Thank you."

He then moved to a table, pulled out a chair for Krista, and excused himself most politely with an, "I'll be right back."

A waitress came by and poured some water for Krista and Blake as well. Krista got the feeling that the work force moved smoothly here.

She sat back in her chair and relaxed. She brought in the items from Gordon and Jan's that she found in one of her sacks the day she had gotten home. She had so many questions. Krista looked around the room admiring the artifacts and smiling over the stuffed animal heads on the wall. That wasn't her thing, but she still appreciated it. A young man in his early to mid-thirties walked past her having washed up in the men's restroom. He noticed her and smiled at her. She returned the smile and thought nothing of it.

Out walked Blake with a cup of coffee and a glass of milk in his hands and he sat down at their table. Following him was a huge, frosted, gooey cinnamon roll—all for Krista.

Krista took a deep breath and said, "Is that all for me?" She kind of knew that already, but she didn't remember it being that big!

"Yessirree. It's all for you. Now that you've got your food all here, I have a better plan. Follow me. I'll get your roll if you can carry your milk."

"No problem. I think I got it."

They wandered off down a corridor and a couple more hallways. The place was massive and greater inside than it seemed outside, and that was saying a lot, for it looked mammoth outside!

~ᐷ~

"Brent. I saw a good looker when I made my way back. She has long blonde hair, just like the girl of your dreams." Darren and his twinkling eyes teased Brent again. After all, she was beautiful to look at. Brent should take a look at her.

"So, are you going to ask her out?" Brent teased right back. Besides, he thought, why shouldn't Darren date?

"Nah, she's not my type. I'm a brunette guy. You're a blonde guy."

Brent rolled his eyes, "I think something happened to your brain when you spilled your coffee. But that's okay. You got me to protect ya. Besides, I'm a brunette guy myself. Not sure why..." Brent trailed off as though he were really thinking about what he said.

"Since I'm all cleaned up from my spill, I think I'll go get myself another plate of hotcakes. This buffet is great. Want some more bacon?"

"The bacon sounds like a good idea. That way, this meal will last me long into the day. Let's do it!"

The guys went for more food and made a morning out of it. Zipper was good for a couple of hours, so Brent wasn't concerned about him. The guys just relaxed before they were going to grab Blake and ask him some questions. Life would get serious enough as the day went on.

Krista and Blake were in his den-like office with rich looking, darker woods for bookshelves and a handsome ornate desk to match. "Blake, I love your window there. Something about it is different. It's rather dark, but I can still see easily out of it." Krista was cocking her head trying to solve the little puzzle of his window.

"Since you love my window, watch this." With that, he pulled a remote control out of his desk and pointed toward the window. All of a sudden, the window became a snowy white mountain scene.

"You like that? Watch this!" He continued to use his remote and the window looked like plantation shutters. Then he pushed the control again and the window turned into a field of flowers.

"Oh, I like that one. I love flowers."

"I never use that one. That is my least favorite. But I'll be sure to remember it for when you are around." Blake finished his show and explained, "I can see out but people cannot see in. Technology is great, isn't it?"

"Yes, it sure is. There is always so much to learn for it keeps changing and advancing." Then out of the clear blue, "Do you think we have much time left here on Earth?" Krista even surprised herself with that one. But out it came anyway.

"Are you asking because technology is so advanced?" He was eyeing her carefully now, as if to get inside her head.

"No, to tell you the truth, that just popped out of my mouth. I'm not sure why I asked, except…" She hesitated, to make sure she really knew why it popped out.

"Except…" He repeated to help her finish her thought.

"Except, I've had a strange feeling lately that things are going to change, on a very large scale, but I can't figure out why. Just, maybe it is getting time for the end of this time. Gordon said you are a believer. What do you think?"

"Yes, I'm a believer," he teased. He knew she really wanted to know his thoughts on God's timing right now. He glanced out his semi-large window they were admiring just a few moments ago and noticed more police cars parking across the street. *"Where did all these policemen come from? It's like an invasion."*

He immediately looked back to Krista who was still in a thoughtful mode when he said, "Krista, I'll come right to the point and answer your question. I do think we are close to the end. I'm not sure how it is all going to go down, but I believe we are close. Let me ask you something. Have you noticed extra policemen around where you live or when you came out here?"

"I don't know if I've seen extra, but I have seen plenty of them on the roads and parked in people's driveways. Why? Why do you ask?"

"Krista, Gordon told me all about you. I know who you are. Gordon also shared with me that he told you a little about the Christian organization that met for centuries until about thirty years ago when they came up with other ways to communicate and semi-congregate. He told me he and Jan gave you something, and I hope you brought it here today."

Krista took all that in. She wasn't used to being found out without speaking about it first herself, and how many people in her life had she ever done that with? None? But Gordon and Jan last week were told because they had all confided with one another. God had revealed in a dream to the three at the ocean that the mission was nearly finished. Those who were on the mission of keeping the maps safe were supposed to take some risks in coming out enough to secure the items God had hidden for all these years from the enemy.

Meeting with Blake was a risky exposure, but Krista was just obeying the Lord and what He had been telling her in His Presence.

Krista bent down for her bag she brought in. She pulled out the exquisite pencil box and the book given to her by Jan. She had looked at the pencil box but had not found anything in it.

Blake got really excited when he saw the pencil box. He reached out for it and handled it carefully. He stopped. Looked at Krista seriously, "Krista, the Lord told me you are to protect His map. I don't know if you know it already, but two of the four maps have been taken by the enemy already. One just last night from a Mrs. Gunther. Does that name sound familiar to you?"

Krista was going to ask him a question that God had given her in the night months ago that He said would protect her and would allow to know if someone was truly sent of Him or not. She threw the question out there. "Before I answer that, I need to ask you a question. What's my dad's real name?"

Blake stood back up and wandered over to the window, facing her. He was still holding the pencil box. Blake wasn't about to just jump out with the name, so he went to a locked drawer in his desk. He retrieved a piece of paper and held onto it. "I think you have something to give to me also."

With that, Krista pulled out of her bag a piece of paper that she had written on just that morning. It was at times like this that she really needed to make sure she had heard from God for this venture. She had. She had to trust God for this moment.

The two exchanged papers and they both had the same name on them, "Jacob Jerusalem Jentssen."

Krista nearly gasped. Tears came to her eyes, but she regained her composure. "One last question Blake; what is so special about his name?"

Blake was happy for that question also. Smiling softly, he told her in a very quiet tone. "The people in God's secret organization all have cities for a middle name. These names only came from the leaders in the organization, and no one past them has ever heard their undisclosed name. Only the leaders know the middle name, but the rest of the organization—and only during the meetings way back when—were allowed to use the first and last name during the meetings."

Blake moved around in the room putting his thoughts together. "Krista, there is only one time that the name can be revealed, and that is upon death. How did you find out his name?"

"My mom told me before she died. I don't know when he told her, but they knew his last mission was going to be seriously life threatening." Krista took a deep breath before she continued. "She gave me Dad's stuff, like logs and journals and things like that. I read all of them and knew his ultimate mission had been passed down to me." She hesitated only for a moment, then added, "I have seen Mrs. Gunther's name in one of those journals."

Krista started to feel the gravity of the time she lived in. She then realized something that was now becoming very obvious. She was surprised she hadn't thought of it before. "Then you knew my dad?"

Blake's smile broadened ever so widely and he said, "Yes. I knew your dad. He was a great man, Krista. He fought the battles of the Lord like the famed secret agent that he was. Thankfully, the one who killed your dad was also killed before he could get out the secret of who your dad was. So, everyone still thinks your dad was a food distributor from the hick town of Maple Valley." He winked when he said hick town.

Yes, Krista could see how easy it was to keep her cover because of where she lived and what everyone thought of her mom and dad. She was seen as just another woman in her thirties with a little dog that came out of nowhere to keep her company.

"Now, the matter of the pencil box," Blake continued. "About the book, we will discuss that at a later date." He sat back down and pushed a little button and asked his secretary to send in his wife. Barely half a minute went by before she was already there.

"Darling, I'd like you to meet Krista. She is the one I told you about when Gordon called. Krista, I'd like you to meet my wife, Milly."

Krista reached out to shake her hand, but Milly brought her into a hug and just loved on her. "Hello, Krista. It's nice to meet you. I hope you are well fed here." She winked and looked at Krista with a lot of love before she turned to sit down.

"I am so well fed, thank you. Your restaurant is a wonderful place to be, Milly. Thank you for the good food."

"You just come as often as you wish. You can come for fellowship as well, hon. We will always be here for you." With that Milly just sat there with a warm smile on her face with all of the poise and calmness one could ever have.

"Fellowship? Do you have meetings here?"

Milly didn't want to say too much, but she made sure Krista felt good by what she asked. "Blake and I are always good for fellowship anytime. If we know of some meetings, would you like us to tell you?"

"That would be very nice." Krista nodded and smiled. She had always stuck to fellowship near her home, but this could also be refreshing out here. She would have to contemplate that.

"Ladies, we have a pencil box to look at."

Both ladies swerved to look at Blake back at his desk, eyeing the box now.

"Watch carefully." With that, he opened the box and removed a plate that was the roof of the top lid underneath. The top lid was rectangular with the rest of the box, but raised and rounded on top, which gave it added character to the beautiful design and marbling. He turned the box around to face the ladies and showed them a sliding piece about as big as the tip of his pinky finger that had been under the plate on the true roof of the top lid. The plate had acted as a ceiling to the inside of the box. He slid the piece about an inch and a half which loosened all four outer sides at the base of the rounded top to simultaneously pop out about a quarter of an inch. Two sides had a piece of onyx that Blake could slide out. He slid the far right side piece and then the left side piece of onyx that was barely a half of an inch in height until he slipped it over half way off the box. The rounded top now rose up like opening a treasure box. Inside this area had been a piece of paper well hidden and secured for centuries. It was one of the maps.

"Oh," came the sounds of the women. It was a sight to behold as Blake unraveled it.

～ Chapter Twenty-two ～

BRENT AND DARREN were just finishing up their buffet and decided to give Zipper a break before they met up with Blake. They had been told in the night from an angel to go talk with Blake this day. They contacted him the moment they got to the restaurant and Blake said he was busy with someone else but to meet him back in an hour. That gave the guys plenty of time to chow down and have a good time, since they had been there for a while.

Outside, the guys walked out to the SUV and when they got close, Brent lightly punched Darren in the arm. "Dare! Look at that!"

Darren followed Brent's gaze to the red sports car they had seen a few times before.

"How about that," drawled Darren.

"Really!" Brent was all excited and ignored Darren.

As they approached the car they heard a little, "Rark!" That sure didn't sound like Zipper, but they couldn't see through the some-what darkened windows at the little black dog quite yet.

"Rark!" This time it was right beside them so they decided to take a closer look.

When Misty wagged her tail her whole body wagged. When Zipper wagged his tail, just the back half wagged. Brent and Darren laughed when they saw how cute Misty was.

"Hi there, little guy," said Brent poking his finger onto the window as if to make contact.

"The little guy could be a little gal, Brent."

"Yeah, yeah, Mr. Fussy Pants. Isn't he—or *she*—cute?"

"Woof, woof!" Zipper was getting all excited. After all, he and Misty had become quite the friends the past hour and a half.

"Now don't you be getting jealous Zip," said Brent as he walked over to Zipper. "I love you more; I love you more, yes I do! I love you more."

Darren had fun just watching and listening. It brought back a lot of memories for him.

Brent took one last look into the red car to see if he could find a hint as to who owned it or why it took his interest so much. He popped open the back of his vehicle with his remote key and Zipper came bounding out. The three of them decided to take a walk in the great expanse of trees and grass that was at this end of the parking lot. That's why they parked there when Zipper was along. It was very handy and easy.

"Rark! Rark!" went Misty to let her pal know she was thinking of him while he was away.

Zipper looked up at his master as if to say, "See, we are friends, Misty and me."

Brent looked back at the red car, and Darren and he chuckled. The guys tried to walk off a bit of the breakfast they enjoyed, and the three of them got way into the thicker area of the woods.

"It was nice meeting you, Krista," said Milly as the three of them said their good-byes.

"Krista, I will look forward to seeing you soon." Blake stood there at the door looking like a pillar of strength. "Don't make yourself scarce, ya hear?"

"Oh, I will certainly try to come by more often, guys. By the way, thanks for the towel for my kitchen! I will consider it a favorite in my collection!" Krista tried to say those words slightly louder than normal in case anyone was listening in. The towel was just a front to throw listeners off track, and she had actually packed one before she got there, but made sure it was showing when she left.

It was all frighteningly coming together, yet adrenaline soared through her while her mind went a hundred miles an hour with thoughts of what to do and what not to do. She laughed to herself thinking, *"What I ought to do right now is give Misty a good walk!"*

She reached her car and decided to glance over at the Retriever she had met earlier. She was instantly shocked that he was nowhere to be found. On the other hand, her owner may have come back and taken her on a walk. Or him, whichever she or he was. She smiled at her silly thoughts and got Misty out of the car. They headed into the front of the woods.

Misty was pure whatever she was and her nose was to the ground. Krista started to go in one direction, but Misty was heading in a different direction. "Hey, Misty, over here!"

Misty galloped five or six feet toward Krista then jumped in the air only to make a dead-run in the other direction.

"Misty! What are you doing?" Krista wasn't too happy about her little doggy at the moment but yielded to Misty's direction. Still she gave a good calling after her in hopes of getting her to come back her direction. Under her breath Krista mumbled, "Don't you be finding more children for me to take care of."

Again Misty would run back half way to meet Krista, then turn around just to dart off in the other direction. Krista knew Misty usually had a good reason, but she was "reasoned" out at the moment. With everything going on, every move she took would be riskier and more dangerous.

A few minutes later, Krista could hear other voices. She immediately went on alert to check her surroundings. She didn't feel alarmed inside, so she decided to keep proceeding. Besides, Misty was up there somewhere. Sure enough, Misty came running back toward her again, but there was another dog following her. When they got much closer, Krista recognized the dog to be the one in the SUV she saw earlier. Well, that was nice! Maybe she could see the owners now.

"Zipper! Get back here boy! Zip!" The last call was a bit sharper as Brent waited for his dog to obey him. Zipper never had a problem obeying. It just wasn't in him to disobey, that's all. Brent hadn't seen Zipper act like that before and credited it all to being with another dog.

As Krista, Brent, Darren, and two silly dogs got a lot closer together, the dogs started chasing around in a circle with the three adults in the middle. Each person had their hands on their hips now watching the dogs act very crazy and entertaining. Everyone was trying to say something or just laughing. It was a sight to see.

Brent bent over and held out his arms to Zipper when he was on his umpteenth round. Zip was having fun. Why would his master want to interrupt it now? Zip just smiled as he went by with his tongue hanging way out of his mouth. He was working up a great sweat and the dogs seemed just a bit out of control.

Brent got brave and stood right in the path of the circle the dogs were making and yelled firmly at Zipper to come to him. Zipper slowed down and came up to Brent with the happiest face Brent could ever imagine on his dog. Brent just turned toward Krista and apologized.

"I'm sorry about my dog, Miss; I don't know what got into him; he is usually extremely obedient and not at all rowdy."

Now Krista knew the beautiful dog was a *he*. "No, I think I should be the one apologizing. Misty acted strangely the moment I got her out of the car, and I believe she started the whole thing. Please forgive me."

Darren's foot kicked a little at the back of Brent's foot hoping Krista wouldn't see. Now they knew Misty was a *she*, and Darren couldn't resist the little secret nudge to Brent.

"So, that was, or is, your red car parked over there in the parking lot?" Brent stammered just a little because he was so curious as to who she was; maybe the nagging of that car that had been in his head for a few weeks could finally be put to rest.

"Yes, that would be me all right. My name is Krista." She held out her hand and the guys instantly acted sheepishly but managed to shake her hand back.

"Oh, sorry about my manners, Kris, Krista. I'm sorry, Krista."

"Good goin' Brent," thought Darren. "Hi, my name is Darren and this is my bud, Brent. So, you ate at Bear Pa's?"

"Yes! I did. I love coming here to eat." *"Cool it, Krista. This is no time to act dumb."* You must have eaten here too?" Then Krista remembered something about waiting for her cinnamon roll. "Oh! You are the guy that I saw who walked by my table and said hello."

She smiled at Darren with her eyes seemingly so bright and happy at her memory returning.

"Yep, that was me all right."

Brent was thinking of the day he saw her drive by, that first time he saw her. He was remembering that little black dog sticking her head out the window.

"Didn't we see you up in the hills a few weeks ago? I'm sure we saw you drive by heading down one of the logging roads. I can't forget your dog sticking her head out the window. In fact, we almost ran into you. You were going by us pretty fast, and the trees ran right up to the end of the road we were coming out of. What were you doing up there anyway? If I may ask..." Brent thought he better tag that last line on, because he thought he may have crossed the line of politeness. Wow, he was getting a shaky start at this meeting.

"Okay, God, what do I say here?" "So, you guys were up in the hills, huh? I remember being there. I was heading somewhere for some reason, but I don't recall everything at the moment." She was trying to politely put them off because she didn't really know these guys. The dogs seemed to like each other, but who were these guys anyway?

Brent noticed himself noticing her hair and the way it fell around her face. Blonde highlights on top of her blonde hair. Nice. He had to clue into what she just said and got the hint she made with her elusiveness.

He graciously started to go onto a different topic when Darren piped in, "Hey, man, we've got an appointment to make. I think we're supposed to be there now, as a matter of fact." Darren raised his eyebrows, and Brent looked horror stricken.

"That's right! We gotta get out of here! Please excuse us, Krista. I just plain forgot about our appointment. Maybe we will run into you again sometime!"

They were all briskly walking back toward the parking lot for Krista had gotten caught up with their excitement and didn't feel like it was closure quite yet.

"That's fine, Brent. It was nice meeting you two, and I loved meeting your dog. He is a beautiful dog, Brent. He is yours, right?"

"Yes, I've had him since he was a little snort. We go everywhere together."

The pace seemed to quicken, and Krista thought she and Misty would walk around the park a bit more as she gathered her thoughts in this lovely place. "I'll see you around then, maybe! Have a nice appointment you two!" With that she stopped, waved her hand, and leaned down to pick up Misty. No more chasing after her until these guys were gone and out of sight.

"Bye!" yelled Darren as he turned around to wave at her.

Brent followed suit and off they scurried to the appointment.

"Brent, I'll put Zip away in the SUV while you head into the restaurant. I'll catch up to you then."

"Sounds like a plan, Dare. Thanks."

Krista and Misty eventually wandered off with Krista deep in thought. "What was that all about, Lord? It certainly felt like a divine appointment, but for what? I'm going to have to call Blake next week and see what God is telling him and find out if he knows these guys." They got further and further back into the woods. Her concentration was so deep that she nearly lost track of where she was.

~ Chapter Twenty-three ~

M R. ADAMS, IT'S an honor to meet you." Brent held out
his hand to this tall figure of a man, who he promptly
liked.

"Please, call me Blake. Don't you have a friend that is supposed
to be with you?"

"That would be Darren. He's coming." Brent turned around and
saw Darren run across the parking lot. "He's running across the
parking lot right now. We took my dog for a walk in the park
behind the lot here, and he ran into another dog. All of that was
unexpected and by the time we acquainted ourselves with that
owner, we nearly lost track of time. Please forgive me, Blake."

"Ah, no problem. You are pretty much on time anyway."

Right then Darren caught up to them a little out of breath.
Everyone made their introductions and walked into Bear Pa's.

After they were seated, Blake offered them food and drink. "Are
you gentlemen hungry? I saw you put away a lot of food earlier, but
there's always more!"

Brent and Darren touched their stomachs letting him know they
were still quite full. Darren just stepped right into the conversation, "I believe we're stuffed but thank you anyway. Your food is
really great, Blake. We come here often, though it's been just about
a month since we've been to Tall Pines. It's a fun place to be to kick
back and relax. Have you been here long?"

"Actually, I've always been here, and my parents, and their parents.
Our generations go back a long way. Since surviving the wrath of
God days in Colorado and up into the hills on this side, my family
has always been between there and here. Many homesteaded here
and never left this place. It feels like we own it, if you know what I
mean."

Brent thought on that. It had been a long time since he felt that way about anywhere. He had always figured his dad's place would be his someday, and pretty much resigned to that.

"How about some coffee or water for either of you?" Blake was eager to serve them so they could get on with business.

Both of the guys took the water offering and when they did, Blake ushered them back to his office. They all sat down and Blake asked the most unusual question. "Brent, how attached are you to that axe of yours?"

Brent couldn't answer at first. He did not know this guy except for seeing him roam the restaurant while he was here eating. This wasn't just any axe.

Blake knew he threw that question out suddenly, so he decided to help Brent out a little. "Brent, I knew your dad. He was a fine man, and I was sorry to learn of his passing when he died. Let me tell you how I knew him."

That got Brent's attention and he sat a bit forward to hear what this man had to say.

Blake propped himself up on his desk and started right in. "There is a very large group of men who have been meeting secretly for centuries…" and Blake told him the rest of the story. Apparently, Blake knew Brent's dad, Allen.

Brent and Darren sat there mesmerized as they heard Blake share about men who were so serious in serving the Lord that they had become the millennium's Round Table of Knights in His service. They all had such in-depth training in things of weaponry, history, geography, and the Word of God. They all had purpose with humility, wisdom, pure heartedness, and fidelity. "Honor in God" was their motto. Certainly they were men of excellence.

Brent watched this man with a new love of those that had gone on before them, sometimes martyring themselves for God's final work on Earth. Who was Blake anyway? He found out listening to him that he too was part of this group and still is. But how high up in this organization was Blake? Brent just sat there thanking God for leading him to such a man and place. What would God require of him next?

"Now, may I ask you about your special axe?" He knew something no one else knew. It was time the right people knew what was going on. The plan of the enemy had been launched, and many of God's people had been told and warned by the Father. They were about ready. Blake's eyes glimmered with love and emotion.

Brent was also filled with a lot of emotion. It's just, he didn't want to open his mouth and share this prize of his. His axe represented his family—his history; it was his life and means. You just don't give that gift away, even if it was just in word only. He sat there struggling.

Darren looked over at Brent. He understood. Every day he was away from the City of God, he yearned for its presence. He felt what Brent must be feeling, that this knowledge about the axe that he was about to share could be like giving up his prized possession; and even if it was for a short time period that he gave it up, it would feel like forever in his heart.

As always, Brent chose to put his emotions aside so he could hear from the Father. He just needed one more assurance. He closed his eyes and a smile crept over his face. *"Thank You, Father, thank You."*

"Blake, I was very attached to my dad and grandpa. The axe is nearly all about them as far as I'm concerned. It's been in my hands for years. It's my connection to those years with them and my ancestry. What do you want to specifically know about it? Why is it of interest?"

"Have I told you about the maps?" Blake grinned so slyly, it was telling all on its own. Blake shared about the maps and their value to the enemy of God.

Darren acted shocked to keep up his cover.

Brent acted shocked because he knew nothing about all of this, but he knew something was up, and realized it was relating to the takeover of God's Great City. When that realization manifested, it was like a direct hit in the stomach. He wanted to throw up.

Blake reached for his intercom button and said, "Darlin' there are a couple of men in this room who could use a soda about now. Bring our special in, okay?"

"You got it, honey," came the reply from Milly.

"So," Brent began after a big swallow to keep things down, "I've been carrying around *the* map?"

"That's right. It had to be that way, Brent. It has had to be so out in the open that the enemy would never suspect. God knew He could protect it by you. Now that the enemy has upped his plan and put it into full force—and in fast gear I might add—God will reveal people to you that will be a part of the guarding of this map. You will continually receive wisdom from the throne. A couple of whopper ideas will come to you yet. It's what the Father has planned, and that's about all I can share right now. Everything has its time and purpose with God. But you already knew that."

Milly walked in with two fresh sparkling sodas that had honey and ginger in them, unlike other sodas. They were calming and revitalizing. Blake did the introductions, and the guys sipped on their drinks. The drinks felt good going down. Brent immediately started to feel better.

"Brent, Darren, it was nice meeting you," Milly said sincerely. "I have to scurry off, but I was glad to see your faces again. I've seen you around here, and you have always been wonderful to work with as customers. As you know, we get some pretty rowdy men in here from the logging company. Thank you for obeying the Lord in dropping by."

Milly turned to go and got to the door. She stopped before she got all the way out and turned to the visitors, "By the way, we have a meeting going on here tomorrow you will want to be here for. Can I count on you being here? We are going to pray and have our own personal buffet in the back of the restaurant. Hope you like barbeque!" She winked and paused for their answer.

"Will it be in the afternoon?" queried Brent.

"Yes, it is planned for two p.m. Will that work for you?"

Brent and Darren looked at each other with, "*Is that okay with you? It's okay with me,*" kind of look. In unison, they answered a hearty, "Yes, we will be there! Sounds good."

"Okay! See you then!" Milly was gone, and the guys turned back toward Blake.

Brent shook his head with the feeling of being overwhelmed. "We knew we were supposed to make a connection with you Blake, but had no idea the seriousness of it all. Do you have anytime today for us to get back with you to tell you what's been happening on our end?"

"How long do you think that will take?" Blake had already figured this day was taken for a lot of this. He had other people to meet as well as make his appearance for the Saturday night crowd. That was the biggest night of the week for his story telling. People that were repeaters—those faithful customers—knew what stories to ask for; they even asked for ones they had never heard before. Yessirree, Blake needed to keep his Saturday evening presence just for his clientele here at Bear Pa's.

"If we're really good, we could keep our visit down to an hour. Is that possible?"

Blake let out a deep laugh. "You tell me, is that possible for you to share everything in one hour?" He laughed some more, and the two young men picked up on the lightness of the moment. It felt good.

Darren reassured Blake they could do it in an hour, while at the same time he jabbed talkative Brent. The atmosphere of seriousness was changing to playful, something they were all comfortable with and decided to keep it that way. It seemed to balance the whole morning out.

Six large angels stood around the three men along with the guys' personal angels. They nodded to each other like their immediate mission had been accomplished. They vanished back through the screen into one of the throne of God's stadiums, awaiting their next assignment.

All day long, the presence of the Father was sent through His holy messengers that wafted through walls, in and out of cars, buildings, and streets all over the world. God had stepped up his angelic activity; for all of His believers knew and understood that when the enemy comes in like a flood, the Lord sets up a standard against that flood.

Brent and Darren made a set time to meet later that day with Blake as he escorted them to the outdoors like he pretty much did with everyone. He liked the idea of never leaving the ship, and each person was his passenger that he cared for. He was a captain in every sense of the word, and anyone with him knew they were covered and protected and loved.

~ℓᕑ~

Deep below the surface of the earth, angels were positioning for trumpet calls. There were angels who did everything concerning the earth's geography. There were also angels who did everything concerning things far above the earth. They too were waiting for trumpet calls. Their trumpet call was different from all of the others. How angels could discern which trumpet call was for what was a mystery God alone knew. As long as God knew, man did not always have to know.

A sound that would shake even the Christians was within days of being heard.

~ Chapter Twenty-four ~

SOME PEOPLE UNDERSTOOD history and didn't want to repeat it. While others looked at it with eyes of bitterness, which caused their vision to be so stained, the lessons of history were lost on them; they really didn't get that "you reap what you sow."

The evil ones who were left on the earth those thousand years ago sought out clever ways to survive. Small numbers of those who had received the mark of the beast found out their doom and took their babies to hide-outs in hopes their children would be spared the devastation that was taking place all around them. Most of the hide-outs had been destroyed, or those in them had died due to lack of food and water. Then there were those who had gone into hiding never accepting the mark of the beast. Most of the rich unbelievers had succumbed to the charisma of the anti-Christ and did not know better to hide away. But there were some that were very smart and did whatever they could to hide and secure their next generation. Only the very rich could put their babies in under-ground facilities with or without them. They had access to finding information about the anti-Christ's plan because they were part of some leadership that gave them that access that helped them get out just in time. Some had used technology to hack their way through to the plots of the ones in charge. As good and secure as many of the hide-outs were, they were not a sure thing. Enough had survived, however.

After a few hundred years of a snail pace of any growth, things started to move forward and population growth looked positive. Although primitive in some aspects, people discovered and redis-covered how to build and make things work. Even those who had knowledge in building those first decades could not obtain resources most of the time. If they did have resources, so much had been destroyed above ground, their efforts were for naught. They had to write what they knew and teach it to their children for the next generation. Even paper was scarce for a long time. Those were frustrating days for everyone. If one didn't know the presence of God, insanity ran rampant, which caused a realm of difficulty no one had anticipated. It was as if hell had come to the surface of the earth the first hundred years. Perhaps it did.

Not all of the evil ones meant to be evil at first. Fear had no bounds, and with the lack of God's presence, greed and control had a perfect breeding ground, which eventually took over, leading to a very evil society. Thankfully, there were many without the mark that grew up and found God. God never let His creation live on without hope entirely. His patience was without understanding or comprehension, for He changed not, nor would He ever. Besides, His ways are without understanding because they are so much higher than man's. He revealed to man what he needed to know, and it was that simple.

Man still had to live by faith throughout the millennium. It took an honest, close relationship with the Father and His son Jesus Christ to walk by that kind of faith. It was never head knowledge that God existed, but a personal—making Christ one's best friend— relationship with Him. One could not be in His will or even hope to know His will if He didn't have that kind of relationship.

Meanwhile in the Great City, the beloved of God were ruling and reigning with Christ. They looked after the millions within the mighty walls of the city, even when they needed to go in and out. They had just heard a trumpet sound, and all stilled to hear the latest call of the Father. This was a chilling call, for AFFLICTIONS and DESPAIRS would be great upon the earth. They had much to do for God's final show.

One other word had flashed in the announcement: MERCY.

On Earth, everywhere that people went there was a multiplication of police-men and agent guards. Agent guards worked with the police but were a level higher in authority over them. Agent guards spied, terrorized, and told law enforcement what to do. Law enforcement didn't mind because it wasn't like it used to be in the twentieth and twenty-first centuries. Officers tried to outshine one another so they could work their way up to be an agent guard and have more control. Salaries were despicable throughout the world that had turned socialistic under the four rulers. This gave the rulers of the lands more control and more money for themselves. In this selfish society, it was a perfect regime.

Police officers and agent guards were on the same page as far as getting rid of the Christians, but had been told for years that there was a time when obliteration would take place, and their job in the meantime was to be prepared and practice control on a few individuals. They also recorded everything they learned from these trials they put upon the Christians.

The four generals were now going to instigate the next step before the obliteration force was to happen. They were going to practice on the people they believed could not commit to one side or the other. They were the weak link in the chain of society and were called "wishy-washies." They were a perfect target.

The Bible referred to these types of people as "lukewarm." God was dismayed with these people more so than those who hated Him. The lukewarm did the most damage in the kingdom of God because they would call themselves Christians, but did not act like Jesus; nor were they close enough to Him to be in His perfect will. They continued in their sins without repenting, and did not want to understand the true meaning of repentance and recompense. They were selfish people only using God as a source of help when they were desperate, or attended church, thinking outside appearances were enough to please Him. They did not walk with a strong conviction, nor did they fear God literally. They were blinded by the enemy, who loved them the most. He could have his way with them, and unbelievers would be turned off to Christianity because of them. There was no clear distinction between how they handled frustrations and trials and how the world handled them. They were religious but lacked relationship with Jesus Christ as their truest and best friend.

Monday was approaching its first dawn in the far eastern part of the world. The evil plotters lost sleep over the excitement of closing in on people they didn't like, thinking of ways to wipe them off the planet. Evil creativity was finding fresh inspiration, and great woes were about to hit the earth. News had come down from the very top (the four generals and their captains) that God's city was finally about to come down and all plans were a go, except for the final blow to God. That would not be far behind.

Timing was everything. The devil knew that if he acted swiftly this time, his plan would certainly not fail. He was more than confident over this fact. This was his time, and he knew it without a doubt. He was giddy and beyond silliness in his thoughts of victory. His plans had already proven to be above God since he now had two maps in his possession. God wasn't as all powerful as He led millions to believe with His fantastic trickeries. If there was really a throne surrounding the Great City, satan knew he would be able to see it. Even if it was for real, he wouldn't let his followers believe it. So, it didn't really matter, except that he had to attack the foundation of the city and get below it at a particular place, which the maps would reveal.

With two maps in his possession, satan was self-possessed with power that caused him to act like a fast-forward button. The taste of blood was in his mouth, as sweet nectar to his ever darkened spirit. He was having way too much fun outsmarting God. And if he could keep outsmarting God, His people were as good as gone. Emuel was putty in satan's hands, as well as his daughter and the four generals. The devil let out a good roar of laughter. He was laughing at himself. What was he thinking? All of his disciples were putty in his hands, and that equaled hundreds of millions. Man didn't need him those thousand years. But they needed him now for the day of showdown and the last minute plans, after which they would need him forever and hail him as the one and only almighty god. It was satan's rule now and nothing was going to stop him.

The lead rulers of satan's domain had done a good job confusing everyone while he was locked up. They had done a good job building hatred, pride and intimidation. They just got messy and out of control trying too hard to outdo the other. Their own pride and deception kept them from having a united front unless they could muster enough hatred and purpose at the same time. It always fell apart, however, but not without some successes. They knew satan would be released when the thousand years were up, so they constantly vied for top power. They had everything to prove to get the highest reward, worship, or authority when their master returned.

The hundreds of millions of people wanted the old boundaries back. How else could they get back at God after what He did to their ancestors? Revenge was on their breath and in their blood from the beginning of the rapture, passed down to their children and all of the generations following. It was their day to shine now, and they would, with their loudest voice and strongest arm. Yet even in their thirst for revenge, rules had been set in place, because the final issue of destruction had to be successful and structured. These days were not days of chaos in the devil's mind, but days of planned annihilation that would bring him all the glory. Oh, how he craved his shining moment that would carry his kingdom through eternity.

~ Chapter Twenty-five ~

THE APPOINTED WEEK for starting mayhem and fright throughout cities everywhere was in full swing, with a determination to strongly and resolutely crush the targets that the leaders had claimed. Fires erupted, car crashes oddly increased, and tens of thousands of people were arrested all around the world. The lukewarm wishy-washy people were the target and fear ran widespread. Only, the lukewarm didn't realize they were the target. Deaths had to be managed, for the leaders over towns and cities only had so many facilities to deal with so many at one time. These facilities did their best to keep up, and thankfully, many had been incorporated before the gauntlet had been released.

Christians were finding themselves in more prayer and seeking the presence. The generals did not overly concern themselves with hard-to-get areas like where Grandpa Gordon and Grandma Jan lived, between the ocean and the mountains. There were pockets of refuge throughout the whole world, but even they had to be careful. Agent guards were everywhere. But one day Gordon made a profound observation.

"Jan, have you noticed some of the police we usually have here are gone, and those agent guards...where have they gone?" He didn't know if he should be happy or not. Was it a plan of deceit, or were they needed more elsewhere? He had to find out.

Without warning, a crash of knockings went on at their back door. Fright tore through Jan as her loudest whisper could get out, "Gordon!" Terror ran its chilly hold through both their bodies. Their first thought was the grandchildren. Where were they? Thankfully, they heard their giggles in their room playing with their coloring sets.

"Jan, stay here. I'll check out who is here."

That was easy for Jan, except she had to keep an eye on her

beloved Gordon. They both prayed in the spirit under their breath waiting for calm to come to them.

"Bang, bang, bang!" The knocks sounded desperate. Somehow they didn't seem angry as originally thought which gave Gordon a bit of reprieve inside of himself, believing God was leading him in wisdom.

Gordon peeked around the edge of a kitchen window to take a first look. His eyebrows furrowed together as he couldn't quite make it out. Then he saw two people. One was smaller than the one in front, like the person was hiding behind the bigger one.

And then it hit Gordon like a tsunami wall. *Luke! Becca!*

Gordon darted to the door screaming out to Jan, "It's the kids!"

Jan wasn't sure what he blurted out, but she came running to his rescue, but there was no rescue for him, just their son and his beloved wife.

The door knob practically got thrown out of its hold, and the screen door went crashing open. Luke and Becca came running in as if to hide and escape from a mad female grizzly bear hot on their heels.

"Dad, Mom! We made it! We made it!"

By this time the grandkids came running to see the commotion they had heard. "Aunt Becca! Uncle Luke!"

Everyone wanted to hug everyone, but they ran into the securest place in the house before going downstairs. Tears blanketed their faces and clothing, and their cries turned into sobs. No one spoke of anything for quite a while, for all they could do was be close, very close, and whisper each other's names.

Grandma was the first to pull herself away to offer food and drinks. She looked at them and knew a hot shower was probably right up there on their wish list. "Children, what can I get you?" Without an answer she absent-mindedly went into the kitchen just because she knew the right things to get.

Gordon ushered them downstairs to a more secure place and immediately offered a comfortable place to sit. "Why don't we all sit down? You look so weary, so tired. Mom will get something to refresh you two, and then you can share all about your travels." He looked carefully into their eyes noticing their desperation and need to talk. But the grandchildren were around, and it would have to wait. The important thing was they were here safe. Nevertheless, Gordon took Luke aside and asked him if there was immediate danger to them or the house. Luke reassured him that they had gotten through into what they believed to be a safe area, but before that, it was frightening, and they believed they barely got away with their lives.

With that settled for the moment, everyone relaxed and tried to feel normal. That would take time, God's Presence of peace, and knowledge of His will in each of them.

Rusty stood holding Aunt Becca's hand. It was one more person closer to his mother, and he felt he missed her very much right then. Even with that, there was such a joy seeing Aunt Becca, it felt like his mother was alive, and what Mrs. McCauley and the angel said was true. He would again see his mom and dad.

Sissy walked up to Uncle Luke and asked gently, "Did you see Momma and Daddy?" Her eyes looked like she was going to break down into sobs if the answer was no.

Uncle Luke bent down and gave her a soothing smile. He picked her up and put her on his lap in the overstuffed chair nearby. "All I know is that they are in a very safe place, Sissy. That's the best place to be except here, isn't that right, honey?"

"Uh-huh." Sissy nodded her head up and down, but no smile came on her face. She looked back into Uncle Luke's eyes piercingly, "Where are they? Are they near here?"

Uncle Luke swallowed hard. He did manage to keep it light for Sissy's sake and said one of those millisecond prayers so he could hear God for wisdom—which only He could give at the moment. With only the slightest delay for Sissy's sake, he looked at her right back and said, "I'm not sure where they are, but I know someone who does."

"Who knows Uncle Luke?"

Luke grabbed her hand closest to him and held it to his chest.

He looked deeply into her eyes so she could read the depths of his heart, "God our heavenly Father knows where they are, Sissy. God knows everything. He is the only person who knows how to take care of them and also protect them all of the time. I believe He is protecting them right now." Uncle Luke tweaked her little nose with the end of his finger, and with a calm smile of confidence said, "I think you should believe that too, Sissy; because I believe that is true. Would you like to believe with me?"

Sissy nodded her head in a yes again, and said, "Uh-huh." Even though she sounded weak and frail, she followed with all of her heart. "Mrs. McCauley and the angel said we would see mommy and daddy again. I know we will."

Luke shot a quick glance at his dad with desperate hope in his eyes.

Sissy buried her head deep between Uncle Luke's arm and chest and decided to stay in his lap with his arms wrapped around her for a long time. She was being fed security and hope the whole time, and she needed it.

Rusty walked up to Uncle Luke and agreed with his little sister. "I believe with you too, Uncle Luke."

Uncle Luke grabbed Rusty to be next to his side, and that gave Aunt Becca a chance to go be with Mom for a little while. She needed the change of scenery and Mom's cheerful countenance while she flittered in the kitchen. It had been a long time, even though it had not been a full week, since Becca was in a kitchen that felt like home. Her home had probably been destroyed like so many others.

Many of God's people had taken what they wanted out of their homes to put it in the trunk of their cars or wherever else they felt it would be safe over the weekend before the dreaded Monday came. God's angels and His leading for the warning was everywhere. Many had no place to go, while others did. Christians weren't supposed to be the target yet, but several got hit by excited supporters of destruction. However, God did not forsake His people.

"Sweety," Mom said to her daughter-in-law whom she adored, "how are you holding up?"

"I'm not sure at the moment, but when we get settled, and perhaps take a nap today, we will tell you all about it. I feel like spilling it all out right now to you, but Luke needs to be with me. We will look forward to sharing tonight after the kids go to bed."

"We will get some good food into you, and you will sleep like a dream. Don't you worry about a thing, honey. God has taken care of you and gotten you here, and He will take care of you the rest of the way."

Jan fought back tears while she grilled up some sandwiches. Becca came over to her and wrapped herself around her and wistfully said, "Thanks Mom. I'm going to believe that too."

The day moved on, and Gordon went out to get the answers he thought would change all of the dynamics for his little town.

~*~

The Saturday before, Brent had excused himself from Darren to run some errands before they went back to meet with Blake later that day. He put Zipper in Darren's control while he did some of his own investigation and shopping.

Krista and Misty drove back to Maple Valley to formulate a plan.

Blake and Milly continued meeting people when they knew they weren't being watched.

~*~

The week the plans went into operation, Emuel gloated in his plush den at home where at the push of a button he could get reports from his generals all over to hear about the plan of destruction and how well it was going. He was pulling the carpet right out from under the God whom he considered more and more to be all fallacy.

Durdana, having conquered each general, was now focusing on this person she had in her dream. She played the dream over and over in her mind, determined to play an upper hand once she found this perpetrator of her body and soul.

While the generals were yelling orders to the captains to keep the destruction in bounds, they also had to stay available for Emuel. The devil kept his hand on Emuel's shoulder for the moment. God, well, He had His own plans.

Chapter Twenty-six

THE CHILDREN HAD gone to bed, and Luke and Becca were refreshed but still shaken. Gordon brought them out to the living room and had the four of them all stand up, join hands, and pray. The gratitude and praises came easily because they were brought through so much, were given a place of safety, and were now together with family. The presence was flowing through them and around them during worship which caused the heavy burdens and memories of the past week to waft away to the One who alone could carry them and deal with them marvelously.

All around the world, God's people were worshipping, praying, and seeking direction and wisdom. No matter what happened, they would trust the Lord. A commitment is a commitment, and there is no turning back no matter how much feelings or circumstances try to drown out any reason. Commitment goes past reason. Commitment seeks out a way to make it happen, forsaking all understanding to do it in your own strength. This was part of the believer's key to victory.

Back in Dad and Mom's living room, the four were sipping on apple cider and enjoying some of Jan's famous cookies. Their prayer time sealed hope and faith in their hearts. Now it was time for Luke and Becca to share what they needed. There was a reason why they went through what they did, but they had to get it out first.

Luke and Becca sat on large couch where they could sprawl out, but Becca had her legs tucked up by her, and the two of them held hands. Another team.

Luke started the sharing. "At work Monday I heard different groups of guys share about what they would do when they got home. A lot of us who trust in the Lord walked around looking at each other because we no longer had the feeling that we were equals in the corporation anymore. Our regular co-workers seemed distant from us, and we didn't know why. We, the believers in the building, tried communicating with our phones, but didn't know if we were being monitored or not. We would give 'the eye' to the other and meander to the copy machine and speak not more than ten words so we didn't give ourselves away. With all of the witnessing we've done at the company for years, over half of the workers know who the Christians are. But we weren't the ones that everyone was chattering about. I went in one room and heard some guys talking about a co-worker that we had been witnessing to for a long time, but hadn't given his life to the Lord yet. Then I would go somewhere else and see some people laughing like it was a private joke while they were looking toward another person we had witnessed to strongly that was about to come over to the Lord."

Dad had a thought to ask, "So, no Christians were the subject at all? No looks were aimed at you or your believer friends?"

"That was the consensus mostly, but we still felt scrutinized to some point." Luke took a sip of warm cider and continued, "But there were those, come to think of it, who say they are Christians and go to some church somewhere, but they don't act like it in the least; I observed a couple of them being targeted. What do you think, Dad?"

"It's difficult to make heads or tails out of this yet, kids. I just know of the dozens of testimonies we've heard—how Christians were warned to protect themselves and leave to go somewhere they thought might be safe. I haven't heard of a lot of them getting hit yet, but a lot of people are getting hit. How did you get here?"

"Becca had packed up everything as much as possible, but we planned on staying in our house! We didn't know that Monday was going to dictate such uproar for everyone all at once! It's pandemonium out there!"

Becca was remembering all kinds of things from that day. "I remember walking back from Madeleine's house, just doing my daily checking on it since they disappeared, and I saw some people hiding behind some of the trees a distance from me. They acted like they had seen me and were just plain hiding! It was awful!"

She tried to gather her calmness and continued her story. "I double checked everything in our house and made sure that if we got ransacked, we had what we wanted out of there. I kept looking out our windows the rest of the day until Luke got home."

Luke's eyes were somewhere else as he spoke up. "The traffic was worse than usual coming home. I can't remember ever seeing such panic on the roads. Accidents were dotted along the way; they must have happened throughout the day. I didn't like it when a police officer had to wave one of our lanes through because two others were closed due to accidents that looked pretty serious."

"By the time he got home, I already had food packed; Luke took a shower and gathered up some last minute stuff, and we got out of there. Thankfully it's light out much later with summer nearly upon us. In a strange way that gave us some security because we could see all around us."

"What was also sad was the smoke in the air," Luke added. "People were on the streets and looters were out everywhere with clubs and laundry baskets for their loot. I'm not sure how the police liked the amateurs out there. I think they were feeling out of control. But it bought us time before many road blocks were up...I think road blocks are up...I'm not sure. We saw one go up behind us when we got five miles out of Preston. It was being set up not far from Tall Pines."

Gordon and Jan looked at each other with grave concern. Then Gordon put a pursed smile on his face and blinked both eyes at Jan while he nodded in a quick jerk to let her know it was all okay. They kept listening.

"Becca was a trooper, Dad and Mom. She kept praying, and I kept driving, and you know how I drive!"

That brought a laugh from everyone, for Luke still had some improvements to make from his racing days on the tracks when he was in his late teens. He was a good driver and quite adept, but didn't always remember to keep the passengers in mind when he tightened up corners too quickly. He was the only one who enjoyed those corners, but no one was honest enough to tell him how they felt, or else when they tried, he ignored them. But as Luke grew in the Lord, even that area was improving. Still, if you wanted someone to get you out of danger, Luke would be the pick any day, for it was like being in the presence of James Bond; he was that good behind the wheel.

Luke and Becca were entirely involved in their adventurous story now, and so were Mom and Dad. No one liked what was going to come up the next few minutes though. Becca started to tense up.

"Everything seemed fine that first night. I feel so badly for those who were in unbelief and stayed behind in their homes. Probably many who left after dark didn't fare well. But more on that later."

Luke and Becca snuggled now and were very close. Dad and Mom didn't miss that, and waited for the rest of the story to unfold.

"We found a sit-down diner the next morning that looked pretty safe. We ate a good breakfast not knowing if it would be our last warm meal for a while. Becca had the TMV full of food, but we were just playing it by the moment. Actually, we thought we'd be here by Tuesday night. Here it is Saturday."

Their TMV was a four-wheel Terrain Motor Vehicle that was semi-low to the ground but had van qualities: it could hold a small refrigerator and had a bed that could be folded out to a double bed in back. There was storage room, and the TMV was able to sit seven easily. It was a great vehicle that could handle the roughest terrain and hold corners like a sports car. It was a must for Luke.

Dad and Mom felt a churning in their stomachs thinking of the possibilities of what could have happened in those four extra days. They didn't dare believe that it could be all that bad, but their gut told them the truth. Mom had an extra-large mug with triple potency English style black tea she was sipping on to help keep her out of shock. She knew some of the old tricks. They listened on.

Luke opened his mouth to say something, but Becca just happened to speak it out first. "I was on my way back from the restroom after breakfast and couldn't find Luke anywhere. I walked over to one side of the diner to look around a corner when three big guys cornered me. They were shoulder to shoulder and formed like a crescent moon around me so I couldn't get away from them."

At that point, Dad's knuckles turned white as his fingers were pressing into the recliner's arm rests.

Luke immediately sensed the tension and tried to ease it. "I came out from the other side where the men's restroom was and saw these thugs corner her. My first reaction was to tear each one apart." Luke laughed nervously while gathering his thoughts but no one including him thought it was funny, it was just a nervous reaction he had. "I looked to see if there was anyone who could help me. The waitress wiping the counter just kept looking down and wiping the same spot over and over. I found another man wearing a zip up coat watching me. He was large and stocky and you know what he did? He just slowly shook his head back and forth in a negative warning for me to leave the situation alone. I was frozen and didn't know what to do. Becca had to survive and not get hurt and that's all I could think about. I have to tell ya, Dad, I was getting really angry. I was scared. I didn't know what to do." Luke dropped his head. He was remembering the moment too vividly.

"What did you do, son?" Gordon wanted to be as gentle as possible. He could tell his son had his insides ripped right out of him when he saw Becca cornered.

"I'll tell you what happened!" Becca blurted out. "Before Luke came out I just started thinking, '*I plead the blood, I plead the blood, I plead the blood of Jesus!*'" She straightened up a bit on the couch. "I finally saw Luke. He was looking like he was going to explode. The men started to put their hands on my face and tried touching the outside of my jacket. I felt like crawling bugs were all over me. I kept pleading the blood of Jesus, and it came right out of my mouth out of desperation. Mom and Dad, I started yelling it! At the top of my lungs I yelled, 'I plead the blood of Jesus!'"

Before Luke could say what he did, Becca beamed and said, "Then Luke screamed, 'Get your hands off my wife right now in the name of Jesus!'" She turned to Luke, and they had a moment. They knew God. They were together, and God had done what He promised He would do in His Word.

"So what did the men do?" Mom was leaning forward groping for the rest of the story.

"This time they were the ones frozen in their spot," said a happy Luke. "I ordered them again in the name of Jesus."

Becca was nodding her head up and down strongly.

"I felt such power running through me, Dad and Mom. I needed the power of God through the name of Jesus to fight that battle. I get it now. There is man's anger that produces sin, and there is God's righteous anger that kicks the living daylights out of the devil. It's not flesh and blood. I get it. I found out."

His dad just smiled and his mom had tears in her eyes.

"Guess what happened next, guys. They walked away! They actually walked away!" Becca still felt the awe of it all.

"And that guy I was telling you about that was discouraging me from approaching the men? He was gone." Luke still acted baffled.

"So, then what did you do?" prodded his dad.

"We hugged." Becca giggled. They looked at each other again.

"Then we took off," Luke chimed in. "We looked all around for more guys to come out of the bushes or something." He laughed again, but this was more of the relief kind. "We looked all around our car and," as if rehearsed, Becca said the last words at the very same time Luke did, "we hurried up and got in!"

More giggles went around the room, and everyone felt a whole lot better.

Dad wasn't satisfied yet. "So, this is Saturday, what happened with all of the days in between? Did you run into more trouble?"

Luke and Becca looked at each other and Becca laughed with her infectious laughter. "Well...yeah, we did." She looked at Luke to see if he should tell it instead of her.

Luke smiled broadly and started right in. "We got a flat tire just a couple of miles down the road from the diner." Luke rolled his eyes. "But, I had a spare, actually two in the back! So, I'm working on getting a spare on when someone pulls up next to us. I look at him, he looks at me. And what do you suppose I see?"

Dad and Mom just shook their heads.

"I saw the man that was in my dream from the night before. This man said to me, 'There's only one route to take and that is through the Olympic Peninsula. You know the one.'"

Dad got a special look with this. He raised Luke and Madeleine on those mountains. They camped, fished, hiked, and took several retreats in the mountains. You had to know where to go, where the shelters were, where the streams were, and where plentiful food sources were. The mountains ran their own weather, and you had to know all the quirks. Thankfully, summer was on and that gave Dad a lot of comfort.

"Exactly," Luke said while looking at his dad, like they had some secret code between them.

"Go on and tell them what happened!" Becca urged.

"Okay." Luke was smiling like he was getting to a good part. "The driver left and of course, I knew which route to take. We fixed up the wheel and turned around to head down Highway 101, which turns into Highway 1 and goes through the mountains; it turned into a dirt path during the wrath of God. Certain men had it in their head to make it a hidden way into the mountains, one that their cars could travel on." He said that last part for Becca. "Who knows about that highway anyway, Dad?"

Dad just smiled and barely bobbled his head; Luke didn't give him time to really answer.

"We got up to the top, but by now it was about to get dark. It took us several hours just to get there. I thought the plans I had would be easy. That was a mistake! No, actually, it seemed to be divine until we got down the mountain, and let me tell you why."

"Honey, you were up in the mountains all this time?" Mom was astonished.

"Pretty much. That night we ate some of our packed food and got a good night's sleep. We were so tired from everything that went on that day. I really wanted her to see a few things the next day, and if it took two days, it was okay. We had a great peace about what we were doing, and God seemed to think it was important enough to give it to me in a dream and have that driver stop by and confirm it. Just think—if we had not had that flat tire."

Luke took a moment to sip more on the apple cider, and everyone felt like now they were having a good time. But Becca just kept quiet.

"Did you see anything different or anything you liked, Becca?" Mom was curious to know what all it was Luke was going to show her.

"Oh, yeah, I saw some really cool stuff. But nothing was as cool as those bears." Becca nudged Luke with her elbow again, giggling because she knew what was coming and could hardly wait until Luke got to that part. "Oh, but first, there was the most pristine lake I've ever imagined. It was," and she turned to Luke inquisitively, "Lake Irely? Something like that."

Luke and his dad both nodded. "That's the lake," Luke said.

Dad was ecstatic. He hadn't been there for a few years since he and some of his brothers in the Lord went up there to fast and pray. "There's nothing like that lake is there, son. I'm glad you got to show it to Becca. Did you see a special friend of ours?"

Again came that secret code look between the two.

"Yup, but let me tell you just how that happened." Luke got all comfortable and prepped himself for a whopper of a story. He loved telling stories and did a pretty good job of it. But this one was something beyond one's normal imagination to believe. But it happened, and he jumped right in there to tell it.

"The next day Becca and I moved the van to a better spot, more hidden in the forest. We put on gear for hiking, all a part of our survival gear, and headed to Irely Lake. We could see deer trails everywhere we went. When we got there, I couldn't see any sign of man having been there for a long while. We may have been the first for the season. We just brought along one fishing rod. I found prints of wild life including those of a grizzly. I didn't like that."

"Yes, he looked pretty concerned when he spotted those tracks. It sure didn't make me feel good either."

"I couldn't really tell how fresh they were because of the light rain the night before, but I felt okay to take a little time to catch us some fresh cutthroats or coho. I managed to get a couple of cutthroats and that was it."

Becca got a little tense, but she had a big smile on her face. "But then we had a visitor on the way back to the car, huh, hon?"

"Yep. We sure did. Dad, remember those stories you used to tell about the big grizzly you nick-named Ben?"

"Oh, yes, son. Is that who you saw?"

"How could it be Ben after all of these years, Dad? I thought it would be impossible that he would still be alive. But you gotta hear this."

No one wanted to wait another second for this. Nerves started to get on edge anticipating something horrible, yet here were their children, right in front of them.

"About twenty yards away stood a tall mature grizzly on his hind haunches looking right at us. It scared the living pa-jee-bees out of me."

"I almost collapsed," Becca added.

"I didn't know if he or she was the only one in the area, and we did some quick praying like, 'Jesus, Jesus, Jesus.' Couldn't think past that. It was like a total stare down between the grizzly and me." Luke managed a grin while remembering.

Becca's eyes were big now. "The grizzly got back down on all fours and walked right toward us! I couldn't move and don't think I was supposed to."

"That's right, Becca, you don't want to run in front of a grizzly or any bear," Dad added.

"I was thinking I would throw the fish as far away from me as possible. I really wanted it to be a peace offering, although I didn't believe it. I slowly raised the fish above my head and threw the fish as far away as I could to the right of the bear, but far away from him so he wouldn't think I was attacking him."

"Good, good." Dad was sitting on the edge of the chair now.

"That stopped the grizzly. He stood back up and sniffed the air. I think he was checking out to see if others were around. Whatever he did, we still didn't move. Then he did the oddest thing, Dad and Mom. He was acting like he was clapping his paws together! Seriously! He did it five times."

"Really!" Becca said. "He was clapping."

"Go on," Dad said.

"He got back down and went for the fish. Then when he got them, we started to walk back on the trail, but tried a different trail that was nearby. He looked at us with a mouthful of fish and nodded his head in the direction we were going as if to say, "That's right, just keep going in that direction." It was weird. Very strange."

"Very," said Becca.

Mom's arms went limp, and Dad, too, relaxed. "So, you got back to your car all right?"

"Yes, without another incident. But what happened when we got down the mountain a couple of days later is the worst thing that happened on the whole trip. That's why we were frantic at your door. We got really spooked."

"I'm spooked just hearing you say that. What happened, darlin'?" asked an eager Mom.

"Gotta have another cookie or two first. They're good, Mom. Thanks for making them."

"Sure, babe. I think I'll take a bathroom break. Can I get anyone anything while I'm up?"

Everyone was just fine and cookies landed in everyone's mouth. Couldn't get enough of Mom's cooking anytime.

Then Dad got up and played with the gas fireplace's intensity while Becca got up to get a glass of milk for her and Luke. It was a long night, but it sure felt good to get the stories all out. It put everything in perspective. Becca could easily tense up still over the last story coming. She wasn't sure where it was all going to end. She was eager to get Mom and Dad's viewpoint on it all.

Mom came back all refreshed, and everyone was gathered again comfortably to hear how their excursion had ended late Saturday morning.

Becca was reflecting on their adventure. "I love the Olympic Mountains and wouldn't have missed this journey for anything in the world. God sure gave Washington state beautiful mountains, and a lot of them! Too bad Mt. Rainier doesn't exist anymore. I heard it was unusually beautiful."

"That's what the stories say that have come down through history. Luke, be sure to remind me to give you a book that Great-Great-Grandma wrote. Survival stories that got passed down through the centuries are in the book, and there is something in there about Mt. Rainier. You both will find it fascinating. I think we were going to give it to you this coming Christmas, but frankly, I don't know if any of us will see Christmas. Personally, I'm hoping we will all be in the City of God by then. I don't like what I'm hearing about what's going on everywhere. Since the devil has been released from his thousand year lock up, he seems furious and unrelenting. I don't know what is going to happen to any of us. But go ahead with your story. We need to hear this."

"Late Friday morning we left to get here, thinking it would just be the day and all would be well. At this point, we were getting rather ready and anxious to get here. I got to thinking about Mom's hotcakes." He winked just then at Mom. It was an event for them whenever he was around. No one made them like her and part of the joy of coming home was woofing down several of her hotcakes, a recipe handed down to her from her ancestors. He and Becca made them at their house from time to time, but it was more fun having someone else make them, like Mom. It was their special thing.

"The road on this side was worse than the road on the other side. We had to take it slowly to get over some pretty bad spots. Then Becca got a check in her spirit. We didn't know what, but it made us very uneasy. We drove about a quarter of a mile until we could find a place to turn out and hide from the road. We didn't know what else to do. You know God, He doesn't always tell you until step by step you've obeyed, and then the bigger picture comes!" Luke's eyes got big for a moment, and he proceeded with his story.

"We got out to listen as well as to watch. It just seemed like the right thing to do. We kept the TMV in sight while we walked a few steps to climb up on a boulder so we could get to a vantage point where we could see what was before us. Then we saw it. Agent guards with their rifles were walking on trails like they were looking for someone. There were maybe three of them. I immediately thought of the old shack about a mile down near the base and wondered if it was a fortified building now with agent guards securing this side of the mountains. They are probably all up and down this west side. But I don't know."

Luke continued, but a worried look was on his face now. "We knew they could see us if they looked up and peered through the trees hard enough, so we got back down and went back to the car. God had brought us through so much, and we were so close, we just couldn't give up now."

"That's for sure," said Becca. "We rolled the windows down just a little way to see if we could hear them approach, and prayed!"

"Then it was obvious to us that we needed to get out and make a run for it. We really hated to do that because all our valuables and items to survive with were in the car. Not to mention a comfortable bed when we are on the road. Leaving the TMV was painful. But our lives meant so much more, so we took off."

"How did you go, son?"

"First, we went up and over like you taught me, Dad. We wanted to get away from them first before we descended back down to the house. We had to find that shack and when we got to another vantage point, we spotted it with our binoculars. Sure enough, it was a little guard house now, but no bigger than say, maybe seven hundred square feet. They just used wood to build it back up, so it wasn't anything fortified, I'm thankful to say."

"We weren't sure if the search party was going to head north, but didn't think so because when we watched them, they were mostly heading east up the mountains. We figured that little guard house probably didn't house more than four at a time, so we didn't feel too threatened by any others being around. Just to make sure, we hung out at our vantage point for over an hour."

Becca was as sharp as her husband, and they could have been detectives together. Details rarely got past them if they were involved in something.

Luke picked the story back up. "When we left the vantage point, we made our way back down the hill a good mile away from the guard house, and where we thought the agent guards were monitoring. If we didn't get off the mountains soon, we didn't think we'd be safe at all. Too many things like beasts and bugs and agent guards that could surprise us. Yet, we kept the confidence that if we stayed in God's will, we would be the safest."

"Yep," said Becca.

"To wind this thing all up, we got curious about the TMV. We had to know if they found the car and what happened to it. I know, it sounds silly, but we felt driven to do this. We did an about-face and went back to the TMV instead. The other sillier thought we had was that we could drive the TMV right through the guard house."

"You thought that, not me," said Becca.

"Well, it's not like I held onto the idea. It was just an idea." Luke said it so matter-of-factly, as to not own up to it fully. He admitted it was a silly idea after all.

"We got back to the TMV, and everything seemed intact. We were really surprised and delighted all at the same time! We just weren't thinking..." trailed off Becca, back in her thoughts.

"We got in and figured we would try a trail around the guard house or drive by really, really fast." Luke sat there feeling a bit sheepish all of a sudden. "The next thing we knew, there were three men with their guns pointing at us ordering us out of the TMV. It seemed like the right thing to do to be back at the car, but we got caught." Luke had the cutest expression while he humbled himself. He never minded humbling himself once he got to that point of resolution. Then he made it cute, and no one could ever be mad at him.

Mom wanted to say something, but held back so she could hear the end of this frightful experience. *"Thank You, God, for bringing them here."* How many times had she prayed that prayer this day.

"They questioned us over and over again. They didn't think we were the people they were looking for and were really upset. All I can hope is that God used us to get them off the trail of whomever it was they were after in the first place. God does things like that."

Luke finally reclined back on the couch, and he and Becca repositioned themselves.

"Son, that's when you have to recheck that peace only Christ can give. If you knew you were in His will, then you have to stay your course until God shows you why. He can't do much with people who follow circumstances instead of His Spirit."

"Well, yes, that is what I did, we did." Luke and Becca took a quick look at each other while Luke continued, "They held onto us through the night expecting to take us into town the next day. We slept on cots on the floor, but they did feed us sandwiches. That was good."

This time Becca rolled her eyes.

"The next morning after we had bowls of cereal I pleaded with them to let us go for a walk. I told them, "How far do you think we could get with your rifle in our back? We just need to walk around, that's all." The guards agreed, finally, and we walked around trying to see where the road downhill would take us. It was pretty much as I remembered it, Dad."

"Good, son." That's all he wanted to add at this time.

"We knew we were goners. Only God could deliver us, and we were clueless, but not without hope."

"Nope," said Becca. They were holding hands now.

"And then—it happened. It really truly happened." He waited for affect. "We were on the back side of the house now. That old bear came around; remember the one that clapped his hands? He was there! I'd say about a hundred feet away. I saw him out of the corner of my eye standing up nodding his head up and down at us. I had no idea what that meant, but I got Becca's attention and told her with my eyes to look in that direction."

"It was so scary," Becca sighed heavily.

"That is was. I can't remember when I've done so much praying in such a short time as I have this past week."

"Me either."

"Out of nowhere I spotted another grizzly standing up about thirty feet away from the other. They were on the higher ground, like sentries standing there on different sides. We watched them get down which put them mostly out of sight, so Becca and I just walked around to the opposite side of the building. Then Becca did the weirdest thing, and I wanted to yell after her, but it would have given everything away."

"Yep, I went right into the little kitchen that was there as fast as I could and pulled out the smelliest food I could find from the refrigerator. There was a cross-breeze going with the little windows open on each side, and I hoped my plan would work. I stuck some meat on the counter and said to the two guys inside, trying to sound really mean, 'I just want one quick bite, do you mind?' Then I tried to sound really defensive to throw them off and leave me alone, so I yelled, 'It's just a bite!' Then I said, 'Oops, I've got to get something outside, but I'll be right back!' I ran like the wind out to Luke who was trying to make conversation with the guard to preoccupy him."

"It seemed to work, too. The guard looked at Becca to see why she was breathing so fast when all of a sudden the roars of the two grizzlies made us all jump out of our skin! The next thing we heard was wood being torn and ripped apart by angry beasts that would take a lot more than four bullets to put down. The agent guard that was standing with us was so scared that he took off running. The two guards in the building were killed, and we're still not sure where the other guard was. We just took off running in this direction! That is why we were out of breath and scared when we got here, because we didn't know if we were followed by man or beast!"

Everyone wanted to laugh, but it didn't come out. They were too deep in thought.

Dad stepped right in and encouraged the both of them. "You both did exactly what you were supposed to do. You were led by His Spirit and you followed Him the whole time. I too believe that God used you because He could trust you, no matter what, to help Him get the guards off of whoever was out there. God planned your rescue before you ever left Preston, and you haven't missed Him one bit."

The atmosphere brightened, and God sent His ministering angels to bring a sense of euphoria to the group. They had been used of God and did His bidding just as He asked them to. Obeying and trusting God was the best high in the world. The family started to praise the Lord and worship Him with high praises. Angels manifested in the town at the strength of the worship that not only this family was doing, but others who were also with loved ones were partaking in because they also had found their refuge there this past week.

All over the earth were tens of thousands upon tens of thousands of these stories and journeys. The destroyer was striking, and God was shielding. Not all were meant to remain, and not all were meant to die. Horrors were out of control, and the devil loved it. He would let man worry about how to control it; satan just wanted death and more death. The more with him in the end, the merrier.

Luke talked with his dad about his car before turning in to bed. "Dad, the TMV is still up there, and unless the bears got it, we could still bring it down."

"I thought about that, Luke. Let's sleep on it, and we will hear from the Lord. I'd like to round up a party to get your TMV. We could probably discover a lot up there of what is left of the facility."

Gordon walked over to the fireplace to turn off the flames.

"It's up to our strange and wild government if they want to rebuild there. They sound like they are busy everywhere else, and I have a feeling their hands are too full now." He patted Luke on the shoulder, "We will just see what God says." Dad wanted to make sure what came out of his mouth next was deeply felt by Luke. He looked him squarely in the eyes, "Thanks for sharing, Luke. More than anything I'm glad you are pursuing the Lord hotly, not like you used to do, halfway. You'd be the one in more serious trouble without much hope of getting out right about now had you not thrown yourself into the Lord whole-heartedly. So many have put their relationship with Christ off, and just like the Bible says, the thief comes when he isn't expected. You are a good testament to being close to Him in all ways. I'm so grateful son, and so pleased."

Luke's eyes misted, and he was more than grateful also. God had given him a great heritage of believing parents that knew how to pray. Luke had a lot to be thankful for, especially tonight. He gave his dad a great long hug and then said good-night. Luke had one more stop before getting to bed. He walked out to the kitchen to say good-night to his mom.

"Gotta have your hotcakes in the morning, Mom!" His eyes sparkled as he gave her his imaginary request.

"They will be there, hon." They hugged good night with awe and wonder at the God of wonders. Mom whispered in his ear, "What is there that God can't do?"

Luke smiled at his mom as they shared a moment of pure appreciation for God and being with one another.

~ℓↄ~

Far away was another wonder happening in spite of all the chaos. People in the city were watching an amazing flurry of angels going in and out of screens more than ever imagined. The angels had told many of the onlookers that there were other stadiums the people had not seen yet, and they too were arenas of increased angelic activity connected with Earth.

One screen would blink out and blink onto another scene, a constant blur of blinks throughout the whole building. People could not keep up with some of the screen changes. Angels never ran out of number waiting to pass through to any need that was called upon of the Father. All of history was recorded, however, and each passing moment added another moment with all of the other zillion moments happening to history in a twinkling of an eye. It was a sight to behold. God's glory seemed to be brighter and brighter on His throne, but it didn't affect the Great City. It was affecting Earth, however, and the enemy hated it.

~ Chapter Twenty-seven ~

NEITHER SATURDAY NOR Sunday was a Sabbath day to Emuel. He rose up that Saturday morning with one intention, and that was to get his generals on the conference phone. At first he wanted to yell at them for their lack of control according to the plan. Then he wanted to congratulate them for throwing everyone into utter confusion, but also rebuke them for not being able to handle the bodies. He didn't know which way to address them, so he decided to hit them from both sides. Generally speaking, he was angry and needed to vent it.

Durdana was miffed because she couldn't come and go like she used to. Everything was in turmoil, which caused her to lose control. Her dad was running everything the wrong way. Destruction should be done stealthily so the rich and powerful could come and go as they wished. She felt confined to her palace for the time being, and that wasn't working well for her. She needed to contact a general or two—or three or four.

The devil was thrilled to have daughter against dad. After all, division was one of his specialties. Red drool dripped from satan's mouth just thinking of it. His meat and drink was dissection of everything he could touch. Besides, Emuel was getting too big for his britches, and Durdana was hooked and increasingly obsessed with the promise of a visit to take place between her and the debonair man in her life, or so she thought. Mr. Debonair was a good name for him she concluded, and until she knew his true identity, that was what she would name him. The devil had utterly and totally captivated her. He had robbed her of her power, but would puff wisps of hatred and disdain in her toward her dad. The devil would craftily blow his breath of deceit on her to believe she was the one with the power. He had also orchestrated her unity with the four generals so strongly that the unification throughout the world to walk out satan's plan was a win-win. He just couldn't lose. He had thought of everything. The trump card and frosting on the cake was offering Durdana—during regular nightly visitations in her dreams—that he, Mr. Debonair, would meet with her in person in the daytime very soon, and they would be lovers forever. Mr. Debonair knew how to thrill her beyond any man's natural ability in those visitations. To Durdana, her mystery man was a high potency drug, and she wanted more. He had her in his grip forever.

~φ~

Brent had finished working on his project throughout the week. The meeting he and Darren had with Blake later on the Saturday before worked out well. That Sunday at the BBQ, Blake said they needed to stay out of Tall Pines no matter what and beware of anything that would to try to lure them in for the week. Brent and Darren took his warning seriously and kept to the firs in the hills.

Krista, too, had gotten the warning while she was at the BBQ. She and Brent got a chance to speak with one another in a more casual setting surrounded with a large number of other people of all ages. It was a comfortable setting and spiritually productive, as many testimonies were shared and a lot of spontaneous prayers were given.

Brent thought back to that day with a broad smile on his face. He kept thinking of that cute dog, Misty. Nah, who was he trying to fool? Himself obviously.

"But, Lord!" he would argue, "It's not the right time to meet the woman of my dreams— is it? It just can't be!" Brent could easily put himself into a tizzy over it. He just didn't understand why he would meet her and be so taken by her. But hadn't he felt something deep inside whenever he saw her or her car? There was some connection to be made for sure, but he didn't see how or why. Blake had said that Brent's dad and Krista's dad had known one another. But what could that mean to them? He would have to get together with Krista and find out. Maybe they could figure it out together. Brent smiled over that thought, and everything felt a whole lot better all of a sudden. A spring went back into his step, and he decided it was time to take Zipper for a walk. Maybe Darren wasn't playing with some raccoon or something, and they could visit with him for a while and try to put a plan together. Whatever either of them wanted to do, they needed to watch each other's back more than ever.

<p>

Krista was pacing back and forth in her backyard. There were no neighbors that could see her backyard, and she was relieved at that. She felt crazy and didn't want someone to see her acting crazy. She threw her arms up in the air over and over again while shouting out questions to God. "Why did I meet Brent? What's that supposed to be all about? Who is this guy anyway, and why would it matter that our dad's knew each other? Why does he have to have such a beautiful dog? Why is Brent so handsome? Why do I care? What's going on?" Misty would walk back and forth with Krista for a while, and then take off running down the pasture between the trees to chase another critter who dared to crawl down a tree for something. The squirrels would bark rebukes at Misty when she was around. They all seemed to have fun and stayed busy with one another. Then after a few minutes of critter control, Misty would make her way back to Krista and follow her around some more.

Krista finally decided to make her way to the hills where Brent worked. She and Blake had a good conversation about Brent, when he had advised her to see him soon and also stay out of Tall Pines. So that settled that. She had a map to retrieve and would just have to forget that Brent was attractive and charmingly boyish. It wasn't like her to get fogged up in personal matters, or was it? Even though for years she had performed some dangerous and clever missions for the Lord, she found herself thinking there was more in that; and wanted to explore this "something more" in life she felt drawn to. It had to be God's Holy Spirit leading her in a different direction. She wanted a family someday, and caring for those darling children those many days had caused her to see that there was more to life than being sharp, witty, and outsmarting the enemy. Relationships were fulfilling and served a different purpose. God was all about relationship. Relationship was a source of anointing which would break the yoke of the enemy. The Bible said that unity brings the anointing, and that anointing breaks the yoke of bondage. Krista understood that she needed to get closer to her friends and allow God to let her yoke up with someone, yet more intimate, that could lead to marriage. Wow, that thought nearly bowled her over. Suddenly, Krista slapped herself in the face and laughed. Get serious, Krista! Get the job done and think about these things later!

Shaking her head to affirm that she needed to refocus, she jangled her keys and Misty came running. "To the hills, Misty! We're going to the hills." And off they went.

~ℓ♪~

Gordon and his band of friends who were wise men with years of experience in "taking care of business" were very able in the mountains, as well as with keeping things protected and watched in their little town. Cautiously, the following Monday, they made their way to the mountain to the shattered facility that once guarded the road across. It didn't seem that they were detected, but they stayed low just in case. Just like Gordon suspected, the building was left there to rot in the ground for it wasn't important enough at this time to watch the few who would ever travel this way. Luke had gone with them to show them the car and drive it back down.

The five men that made up the group, plus Luke, inspected whatever they could find. Papers strewn about in the mess with recorded sightings of people in the valley below were discovered, which made the men look all the harder to see what it was that the agent guards used to spy on the people below. In one bottom drawer was found a pair of high-powered binoculars. A couple of men who were roaming outside found a hideout in some boulders that had a covering protecting it. Inside they found a telescope and other items revealing how they got such accurate recordings. This sent chills up men's backs. You could hear them walk around thanking God under their breath for this victory of discovery.

One of the guys came back toward the building shouting, "Hey! I found something here!" The men knew they were all meant to see this, so they all ran out to see what the one of them had found. There was a dead body there, and Luke figured it the one who was talking with him outside that day the bears attacked because of the color of his hair. This find was not far from the boulder fortress with the telescope. The men dispersed around the area looking for that fourth man Luke told them he and Becca had seen, but didn't know where he was during the attack. It made sense that he would be near this area. Sure enough, just yards away was the other body lying in parts here and there. It was pretty torn up from the grizzlies, and clearly some other animals had been there feeding. It wasn't a pretty sight.

Luke had a funny thought. Dare he share it with the group? "Hey, I had a silly thought." Luke was shaking his head already like it was silly, and no one would take it seriously. He looked up at them and just went for it. "Do you think these bears could ever be angels? They seem to protect God's people, and after all these years of your stories, Dad, and what happened to Becca and me, it has occurred to me that the bears never attack Christians. Could there be anything to that?" Luke waited for the laughter to be hailed at him, but no one laughed.

The men looked at each other raising their eyebrows, not eager to speak, but looked at Gordon to give the answer.

"It seems you remember, then, all those stories I told you about a grizzly we called Ben. Remember that book I told you that we were going to give you to read? There are stories about Ben from as long as we can remember in that book. He is always called Ben. He always looks the same. He has the same markings and has identical mannerisms with every generation that has witnessed him and got rescued in some way by him. Son, we absolutely believe him to be an angel of God. There is too much evidence for it to be any other explanation. We don't know about any other bears, but we do know about him."

One of the other men, the senior one of the group, spoke up. "Son, did you ever see Ben slap his chest with his right paw then hold it up beside him as if to make an oath and just stand there looking at you?"

Luke was shocked. He hadn't told anyone that. He saw it the day he and Becca first ran into him, then on the day he saw him higher up on the mountain before the two grizzlies came down and smashed the building. He just thought it was way too ridiculous to share that with anyone. It was silly and, literally, unbelievable. But, guess not.

"Yes, actually, that's exactly what the grizzly did. So, that was really Ben, huh?"

All of the men nodded in affirmation.

"Would these wonders never cease?" thought Luke. He hoped not.

The men stated it was time to find the TMV, so Luke led them all up the mountain the other mile.

There it was, unscathed, but a note was lying on the front seat. This is what it read:

"Thank you for the use of your vehicle. I had come a long way, and I was impatient to get to my home near the ocean. I was so bitter and full of hatred and fear I didn't even think to look up from the trail when right before me was the dreaded facility with guards there eager to run after me. They would have shot me had I not had such a distance on them and could get down to hide often. I saw you drive here, and watched you get taken by the agent guards who were out after me. You saved my life. I didn't stay in the car until the next day after I heard the commotion down at the guard facility. I saw they were all dead and headed back to the TMV for food. I was afraid to go down the valley until I knew that no one was going to come up here after the guards or after me. I found a Bible in your car and knew I should pick it up and start reading. I was humbled that God would protect me for I have done a lot of bad things in my life. I was running back here to my mom and dad and ex-wife who had been treated horribly by me years ago. I feared for my life and this is where I ended up. I spent two days reading your Bible in the car. After doing much crying and repenting, I felt a peace to come down the mountain and find my folks and ex. I am going to make things right with them.

Thanks again. I hope we will meet someday, and I will repay you.

Sincerely,

Jason Cumberland.

P.S. I nearly ran into a bear. I was scared half out of my wits! I didn't know if I'd ever leave the vehicle, but the strangest thing happened. I swear to you, I'm not crazy, but this is what happened. The bear held his right paw in oath style to me after he hit his chest. He then nodded with his head for me to get going down the mountain. Have you ever seen this bear? My Dad told me of him once. That's the only reason why I have the nerve to share that with you. Watch out for him if you ever get back to your car.

In your service, Jason.

~ Chapter Twenty-eight ~

I WANT ALL THE prisoners taken to the islands for mass slaughter! I don't care who is escaping. Just get them rounded up and out of our cities! And get me those maps!"

Emuel slammed his hand down by the conference phone. After he swore for a few minutes, he still fumed. He paced back and forth to his window overlooking a peaceful garden which gave a false sense as to what was happening out in the real world. But he knew. Things had really gotten out of hand, but he would use it for the good. He ordered all of the looters and anyone who looked like a lowlife to be taken with those he called the "wishy-washies." He'd get rid of them all. It was way past time to scour the earth of the little people anyway.

Just yesterday he ordered the hundreds of millions of soldiers run by captains of the generals to start converging on the city. It would take a little more than a few days, but it would be a great time to strike. There was no way the peaceful, quiet little people of the city would be expecting what was about to happen to them. Peaceful, peaceful, peaceful. Their peaceful ways made Emuel sick to his stomach. They were naïve and stupid. They were way too nice for a war. They didn't have a weapon around. Emuel had them. It was all falling into place. Emuel's evil grin took over his face. It looked like satan's grin, and most likely was. He just slipped in and out of Emuel and his generals at will.

Krista knew the back roads and hills like the back of her hand. She knew her Father God's voice well, too. She prayed, God led. She pulled up to a cabin; it was about six o'clock. She wondered if this was Brent's place and believed that is what the Father showed her.

188

The two got out of the car, and Misty immediately had her nose to the ground trotting all over the place. Misty ended up two steps onto a porch in front of the cabin and up to the door. "Rark! Rark!" Her tail wagged fiercely.

"Yup, this could be the place."

~ʔ~

Brent had found Darren in the back whittling on some stick and whistling some worship song. He convinced Darren to go back with him for he had a good sized freezer and wanted to start emptying it. It was steak on the grill tonight!

They showed up in Brent's driveway in Darren's truck when all of a sudden Brent's heart nearly fell out of his chest. Darren just smiled. What was that red car doing there?

Krista came from behind the cabin with Misty, and Zipper jumped on top of Darren as his feet and claws did a great twist and turn on his thighs.

"Ow!" Darren's body stiffened, and he quickly opened the door to relieve his legs of an over anxious big dog. Darren didn't really hurt, but he still had to make Brent believe he was mortal.

Brent looked straight ahead fighting for composure. *"I can do this,"* he thought.

"Hi guys!" waved Krista. Misty and Zipper were already around the house once and heading off down a dozen trails together.

She held out one of her hands to shake to help put them at ease. Darren was always at ease, but he just watched Brent and chuckled to himself. Here is a man in his thirties who gets all goosey-legged every time he's around Krista. Darren couldn't help but laugh silently. Oh, this was going to be good.

Brent wasn't dumb at all. In fact, he was the total opposite, but when he thought of Krista or was around her, he felt all blather-scattered. He'd really have to reign in his emotions and take charge of them. What kind of impression was he giving her anyway? It couldn't be good.

"Krista! What are you doing around here? How did you get here?

How's Misty?" He realized he was just chattering and needed to reel it in. He looked at Darren for support.

Darren just looked back at Brent with a blank stare.

"*Oh, thanks a lot, Mr. Cool.*" Brent was overreacting but then remembered the steaks and grilling. That thought came to his rescue, and he pulled himself together.

"Well…" Krista paused as to not sound too silly, for she still didn't know these guys very well. "I prayed how to get here, and God showed me how! So here I am!" She smiled with an adorable smile, and Brent found his legs getting weak again. He was hopeless.

"I, uh, got some steaks—a half dozen as a matter of fact—that I was going to grill up for ol' Darren and myself. Would you like to join us?" "*See Brent, you're not all out to sea.*" Brent encouraged himself and was pleased he could actually get something intelligent and polite out at the same time.

"Yeah, Krista," Darren added, "Ol' Darren here would love to be in your company for some good steak eatery." He passed an odd look over to Brent as if to say, "'*Ol' Darren is it now?*"

Brent literally waved off Darren and approached the porch. "Come on in everyone and let's get this party a'goin'!"

The ice was broken, and they all went in and started to let loose with one another. Krista could keep up with Darren, and he loved having another wit around him. In fact, it spurred him on to be crazier than normal, and Brent was right in there with the both of them. Laughter increased as the time went on, and it was nothing to see Krista or one of the guys doubling over with their arms across their stomach because it hurt so much to laugh so hard. It was great and they loved it.

They got to know one another better and had a better sense about each other. About an hour or so after the steaks, the tone of the conversation started to get serious, and what Krista went there for needed to be shared.

"I had a good talk with Blake. It seems his restaurant is one of the safest places to be, but I'm concerned for him and Milly."

The guys nodded in agreement, and she continued.

"Did Blake share with you about some maps?"

This threw Brent off a little, but he half suspected it. Something about their dads and what Blake shared made him listen on with respect.

Krista shared about what she had in her possession and let Brent and Darren know who she was and what she had done the past several years in the service of the Lord. She gave some background about her dad and mom, and Brent completely related. Blake had told her to share, and she was eager to hear what Brent was supposed to share. She knew about the map he had with him.

Brent showed her what he had and she was taken by surprise. *"This guy is really smart or knows how to hear the Spirit, or both!"* Her eyes were as wide as saucers. "That will do," she replied in awe and high esteem toward him.

She glanced over at Darren, and he sat there smiling and said, "Yep."

It wasn't a silly moment to them, but a moment of reverence on how God moves and leads His people.

~ Chapter Twenty-nine ~

Brilliant angels holding on to fault lines for years and scores of years at a time were getting more brilliant. They reflected the brilliance of the Lord God Almighty. Some short blasts from the Trumpets of God's Throne were sounded. These angels in particular smiled knowingly. It wouldn't be long now.

Several days had passed and the troops had encroached upon the city within a day's journey. Supplies could only last so long, and satan had to keep the troops motivated and strong. He held them there for just a short time longer. He knew God could see them, but also thought God didn't know his private thoughts and ultimate scheme.

Rumors from satan's rulers had reported that they had located the maps and would soon obtain them. Auras of bloody dark brown vapors emanated from satan's presence representing all of the dried blood from the great slaughters that had taken place all over the world. When it was reported that some of the Christians had gotten mixed in with the wishy-washies, satan could only laugh. That was fine with him. The wishy-washies would probably pull them down and turn the Christians into them which would please satan all the more. Not everyone could stand against numbers of angry confused people without compromising themselves. It would turn out just fine. His darkened vapors would leave trails of choking fumes in his wake when he was about roaming. It was time to implement the last plans.

~℘~

Blake and Milly had been arrested for protecting people in their restaurant and for Blake confronting the police, which he did just for fun. He got a lot off his chest, and it was worth it all. He laughed all the way to jail. Why they didn't throw a fuss like most of the hostages was indifferent to the agent guards who discovered them. They were too busy to care. The police, however, who handled them the rest of the journey from jail to the island were perplexed. Some of them secretly came up to Blake or Milly asking them for prayer.

Regardless of what line of work that existed on the earth, terror was running rampant. Many of the die-hard atheists observed the real Christians who exuded peace and calm, and whatever it was that was making them that way, there were those who hungered for it and became Christians secretly.

~℘~

Emuel had planned another conference with his generals and had them fly in for an evening meeting. That Friday, the islands were going to be systematically blown up, ridding the earth of scum and filthiness. The day after that, on the Sabbath day—the day that was Holy and precious to God—the City of God would no longer be under God's control and command.

Satan had his men lined up to obtain the last two maps, and Emuel had to be heavily sedated to get any sleep at all. His excitement could not be contained. He and his experts had studied the first two maps and realized they actually came together, and what would be the center circle would not be a map, but probably instructions. He hoped that about the circle. But he was certain the third map would be as the first two. The plan satan had should be happening right about now.

~℘~

Krista was asleep at Brent's cabin with the two dogs. Brent had gone over to Darren's to stay starting the first evening Krista arrived. The two guys had thought of this for some time now, so it was planned and easy to do. They all agreed this was God's direction and had a great peace.

The dogs were outside now and preferred the outdoors at this time of year. Krista stirred in her sleep as evil beings were attacking her spirit. She fought them off trying to yell out "The blood of Jesus! Jesus! Jesus! The blood of Jesus!" In previous dreams of warfare, it seemed that having to form those words was nearly impossible as her mouth would feel sealed closed. Then when she could make noise, it came out as nothing more than a weak and wimpy whisper. The intimidation was always overwhelming and the feeling of exhaustion was prevalent in each of those dreams. Her body acted weighted down and unable to move. She thought she was awake when in reality she was between the dream world and the real world. It was a realm of the supernatural, and she never liked it. This experience was no different than the others, but it seemed this one took a bit longer. Several moments went by before she could force herself to get the words of her Savior out of her mouth with any power at all. She bolted up like a heavy spring had been released in bed and looked around to see if she was truly awake.

She could barely make out that the front door was open, so she turned on the lantern Brent told her about next to the bed. She peered through the cabin and could not hear or see anyone. Something horrible had happened, and she didn't know what. Shaking, she got up and tip-toed around to see what she could see and saw something that spread trepidation all through her. *"No, no, no!"* As fear clamped around her throat, she found Brent's axe gone. It was in a chest next to the freezer, and it was gone. She put a hand up to her throat to subconsciously relieve the tightness, but all she could do was gasp out sobs.

Minutes later ticks on an old clock started to register in her ears as the numbness slowly receded. *"The dogs!"* She ran around frantically. Where were the dogs? They were staying with her, right? The map! Where was the other map? She clumsily put some slippers on out of haste putting them on the wrong feet, but she didn't care. She ran outside calling the dogs but went straight for her car. She forgot her keys and started to go back when it occurred to her that if they had broken in, she wouldn't need them. She went back toward the car and sure enough, it had been jimmied open. More like a rough, forcing in. The door was in awful shape, but she didn't care. It was the map she was supposed to guard, and the map she had to find!

She went to the back seat where she had a covered area that, when pulled down, exposed another cover that hid a locked compartment. It had been busted. That beautiful pencil box had vanished. She fell into the back seat and sobbed for a long time.

~*~

Durdana had managed to see each general and gave a final dose of admiration, devotion, and intimate promises that she knew she would never keep. She fulfilled their craving desires for her, and as a result, each general was proceeding with what they thought was their own personal plan for their ultimate power takeover. Whatever it took for the demise she and Mr. Debonair came up with the past two weeks was all that really and truly mattered to her. She was purring like a kitten now.

~*~

The next morning the guys awoke to a lightly rainy, misty day. It felt good, and the air smelled fresh. They were going to head over to Brent's place for breakfast to be with Krista. It was Friday, and they had put in forty-four hours that week already, so they did the Friday-off plan. They began this plan a few weeks ago to avoid the Friday night pressure to head to the bars.

Brent turned to Darren while they were in the living room finishing getting things together when Brent said, "Hey, have you noticed there has been no Jason the past week or two? I wonder where that miserable guy took off to? Maybe they transported him. Mal hasn't said a word."

"Right, Mal hasn't said a word except, 'Hey, you two bums, work faster, play less!' Yessirree, Mal hasn't said a word."

"Well, Mr. Funny, you know good and well what I mean. I wonder what happened to Jason? I can't say as I miss him at all. That's probably why Mal hasn't been around as much. He's been covering twice the territory and acting twice as mean and grumpy."

"That's for sure." Darren looked at his jacket but knew quickly the temperature would be going up, and he didn't want to have to remember it or lag it around. He decided against it and looked at Brent. "Ready?"

"Yep." Brent headed toward the door Darren had just opened. Right smack dab in the middle of the door on the outside was a huge piece of note paper that read: "You guys aren't working here anymore. Pack up your things and get out of here."

That hit like a ton of bricks. Brent and Darren looked at each other and instantly thought about Krista and her car at the cabin. Was there a sign there too, and did Mal suspect anything? They hustled out to the SUV, and Brent had a quick thought. "Hey man, let's each take our vehicle over there. I don't like the feel of this."

"Neither do I," replied Darren, and off they went.

~ Chapter Thirty ~

A TRUMPET BLASTED THAT told the angels holding some of the earthquake fault lines to be prepared for the last trump for their mission. It was a countdown to them which started at the blow of that trumpet. It was beginning.

~ ℘ ~

Durdana had told each of the generals to tell the other generals of the plan she had worked on with each of them individually, but now, not to worry about it, because she had already told them. They were relieved they didn't have to sound like the traitor. Rightly, Durdana was a dream and answer to their visions.

~ ℘ ~

"Gentlemen, this weekend is the culmination of centuries sought for by our people. It has come." Emuel walked around the room and repeated himself because it felt so good to hear it out of his own lips. "Finally, it has surely come."

He walked over to an exquisitely built-in cabinet that had marble overlays on sections of rich dark wood that showcased bottles of delicate craftsmanship and design that held the world's most expensive liquors. He had his own personal stash in his living quarters, but what he had in this room was to equally impress any and all of his visitors. He opened up one of the cabinets and brought out a fine Cognac that was decades old. It was reserved for this day and this weekend. He had several cases tucked away in a room with many other tasty alcohol concoctions that would serve him liberally as soon as this weekend came to an end. His mind would spin at the taste of this victory that was only hours away. Today, in salute to his generals, he brought out the best and promised more for the end of the victory.

Later in the evening, he and the generals would fly to their bunker situated on a hilltop just a mile away from the Great City, so they could view the falling and destruction of the foundation of that city. This would be enabled from cameras set up everywhere and at every angle to project on Emuel's mammoth sized screen in the conference room, and a special lens was created to record the spectacular show for whoever wanted to individually watch it on that day and forever. Stewards, servants, and caterers were already setting up for the event. All was in place. His plan was ingenious, hitting God on His day of rest.

For now, Emuel was to watch his generals each call in their order to their rulers under them to blow the islands. Their phone devices were connected to each of the commanders on every island in their region across the planet with orders to set off the bombs. Each wishy-washy soul, and each Christian that had been reined in with them, were about to wake up to another realm.

The devil no longer paid any attention to the weak and feeble minded he had ordered to the islands. They would be destroyed, and the final destruction was next. If a few came to the Lord, what of it. They would end up at the City of God which was about to be turned over to him anyway. This day wasn't the bigger picture, and besides, one week wasn't going to start a revival. He had good cause to celebrate for everyone that worked for him had done a good job. Didn't they take care of business for the last one thousand years? What was a week? He kept his mind on the final destruction, believing his captains and generals had done their job. The devil strutted and jigged across the room.

Emuel nearly danced in the room much to the generals' surprise. But they understood. Soon they, too, would feel like dancing.

~𝓮𝓭~

"Sixty-two! Sixty-one! Sixty! Fifty-nine! Fifty-eight! Fifty-seven..."
The earthquake angels under hundreds of islands counted down
the seconds for the last blast of their mission to sound.

~𝓮𝓭~

There were many Blakes and Millys God had planted that ended
up on those islands everywhere. But their names were different,
like Dave and Zoanne or Don and Danielle. They had been in jails
and prisons but carted off to the islands. All prisons were cleaned
out for a future holding of rebellious City of God residents. Emuel
would decide then what to do with those people. He wanted to see
them, talk to them, and discover the city he was about to take over.
Then he would know better what to do with the believers who were
about to be crushed and realize they had only followed the God
of deceptions. He figured they would make excellent slaves for his
kingdom. The more he thought about it, the more he liked that idea.
It was as good as done.

"Forty-four! Forty-three! Forty-two..."

But what happened on those islands took place in a matter of
hours. There were more conversions that took place than if satan
had not ordered such an edict for all of the wishy-washies to be
taken away. Because of their sheer terror, they were finally eager,
ready, and willing to accept Christ as their Lord! All of the Blakes
and Millys knew how to handle the crowds and brought them all
into salvation by leaps and bounds. God's display of mercy against
the flood of destruction was never ending! They may have lost their
houses and cars and jobs, but were about to enter into the most glorious spectacular and magnificent realm with mansions they could
not have dreamed of waiting for them. God was ready for them.

"Twenty-one! Twenty! Nineteen! Eighteen..."

"Gentlemen, are you about to place your calls? Have the connec-
tions been made?"

The generals held up their phones, connected to their captains of
the islands.

"Five! Four! Three! Two..."

The final blast sounded.

"Now, Gentlemen!"

The command went forth.

It was a spectacular sight to some. To the enemy, they saw the losers of the world disappear before their very eyes.

To the ones in hiding, it was horrifying, for when they found out, they had no idea what God had done. All they knew was what they either saw or heard from the news and others. Their faith was tested to the very limits.

To God, it was another checkmate. Before the labeled wishy-washies could change their minds, God in His mercies took all of them home without one having to cry out in pain. The earthquake faults under them had swallowed up the islands with the people who were changed in a twinkling of an eye a second before the explosions had gone off. In reality, it was less than a half a second. It all happened so fast, that the captains in charge of the bombs were putting out of their minds the initial double take they did when it seemed the bombs were released as their hand was about to grab the detonators instead of when they pushed them down. They attributed the reaction to Deja vu.

The greatness of God's loving kindnesses never ceased. Never did, never has, never will.

~-?)-~

A small town on the coast of Washington, just on the other side of the Olympic Mountains, was holding prayer vigils for Krista, Brent, and Darren. Jason, who had fled from the wickedness of Mal in Tall Pines, and found the Lord in Luke's vehicle, had told everyone at the town meeting what the enemy was up to for the bigger plan against the people contemplating turning their lives over to Christ, the islands they were sent to, and the plans for the City of God. Then he shared about the plans he knew Mal had for Brent and Darren.

Gordon had learned from Blake, before he was captured, that

Krista was going to meet up with the young men in the hills. He knew she was with them.

Emuel poured the Cognac and toasts abounded. "For the day of victory!" That was their favorite toast, for each general had his own victory in mind.

Chapter Thirty-one

IT TOOK ABOUT two minutes for the guys to get to Brent's. They both saw her car door opened and damaged. That put more alarm in them, and they ran up to the door. Brent barged in forgetting that she might not be decent, for he was just thinking of saving her. There she sat at the kitchen table with a steamy mug of coffee for herself and two more like it for the guys. She smiled.

Brent and Darren let out huge sighs of relief to see her sit there looking lovely, peaceful, and very happy! The dogs were carrying out one of their favorite pastimes—sleeping. They were curled up next to each other like best mates would.

Krista looked at their shocked and perplexed faces and said, "Hey guys! Come and sit down. Have I something to tell you!" After sitting down, Krista started to share about what happened to her. The guys were nonplussed and in pure amazement over it all. They hadn't even had the slightest twinge that anything wrong was going on in their spirit that morning before going out the door. God came through, for Krista was safe, but they were sad at the same time for what had to happen to Brent's axe.

They sat down to a good breakfast Krista had warming on the gas stove that consisted of eggs, hash browns, and bacon.

At the end of the meal, Krista excused herself and went merrily out to the car to get something. Moments later Brent and Darren heard a "Pop-Pop!" gunshot!

The dogs jumped up immediately and ran out with the guys to see what happened. They saw Krista dead under the car. Mal stood there with his automatic rifle in his hands and had the biggest smile smeared across his face. "At least you can't say I didn't warn you." The dogs were already half way to charge Mal, but it wasn't close enough. He shot them first and glided the gun right up to Brent and Darren who were on their way to put him down as well. Mal didn't miss.

Mal looked at each one of them and said snickering, as an evil black vapor mixed with crimson reds drifted around him, "That takes care of you guys at last. Thanks for the maps." He turned to go and vanished off into the woods, which he had been in and out of all morning with some of Emuel's agent guards.

Brent lay there not quite dead. He managed to look over at his dead buddy, then so very slowly he managed to turn to see Krista laying there in a pool of blood. He had such hopes for the two of them. Between them lay two beautiful dogs that knew nothing but unconditional love.

Goodbye, Zip, my ol' Blue Ox, my ol' buddy. Brent slipped into unconsciousness for a short while, then off went his spirit to a lovely place that the whole earth groaned for since the beginning of its creation. He was really home now.

~ Chapter Thirty-two ~

DURDANA WAS DRESSED to the nines on this day. She and her dad boarded their jet for the short flight to be near the City of God. She had always heard about it, but had never seen it. This would be one of the greatest days of her life. She had pledged her loyalty to each general, and each had pledged his loyalty to her. The generals boarded shortly after she and her father, and all were set to go.

The devil was filling Durdana as promised, and this was to be the day he would meet her as a man. Through her eyes, he looked at each man and contemplated such lowlifes. But that's what it took for him to show himself as ever powerful.

When they arrived at their destination, they commented on the millions and hundreds of millions of trained people and soldiers just a few hours away from the City of God in all directions. It was an adrenaline maker. The exhilaration of it all justified the notable confidence each person had when they got to their glorious and luxurious bunker.

Emuel had been right about the third and fourth map. They were studied for the last time by the experts after they had gotten them from Brent's property. They were flown out of there to land safely in Emuel's hands. *"God certainly has lost this battle,"* thought Emuel when he beheld the maps put together. The circular map read on the outside, "How to destroy the foundation of the Great City." Emuel's countrymen of a thousand years ago had thought of everything. The supplies were already anticipated after years of study, and the circular map just confirmed the necessities for the final destruction. Emuel's armies had the weaponry in full.

The sly fox devil had rejoiced over the maps for they were just as he had hoped. The city hadn't been dropped from heaven until he was enchained. But the city had been anticipated for years by those who researched the Bible for any clue to further its destruction, for the enemy didn't want to take any chances. It was a done deal now!

The devil's hordes were all slobbering as they now flicked their swords as they savored the victory and slaughter that felt just moments away. Miles of them were lined up horizontally and vertically as they waited for the last sound from their leader Lucifer to take them into the final battle and war of all wars.

With less than an hour for the city to be packed and run over by its enemy, Emuel checked with some of the commanders while the generals were doing the same. Durdana had given the eye to each general when she knew no one else was looking. Everyone was prepared for his moment.

Jets equipped with bombs of stellar performance, able to melt a hundred and fifty feet of any precious stone or ore was the heralding technology of the day and had been kept top secret.

The devil's plan was so perfect. He couldn't wait. The bombs would drop at specific designations at specific interims. So what if the first ten thousand soldiers would die at different points around the base, being so pressed up next to the city's entrances; it didn't matter. They would melt into nothing also, and the armies behind were strictly trained to proceed no matter what they saw or felt, or the reward for their mission would be forsaken. The comrades that were brave were given permission to kill anyone who did not keep moving forward. This was great incentive and a total successful stratagem.

Durdana was all about drama and all about control. Just watching an event come together that she had planned gave her a sinful rush. Now it was time. Satan surfaced in her eyes and breath as she approached the conference table where each of them was sitting.

She walked over to her dad, looked lovingly and directly into his eyes, and spoke to him tenderly, "Dad, thank you for all you have taught me. It has been my life and joy to learn from you. You've been an excellent teacher, and I hope you will see Mom, whom you had destroyed all those years ago, soon. I think she is waiting for you."

"What do you mean, daughter?" Nothing but inquisitive confusion showed on his face when Sabtah walked up to him and put a bullet in him with a silencer. Aram came up next and did the same thing. Jerahmeel followed, and then lastly, Omar finished him off.

"Hail queen and ruler of our souls," spoke each general. She bowed in mimicking adoration and waved her fingers to a couple of men who stood by in the corners of the room, protecting them all. They had been easily bought by each of the generals who regularly hired them to do their dirty work. Emuel was closed up in a bag and quickly dispersed of. His life was snuffed out just like that. No warning, no nothing. Just gone.

"All right, men; let's get the show on the road!" The chair her dad had been sitting on got taken out of the room and destroyed. Another had been ushered in that looked more like a throne adorned in gold, gems, and purples. It really was becoming of her.

The generals took their seats, and all eyes were on the screen before them. Cameras were feeding into the picture, and if anyone wanted to peer into the city, they went out to the special lens set up. The technicians on the magnified giant binoculars could not figure out why they couldn't see into the city. They could see the walls close-up, but were not able to pierce through the windows and openness on each level. They would have to report it to Emuel any minute now, except, they hadn't heard about his death yet.

Durdana didn't care about that special lens her dad had arranged. She was more interested in the death and destruction about to take place. She could now witness the millions pressed up against the stairways of the city for hundreds of miles all around. Some fell on the stairs and out of sheer fright, screamed. They hadn't gotten hurt, they were just scared. She got a big kick out of watching that. With her headset on to direct cameras, she would tell the producers, "Go here," or, "Over there! Get that scene!" If a producer dared ask where her dad was, she would tell him he got sick over something he had eaten on the plane, or he had gotten airsick and was away for the time being and to not be concerned, but just to do what she said.

Commanders of each jet carrying the destructive bombs called in ready for position. Durdana gave them a go. "Checkmate!" she said out loud, knowing she had conquered all there was to conquer at last. In reality, it was Mr. Debonair, the devil of all the ages who used her mouth to show God it was he who had won at last; not God, or his precious Durdana.

The generals kept remarking how they had never seen a plan so ingenious and overwhelmingly magnificent. The bombs were going to make all of the difference. Never before had there been such a weapon of finite excellence, of destruction and control. The bombs were everything a general's dream could be for such a battle that was made especially for this time, place, and purpose.

The bombers had just entered into their zone to start releasing their weapons when a deafening trumpet blast that could be heard throughout the whole earth sounded with the roar of the Lion of Judah. The blast was so powerful that its reverberation was like one hundred sound barriers coming against the jets. It knocked them back in utter destruction when, simultaneously, volcanoes were released by thousands of angels who had kept them under cover for such a time as this. They erupted and spewed ruby red lava and fire balls of magma over the multi-millions of soldiers surrounding the city. Then, what was even more of a stunning sight to behold was the liquid fire pouring down from heaven and God's heavenly realm. The liquid fire looked like gold spewing out of a fiery furnace, vomiting its fury and rage upon those who dared to defy God and His beloved.

Durdana and the generals sat aghast at the site. Cameramen that were close to the city were disappearing, and producers scrambled to see what cameras did work. The evil leaders were thrilled they were a mile away and safe from this destruction. But they were deceived. Five minutes into the rain of fire, it expanded and kept expanding. The little mountain the bunker was positioned on started to shake violently. Durdana, the generals, and everyone who was frightened, ran for their lives to the underground safety hold with assurance they would be safe there.

Angels of God in that mountain heard their blast from God's trumpet and released their very own fault lines, which they had held onto for years.

The bunker groaned and moaned trying to maintain its solid construction for which it was built. Durdana pushed others out of the way while clambering for safety. Aram was close by her side, never failing to be the proper gentleman for her, but brutal to all whom got in their way.

The shaking got more violent until it was impossible to walk or run. Most of the people had made it to the lowest floor where they were not so sure about their safety anymore. Everyone was holding onto something when all of a sudden the shaking seemed to stop! Durdana took this moment to establish control and order. She made her way to a podium and announced to all the passing of her dad during the earthquake. There were gasps and some sobbing broke out. Durdana smiled tenderly as she allowed them to express grief and release from the sudden catastrophes that had just been upon them all. Durdana quickly reflected and was happily amazed at how conveniently this unexpected lie would fit her plans, being even better than her original plan! The generals were at her side to support her and affirm her position to take over her dad's position so that the world could keep progressing forward in the light of the sad news. They had prepared to show Durdana as queen, and Aram was the first to approach the podium.

Suddenly, the sound of God's hand slapped against the back, reinforced concrete wall. Durdana and the generals turned around to see a crack form from the top of the wall steadily down to the floor as the noise of the splitting roared in their ears.

With a surprised look on her face, Durdana grabbed Aram as the floor below her feet opened to receive her, Aram, and the other generals. Soon, the whole room of people was swallowed into the steamy dark below.

The angels who released the last turbulent volcanic fault watched the bunker sink deeper down into hungry crevices, opening wide their mouths far below the surface of the earth, gripping all into its pit.

The devil let out the most hideous, piercing scream.

After God's ultimate checkmate, He took the devil and threw him into the lake of fire and brimstone where the beast and false prophet had been thrown a little over a thousand years earlier. There is where the devil would remain forever and ever.

~ Chapter Thirty-three ~

B RENT'S ANGEL BROUGHT him to the River of Life. Brent's eyes
went upward and beheld the City of God. The last tears of
sadness came to his eyes as he realized, like everyone else
who came to this edge from the past darkness to the future of
light, that he was not worthy to cross over. "No one is," said his
angel softly, knowing Brent's thoughts. Brent looked at his angel
and was taken by how much the angel looked like him and knew
what he was thinking. All of this was too wonderful. But where was
he to go if not across? He fought back sobs of humility and truth
of his past. His angel put his hands on each of Brent's shoulders
behind him and said, "Look over there." His angel directed his gaze
to a group of people waving and hollering, but he couldn't quite
make it out. "Your dad and mom are waiting for you, Brent." Brent
couldn't contain himself now. His sobs broke into wails of grate-
fulness and sadness all at the same time. He wanted to cross over
now. He looked at his angel once more who was standing beside
him. "There are others..." Brent darted a look back over. "*Was that
Krista and Darren?*"

Brent looked at the river in front of him, gleaming and beckoning him. "Go ahead, go." Those were the last words his angel
spoke to him on this side.

Brent walked in, and the further he got, the deeper he got. The
river drew him in gently as cleansing and purging was flawlessly
and surgically performed over and throughout his entire being:
his body, soul, and spirit. Washing and more washing took place
in Brent's being as the river was now over his head. It took minutes to walk through as elation took over his spirit and his body
became brand new. Thoughts of the past were vanishing, and his
only thought was to see Jesus. Jesus was his mighty warrior, lover of
his soul, and best friend. Jesus stood by him in everything that ever

happened. Jesus fought for him and protected him. Jesus carried him in the bad and the sad moments, and guarded him always in the in-between moments, as well as the confusing and happy times. Jesus was *always* hope, always strength, always faithful for Brent. Simply said, Jesus was his everything.

Jesus greeted Brent first on the side of life. They hugged for a very long time. Brent whispered in Jesus' ear, "Thank You. Thank You, Thank You." Brent was amazed during this moment how his body and mind continued to get stronger and stronger. Jesus led him to a special tree.

After he and Jesus spoke some words together, Brent turned to find his dad and mom beaming from head to toe, eager to hold him again in their arms. That lasted for several minutes. Time wasn't a press anymore in heaven. Brent was light as air just thinking this new thought of reality.

Brent turned around and Krista and Darren were longing for their hugs as well. He hugged Krista and touched her hair. "You are so beautiful."

She smiled and said, "You are too." They laughed and Darren piped in with, "And then there is me!" Now they all got a good laugh and stood staring at each other for the joy they felt.

God didn't take away people's personalities, for He is the One who gave them that to begin with. But He did purify each of them when they walked through His River of Life.

Brent remembered a noble calling of the Lord, for such things were always remembered in heaven. "We fought and died protecting God's map, didn't we?"

Krista and Darren nodded.

"I thought for some reason we would succeed. But we do trust God for everything, don't we!"

The two smiled hugely in the "yes!" they proclaimed loudly.

Krista stepped aside for there was a surprise standing behind her. Misty jumped up in her arms, and when Brent thought he'd jump for joy, a yet bigger surprise was there for him.

Zipper! Zipper came wagging his tail up to him with something very special in his mouth. Brent recognized it right away. There was his axe that God had used for all of the centuries to bring about a special plan for the end of days.

But how did it get there? Brent was about to form the word "How" when Darren spoke.

"Remember you told me about people coming into the City of God with something in their hand that was extremely important to them?"

"Yes, I remember, and I also remember I did not have it in my hand when I died. I don't get it." He looked questioningly wanting to know how it got there.

Krista could not keep from smiling from ear to ear when she said, "When I got shot by Mal, I had the axe in my hand. I kept it hidden in a locked box that could not be detected from inside the car or seen by just looking under the car. Our plan of planting the fake axe that you had made to look just like the real one worked! That's why I was so happy when you showed up because our plan really worked! God's plan actually! I had cried sobs of relief in the car that my mission was finally finished and that we had succeeded. We really did protect the map! I ran out to the car to bring it back in to show you when Mal showed up being gun happy."

Tears of great joy were about to flow when Darren said, "We died while fulfilling God's commission, protecting His true map."

Brent was overflowing with deep, deep joy.

Darren continued with such an eager heart to bless Brent, "You see, Brent; I had died hundreds of years before in the Civil War of America. God sent me down to protect you and encourage you. Of course, He used the skill He had given me to forge the false map. The devil fell for the plot—hook, line and sinker. How sweet is that!?"

Brent was overwhelmed. He could get used to this type of jubilation. It's a good thing, because he was going to be living in it forever and forever.

"But, Darren!" Brent had a memory flow to the front, "The bloody cloth on your hand from the raccoon! You couldn't be one of the believers from here!"

Darren got a good laugh on that. "Oh, *that*... it was blood from the raccoon. She had given birth to her babies in my warm and dry laundry room." Darren let out a large chuckle. "Nah, that blood was from mopping up after the birth and all. I just put it on my hand to make you think I was bleeding. Pretty sneaky, eh, Brent?"

As if that all wasn't enough, Darren turned to Brent and motioned to his friend standing by, "Brent I'd like to introduce you to Nathaniel, famously known as Blake in our day!"

"*What?*" Apparently, Nathaniel too had been commissioned to be a watch tower over the area where the maps were hidden. God chose Washington state because of its unpopularity of being on the coast and way out of everyone's way. Certainly far away from where the enemy searched forever.

"You get to see Milly later, Brent." Nathaniel gave Brent a big ol' bear hug and shake. Brent laughed, and they went on to the City of God a bit further as he got to see his sister and her precious family. Different people came up to Brent and explained who they were. When he saw Jason, he was pleasantly surprised. "How did you get in here, bud?" More laughter, then Hank suddenly appeared and gave his entire testimony to them all. It was a great reunion. It was a God thing.

Krista had been in heaven for a short while before Brent. She had gotten to see her family and friends also. God brought all of His beloved kids home where they would live eternally in His protection and blessings after blessings after blessings that would never stop. The unbelievers throughout the world were dead.

Jesus had told Krista that it wasn't so much guarding the maps as it was just obeying Him. Some people were only given casual things to obey in, but obedience is obedience, faith is faith. He told her that no one could obey Him if they didn't truly trust Him. That was why obedience was so important, because it showed a trust and working relationship with Him. The faith that it took to trust Him in all things is what was and is counted to them for righteousness.

He pointed out to her the moment by moment incidences in everyone's life on a constant basis that revealed either trust or doubt. There was no middle road.

He then told her that the map was only to distract the enemy for the perfect time to approach the Great City for his utter and ultimate destruction. "Good job," He had said to her. He hugged her again before He left.

Krista could see it all clearly, what He shared with her.

"Kissta, Kissta! Krista!" Two children ran over yelling out her name with great joy. They were thrilled to see her again. They got to her and the three of them held onto each other tightly. Misty jumped up to get in on all the loving. Everyone giggled and hugged more and more.

"Oh, dear Lord, have I told you lately how much I love you?" Krista just had to tell Him again.

They meshed into one another as closely as they could when Sissy tilted her head way back and looked up into Krista's watery blue eyes and said, "Look, Kissta," Krista looked up. All of a sudden, two people behind her stood there watching and ready for their turn to embrace. Rusty spoke in his sure and confident way, "It was just as Mrs. McCauley and the angel said; here are my mommy and daddy."

ABOUT THE AUTHOR

Stephanie is a lover of souls who has lived in the great Northwest all her life. She and her husband Jonathan are in the ministry and have the heart to see the captive set free and learn the riches of God's Word. Stephanie is a musician, artist, and had been the owner of a retail store for years. She was heavily involved in politics and has been very involved in the prophetic for years. She spent nearly two years toward a degree in Psychology, and over four years in Criminal Justice. God constantly works miraculously in her life, which is written in a previous book she wrote years ago entitled *Practical Faith for Practical Miracles*. Being Mom and Grandma is her joy. In her leisure time, she plays with the stock market and tennis, and loves to swim.